Wherever She Goes

OCT - - 2019

WHEREVER SHE GOES

KELLEY ARMSTRONG

WHEELER PUBLISHING
A part of Gale, a Cengage Company

GALE
A Cengage Company

Farmington Hills, Mich • San Francisco • New York • Waterville, Maine
Meriden, Conn • Mason, Ohio • Chicago

Copyright © 2019 by KLA Fricke Inc.
Wheeler Publishing, a part of Gale, a Cengage Company.

Wheeler Publishing Large Print Hardcover.
The text of this Large Print edition is unabridged.
Other aspects of the book may vary from the original edition.
Set in 16 pt. Plantin.

LIBRARY OF CONGRESS CIP DATA ON FILE.
CATALOGUING IN PUBLICATION FOR THIS BOOK
IS AVAILABLE FROM THE LIBRARY OF CONGRESS

ISBN-13: 978-1-4328-7040-9 (hardcover alk. paper)

Published in 2019 by arrangement with Macmillan Publishing Group, LLC/St. Martin's Press

Printed in Mexico
1 2 3 4 5 6 7 23 22 21 20 19

For Jeff

ONE

I have made mistakes in my life. Mistakes that should loom over this one like skyscrapers. But this one feels the biggest.

This one hurts the most.

I lie in bed, massaging the old bullet wound in my shoulder as I try not to think of what used to happen when I woke in pain. One of those tiny things that seemed such an ordinary part of an ordinary life, and now I realize that it hadn't been ordinary at all.

I used to wake like this, my shoulder aching, heart racing from nightmare, huddled in bed, trying to be quiet so I didn't wake Paul. He'd still stir, as if he sensed me waking. He'd reach for me with one hand, his glasses with the other, and I'd hear the clatter of them on the nightstand, never quite where he expected them to be.

"Aubrey? You okay?"

"Just a nightmare."

7

"The car accident?"

I'd murmur something as guilt stabbed through me. The car accident. Yet another lie I'd told.

"Do you want to talk about it?"

"No, I'm fine."

The memory flutters off in his sigh, and I want to chase it. Go back there.

No, I want to go back to the beginning, before "Will you take this man," before Charlotte. Back to the first time a nightmare woke me beside Paul, and he asked if I wanted to talk about it, and this time I will say, "Yes. I need to tell you the truth."

It's too late for that.

It'd been too late from the first moment I dodged a question, hinted at a falsehood; I placed my foot on a path from which I could not turn back. Those lies, though, hadn't ended our marriage. I almost wished they had — that I had confessed my past and our marriage had imploded in spectacular fashion.

The truth was much simpler: water wearing down rock, the insidious erosion of secrets untold. All the things I should have said from the start, but the longer it went on, the more I *couldn't* say them. A vicious cycle that pushed us further apart with each revolution.

Pushed us apart? No, that implies action and forethought. In the end, I'd felt like we were on rafts in a lazy river, Paul drifting away, me madly paddling to stay close, telling myself he just didn't realize he was floating away from me and then . . .

Well, there comes a moment when you can't keep pretending that your partner doesn't notice the drift. It had gone on too long, my floundering too obvious, his unhappiness too obvious.

I'm going to take Charlie to the company ball game. Give us some daddy-daughter time while you enjoy an afternoon alone.

I can't go away this weekend after all. I'm in court Monday, and I need to prep. We'll do it another time. Maybe in the fall.

I think we should stop trying to have another baby, Bree.

Even the ending had been so . . . empty. I told Paul that I could tell he wasn't happy, and it was better for Charlotte if we realized our mistake now. I said the words, and I waited for him to wake up. To snap out of it and say, "What are you talking about? I *am* happy."

He did not say that. He just nodded. He just agreed.

So I set Paul free. I took nothing from him. It was all his, and I left it behind. He

9

asked only one thing of me — that I leave Charlotte, too. Temporarily. Leave her in her home, in the life she knew. We would co-parent, but she would live with him until I was settled and we could agree on a long-term arrangement.

I agreed.

The mature and responsible decision.

The naive and unbelievably stupid decision.

Two

As I hang from the exercise rings, two women turn to stare. I could tell myself they're wowed by my enviable upper-body strength, but their expressions are far less complimentary. That may have something to do with the fact that the rings are in a playground, and I'm dangling from them, knees pulled up so I don't scrape the ground.

It's Sunday. The end of my weekend with Charlotte. It's been six months since Paul and I split, and he's still not ready to discuss joint custody. I've begun to realize he never will be ready. I'm going to have to push him — with divorce proceedings and a custody battle. I'm not ready for that fight yet. But I'm getting there.

As I dangle from the rings, Charlotte hangs in front of me. "Ten, eight, nine, seven . . ."

"You keep going," I say.

"No! Mommy stay! Three, two —"

I drop onto my butt, and Charlotte lets out a squeal of laughter, her chubby legs kicking so hard one sneaker flies off.

Then she lets go. I catch her, and she giggles, wrenches out of my arms and tears off.

"Charlie, wait!"

As I race after her, scooping up her abandoned shoe, I hear the women behind me.

"Recapturing her lost childhood?"

"I'm not sure she ever left it. Look at her."

I let Charlotte braid my hair this morning, the result being exactly what you expect from a three-year-old, complete with crooked plastic barrettes. She also picked out my shirt, a ragged Minnie Mouse tee I only keep because she loves it. I brought a jacket for camouflage, but I'd discarded that when the blazing sun heated up a cool May day, with only a hint of Chicago's legendary winds blowing into our suburban city.

As I'm trying to remember where I left my jacket, Charlotte runs for the slide. I take off after her, and I help her onto the rungs. Then I climb behind her, mostly because it's the only way I can ensure she doesn't fall off the top or slide down backward. I sense eyes on me, I see bemused head shakes, and I feel the prickle of embarrassment.

I don't know how other parents do it. I honestly do not. They sit. They chat. They answer emails. They read books. And somehow, their children survive.

Motherhood does not come naturally to me. My own mother died when I was very young, and my father never remarried. I grew up on a string of army bases, cared for by whoever happened to be available. So when Paul and I decided to have a baby, I knew I needed to prepare. I did — with endless classes and books. Then Charlotte came along, and I felt as if I'd walked into a math exam after cramming for history.

When I used to confess my fears to Paul, he'd hug me and say, "You're doing awesome, Bree. Your daughter is bright and happy and healthy. What more could you want?"

What more could I want? To feel like *I'd* achieved that. Not like Charlotte managed to be all that in spite of me. Because of Paul.

Now I'm damned sure that when it comes time for a court to decide custody, Paul is not going to tell the judge that I'm "doing awesome."

So no more floundering. No more muddling through. No more being the "quirky" parent. I must be the most normal mom

13

possible. That means I need to learn how. Observe and assimilate.

When we head to the swings, I try to just stand behind Charlotte and push her, like other parents. That isn't what she wants, though. She wants me to swing beside her and see who can go highest.

Paul doesn't swing with Charlotte or climb the slide or hang from the rings. The very image makes me smile. Nor, however, would he be on a bench reading the paper or checking his phone. He stands close, keeping a watchful eye, ready to jump in if she needs him. And that's fine with Charlotte, who never asks or expects him to join in. Joining in is for Mommy.

I remember when I'd bring her back from the park with grass-stained knees and dirt-streaked face and hair that looked as if she stepped out of a wind tunnel.

"Someone had fun today," Paul would say.

"She skinned her knee again. I'm sorry. I don't know how that happens."

He laughs. "Because she's a little cyclone when she's with you. She knows Daddy can't keep up." He swings her into his arms. "Did you have fun, sweetheart?" he asks, as they walk away, Charlotte babbling a mile a minute.

If I fretted later, he'd say, "She had fun. That's what matters, Bree. Skinned knees

14

heal. It's good to see her active."

Does he still think that? Or does he remember those skinned knees and see them as a sign that I hadn't watched our daughter closely enough?

"Mommy, jump!"

I react without thinking, swinging high and then jumping. I hit the ground in a crouch, and as I bounce to my feet, her gales of laughter ring out.

"Mommy, catch!"

Again, I turn on autopilot, my arms fly up as Charlotte launches herself from the swing.

I do catch her.

I always do.

Always, always, always.

This is what I want to be for you, baby. The mother who will always catch you. The mother who knows what dangers you face, and will be there to stop them. To fix the problems, even when I cause them myself.

"Is it time for tea?" I ask as I set her on the ground.

"Yes!"

As we drink our apple juice and munch cookies, I watch the parents in the playground, analyzing how far they let their kids run without giving chase, what they allow their children to do without interfering.

I gaze longingly at the groups of chatting parents. As much as I love playing with my child, I feel like I should be *there,* getting the support and answers I need. I've done all the things that parenting blogs recommend for meeting others — *join mom-tot groups, hang around at the playground, just put yourself out there!* — but I always feel like I used to when I switched schools midterm. The cliques had already formed, those doors slammed shut.

When I first had Charlotte, I tried joining the suburban mommies in our neighborhood, but their life experience was a million miles from mine. They seemed to sense my "otherness," like a bevy of swans with a goose intent on sneaking into their ranks. As invitations to playdates dried up — and my own were refused — I saw myself condemning Charlotte to the same kind of life. An outsider by association.

That changed after I left. Apparently, the mommies who didn't have time for me had plenty of it for my poor abandoned child and her doting single daddy.

As I gaze across the playground, I notice another woman by herself. She's with a little boy near a patch of forest, maybe twenty feet away. They're playing a hiding game, where one of them tucks away a small object and the other finds it.

At first, I think the woman must be a sitter or older sister. I'm thirty, and she looks nearly a decade younger, the boy maybe five. But then he gives a delighted shriek, saying, "Found it, Mama! That was a good spot."

They both seem to be enjoying the game, and I take note. Charlotte would love it, and it's definitely a more dignified way of playing with my child.

Speaking of dignity, when we finish our tea, Charlotte wants to do cartwheels. I try to just help her, but she insists I demonstrate. I do a double, ending up by the woods, and as I thump down, the little boy says, "Whoa, did you see that, Mama?"

"Very cool," his mother says, with a careful smile. "You must have been a cheerleader."

I laugh. "Not exactly. But thanks."

"Can you do that, Mama?" her son asks.

Now it's her turn to laugh, relaxing as she squeezes his shoulder. "I could when I was your age. Not since then, though. I was *definitely* not a cheerleader."

She passes me a smile, and there's a spark of connection as we both look over at a gaggle of suburban mommies, as if to say *they* were probably cheerleaders, but not

17

us. Never us.

She isn't much older than I first thought. Maybe twenty-three. Slender with a blond ponytail and no makeup except for thick black eyeliner. Is that eyeliner a remnant of another life? She wears long sleeves, but one is pushed up, showing what looks like the ghosts of old track marks. Dark circles underscore her eyes, and there's a strained, distant look in them, as if she's exhausted by the stresses of what might be single motherhood, given the lack of a wedding band.

"You do car-wheel," Charlotte says to the woman. "Mommy show."

The woman smiles. "Not me, hon. My body doesn't do that anymore."

"Can I try?" her son asks.

"I show!" Charlotte says.

We stand and watch Charlotte try to instruct the boy in a proper cartwheel while I give pointers. I tread a fine line here. I don't want to seem like the new girl at school, puppy-eager for attention, even if that's how I feel. I glance at the other woman, and then I look at the poised suburban mommies on the benches, and it doesn't matter if I'd been one of them six months ago. I'm not anymore and, really, I never was, even when I wore the title.

I see this young woman, with her old needle scars and her worn jeans and her shabby sneakers and the way her face glows every time her gaze lights on her son, and she's the mother I connect to.

Still I am careful. Years of new-kid-in-class life has taught me how to tread this line. Snatches of conversation mixed with quips and laughs as I show her son how to do a cartwheel.

I'm holding up his legs when her phone rings. She looks down at the screen and blanches. Then she murmurs, "Sorry, I have to get this."

She steps away to take the call. I can't tell what she's saying — she isn't speaking English — but her tone tells me enough, rising from anger to alarm.

She keeps moving away, lowering her voice while keeping her gaze on her son.

Finally I bend in front of the boy and say, "We should go, so your mom can finish her call. Tell her we said goodbye. It was very nice meeting you, and I hope to see you both again."

When I extend a hand, his thin face lights up in a smile. He shakes my hand vigorously, with a mature "Nice meeting you, too."

Charlotte shakes his hand as she giggles a

goodbye. Then we quickly gather our things and leave.

THREE

Two days later, I'm taking my usual lunch-time jog in the park where I played with Charlotte on Sunday. After a couple of laps, I slow near the playground and circle to a forlorn bench, too far from the equipment to be of any use to watchful parents.

I put up my leg and begin stretching. As I do, I tug out my earbuds so I can listen to three mothers sitting nearby.

Eavesdrop. Spy. Learn.

As I stretch, a middle-aged jogger pulls over to do the same, sharing my bench. I keep my attention on the lesson unfolding ahead.

I contemplate the trio of moms. They don't seem to be watching their children at all, engrossed as they are in the scandal of another parent who let her child play with an iPad. Is that a problem? I have several educational apps on my phone, and Charlotte and I play them together. I *thought* that was a good thing, but —

A child shrieks. I wheel to see two kids fighting over the slide. As I peer around for the parents, the kids work it out on their own, and I suppose that's the way to handle it — watch and see if they can resolve it before interfering.

The war for the slide ends, but it calls my attention to a boy swinging by himself. It looks like the boy from Sunday, the one we'd shown how to do cartwheels. I squint. Yes, that's definitely him. His mom is nowhere in sight.

The boy jumps off the swing and starts gazing around. Then he heads for the path. Leaving the safety of the playground. I look around anxiously, hoping Mom will notice.

"You're doing your quadriceps stretches wrong."

I jump and glance over to see the middle-aged guy who took up stretching at my bench.

"You want to do them like this," he says, and proceeds to demonstrate . . . with a hamstring stretch.

I know better than to point out his mistake, so I murmur a thank-you and glance back at the boy.

He's still walking. Getting farther from the equipment, with no sign of anyone giving chase. So I do.

I stay at a slow jog, no panic, just keeping an eye on the child. Mom will notice. Mom will come after him, and she doesn't need me making her feel like she's failed her parental duties. So I stay back, subtly watchful.

"You hit the ground a little hard."

The middle-aged guy jogs up beside me.

"You have really good form," he says, "but you're hitting the ground too hard. You'll injure your knees. I've seen you before — we run at about the same time — and I thought I should mention it."

Don't get distracted. Remember the boy.

I turn my attention back. The child's gone.

Damn it, *no.* Where —

He appears, walking out from behind a trash can. That's a relief. The not-such-a-relief part? He's heading straight for the parking lot.

Where *is* his mother?

It doesn't matter. As much as I hate to embarrass another parent, that's a busy lot with an even busier thoroughfare beside it.

I kick my jog up to a run.

"You could just say no thanks," the guy shouts after me, and then mutters, "Bitch," under his breath.

23

Aubrey Finch, making friends wherever she goes.

Forget him. The important thing is the boy, and in that moment of distraction, I've lost sight of him again.

Tires screech, and my chest seizes as I look about wildly. A vehicle has slammed on its brakes in the parking lot, and I can just make out a roof rack over the sea of parked vehicles.

I spot the boy. He's still at the edge of the lot, standing on his tiptoes, as if looking for the source of the screeching tires.

A voice calls from the direction of the vehicle. It's a single word, but I can't make it out. The boy hears, though, and starts running toward it.

Seeing him dash into that jammed parking lot, I cringe and have to chomp down on a shout of warning. Fortunately, the lot is silent except for the rumble of what I can now see is a big SUV.

Mom must have gone to fetch the car, unable to find a spot in the lot. She's told him he could swing for a few more minutes while she brought the car around. Not the choice I'd make but —

A sharp boyish yelp of surprise. Then, "No!"

I burst into a run as a man's low voice

says, "Get in," and "Stop that."

The boy shouts, "No! Let me go!" Then he screams "Mama!" at the top of his lungs as I run full out.

A door slams shut, muffling the boy's cries.

An engine revs.

I grit my teeth and will my body to go faster, just a little faster, damn it.

The SUV takes off, speeding through the lot, and all I see is that damned roof rack.

Faster! Harder! I hear my father's bark. *Dig deeper. Work harder. You can do better, Bree.*

You can always do better.

The SUV has stopped at the roadway, engine idling as it waits for a break in the heavy traffic. If I can just get past the next row of cars, I'll be able to get a plate number.

I jog across the lane. A solid flow of traffic still blocks the exit. I can do this. Twenty feet more, and I'll have a clear sight line to the SUV, and there is no way it can pull away before that.

Get my phone out to snap pictures. Even if I can't see the license plate, I can enhance the photo.

The SUV is just ahead. I lift my phone while fumbling to turn on the camera. It's fine. Steady traffic. I have time. I —

A horn blasts. A long, solid blast.

Tires squeal.

The SUV cuts into traffic and roars off.

I race toward the road. No time for a photo. Just get a look at the license. The SUV is pulling away, the rear bumper visible, the license . . .

The license plate is mud-splattered and unreadable.

The vehicle then. Stop squinting at the plate, and get the vehicle make and model —

The SUV cuts into the next lane before I can see the emblem. It's a large SUV. Dark blue . . . or black . . .

Not good enough. Not good enough at all.

I keep going, but the SUV is already at the next light, turning left and . . .

And it's gone.

I inhale and look down, feeling the weight of the cell phone in my hand.

Uh, yes. Cell phone?

I hit numbers as I head back toward the park.

"Nine-one-one, what's your emergency?"

"Kidnap —" I struggle for breath, like I've run a marathon. "Kidnapping. I witnessed a kidnapping."

26

"Slow down, ma'am, and repeat that please?"

"I just witnessed a kidnapping. I saw a boy pulled into a car — an SUV. A dark-colored SUV on . . ." *Street. What is the street?* "On Cliff View. Near Grant Park. The children's playground. There's a parking lot off Cliff View into Grant Park, right next to the playground. It happened there. Just now."

"You witnessed a young man —"

"Boy, child, maybe four or five years old."

"A child being pulled into a dark SUV in the parking lot . . ."

The dispatcher continues rhyming off the information, and I want to shout, *Yes, yes to all of that, now just get someone here.*

When the woman finishes, I say, calmly, "Yes, that's right. Please hurry. They just left."

"I've already dispatched a car, ma'am. Can you remain on the scene, please?"

"I'll be here. In the playground. I know what his mom looks like. I'm going to find her. You can reach me at this number or just tell the officers I'm wearing a gray sweat suit, and I have a dark brown ponytail. My name is Aubrey Finch."

The dispatcher signs off, and I'm on the move again.

27

I pass two mothers leaving with children and I can't help wishing they could have been five minutes sooner, extra witnesses who might have seen more.

Someone *must* have seen more. There will be a CCTV camera or a street passerby or maybe even that guy who pestered me about my "form" — he can't have gone far.

Someone will have seen something.

I reach the playground and scan it for the boy's mother, expecting to see her anxiously searching. She must have turned her back, maybe talking to another parent or engrossed in a book.

It only takes a moment.

Just last month, in the mall, I let go of Charlotte's hand to adjust my shopping bag, and she disappeared. It only took two seconds to spot her dark curls bobbing toward the pet shop, but even as I raced toward her, I imagined showing up at Paul's doorstep and saying, "I lost her."

I lost our baby.

Now I am about to inflict that hell on another woman.

I saw your baby get taken. I know, you only looked away for a moment.

But it only takes a moment.

I can't see the boy's mother. The playground is even busier now. I spot a blond woman reading a book and take a step her way, only to have her look up and reveal the face of a grandmother.

Another blond woman stands at the side, but she has a baby carriage.

Another blonde, heavyset and tending to a girl Charlotte's age.

I spin, skimming faces as they blur before me.

"Are you okay?" a voice asks.

I look into the concerned face of a young dad. I nod and walk away, searching the crowd.

Then I spot her. Off to the far side by that patch of forest, a woman with a blond ponytail hurries from tree to tree as she calls for a child.

As I jog over, I rehearse what I'll say.

Should I be the one to do it? The police will be here any second.

No, I'm a fellow mom, and we've met, if briefly. The news should come from me.

I take a deep breath and walk up behind the increasingly frantic woman. I open my mouth and —

"Found me!" a little girl squeals as she launches herself from behind a bush.

The woman scoops her up. "Don't *ever* take off on me like that, Amber."

"I was hiding."

"You need to *tell* me you're going to hide. You can't —"

The woman nearly crashes into me. I murmur, "Excuse me," and she continues past, still scolding the child.

"Ms. Finch?" a voice says.

I turn to see a uniformed officer. He's nearing retirement age. Bulldog-faced, his eyes and jowls and belly drooping, like someone who's been pulling double shifts all his life and has resigned himself to permanent exhaustion. His nameplate reads COOPER.

Three younger officers follow — two men and a woman — but they stay back as Cooper approaches me.

"Oh, thank God," I say. "I can't find the boy's mother anywhere."

"It's okay, ma'am. We're here now. You said you saw a boy taken from the playground?"

"No, the parking lot." I point. "He was on the swings and wandered that way."

I explain. Slow and relaxed and careful. Step by step, despite the voice in my head screaming that they need to find that SUV, find it now.

This is how they *will* find it. By me staying calm and explaining.

When I finish, Cooper says, "So you saw

30

him here with his mother, and she didn't follow him when he walked off."

"No, I only saw *her* on Sunday, when I spoke to them both."

Cooper's brows shoot up. "You were jogging through the park Sunday and saw them then, too?"

"I was here with my daughter on Sunday. I jog on my lunch hours. I work nearby."

"Describe the boy, please," he says to me. "In as much detail as possible. We'll ask around, see who saw him, figure out where his mom is."

"He's school age, but just barely. About this tall." I motion. "Thin. White. Short blond hair."

He pauses. When I don't continue, he says, "Anything more *specific?*" He points to another boy, fair haired, about the same age. "How would he be different from that kid? Taller? Thinner? Hair darker, lighter, shorter, longer?"

"Thinner in the face. Maybe a bit taller."

Cooper points to another child, who also looks similar. In this neighborhood, tow-headed white kids are as common as German-built cars. As I struggle to remember distinguishing features, my heart hammers. What if it *wasn't* the boy from Sunday? I only saw him from a distance today, and several of the kids Cooper points out do look like him.

That doesn't matter. A child is still missing. Just limit my description to what I remember of the boy I saw *today.*

"What's he wearing?" Cooper asks.

I pull up a mental picture, and . . . it's blank.

Stop that. I saw him. I *chased* him. Surely I can remember —

"Jeans," I blurt. "Jeans and sneakers and a T-shirt."

Cooper casts a pointed look at the playground, where nearly every child is in jeans and sneakers, and at least half are in tees.

"The shirt was blue. A medium shade. Like that." I point to a woman's blouse.

"And his mother?"

"Young, early twenties. She's blond and wears her hair in a ponytail. Well, she did Sunday and . . ." Deep breath. "Just focus on the boy, please. Even if it's not the same child, I did see a child get pulled into an SUV."

Cooper nods. "Okay." He turns to the officers. "Don't let anyone leave before speaking to you."

As they walk toward the playground, he says, "You mentioned being on a lunch break. Are you late for work?"

32

"Yes, but I can stay —"

"We have this. I'll take your contact information and be in touch."

"I just work over at the library. It's a few blocks away. If you need to stop by, I'm there until five."

"A phone number and home address will be fine, Ms. Finch. Thank you for your help. We'll take it from here."

FOUR

The police don't show up or call during my shift. I have to grab a few groceries on the way home, but I keep it quick, in case they stop by. As I enter my building, I'm well aware of how it will look to Officer Cooper. My apartment is affordable. Very affordable. I could do better, even with my part-time job, but I want a down payment on a condo before I fight for Charlotte, so I took a cheap downtown apartment while squirreling away the extra.

I do have money, from before, but I can't access much of that. Not without raising questions I don't dare answer.

I've lived in worse places, and I'm comfortable here. There are a few veterans on disability that I run errands for, while cursing the system that put them into this situation.

Once inside, I tidy my apartment. It's never bad — I grew up fixing my bed the moment I rolled out of it. But I want to make the best impression possible, overcoming any negative one left by the old building itself.

I'm washing the breakfast dishes when a knock comes at the door.

I open it to find Officer Cooper and the female coworker who was with him earlier. I invite them in and offer refreshments. They don't accept the latter. We sit in the living room, and Cooper looks around.

"Is your daughter here?" he asks.

"She lives with her dad."

I catch their reactions and wince. I need to stop saying that. I really do. *She's with her dad today.* That's the way to phrase it. Otherwise, I get this — both of them looking up sharply, like I've just confessed to armed robbery.

Cooper's brow furrows, as if the concept of a three-year-old living with her father confuses him. The younger officer — Jackson — compresses her lips.

When Jackson's gaze scans the apartment again, I say, "Yes, this isn't the sort of place I want my daughter full-time, which is why she's with her dad on weekdays. It's a recent separation. I'm saving up for something better."

Her expression judges me for my decision.

35

I bristle at that. Kids *do* live in this building. Sometimes you don't have a choice.

I do, though. I live here — and bring my daughter here — voluntarily.

"Have you found the boy?" I ask.

"No one is missing a child," Jackson says.

"What?" I say.

"Some parents said they saw boys matching your description," Cooper says. "They just didn't see one wander off."

"Because it was busy. A packed playground with plenty of kids who look like him."

Jackson opens her mouth, but a look from Cooper stops her.

"I know what I saw," I say.

"A boy pulled into an SUV," Cooper says.

I relax. "Yes."

"You heard someone call to the boy from an SUV. He ran to it. *Willingly* ran to it. Yes?"

"Right, but then he freaked out. He shouted 'no' and began screaming for his mom as a man dragged him into the vehicle."

"Is it possible . . . ?" He shifts on the sofa. "You have a little girl. I'm sure you've needed to carry her to the car once or twice, when she's overtired, overstimulated, kicking and screaming bloody murder."

"That's not —"

36

"Kids love the playground. They hate to leave it. There can be screaming. A good parent doesn't drag their kid into the car like that. Unfortunately, questionable parenting isn't illegal."

"That's not what it looked like at all. Are you sure no one saw *anything*?"

"A couple of parents saw *you*," says Jackson. "They noticed you jog past. With a man."

"What? Oh, right. I wasn't *with* him. He was just . . ."

"Just what?" Jackson says when I trail off.

Hitting on me. That's what I was going to say. Then I realize how it sounds. *Yeah, so this guy told me I was stretching wrong and running wrong, but I'm sure he was just coming on to me. Really.*

These officers already think I'm delusional. *That* won't help.

"He was talking about stretches," I say. "I was busy watching the little boy, so he took off." I stop and look at Cooper. "He would have seen the boy. He must have. He said he jogs through the park at lunchtime, too. I could —"

"Parents said they see *you* there quite often," Jackson cuts in. "Hanging around the benches, watching them, watching their kids."

37

That throws me, and it takes me a second to recover and say, "Yes, like I said, I work nearby, and I jog through the park. I do my stretches near the playground. At the benches."

"There are other benches in the park, Ms. Finch."

I cut off a snippy reply and say, evenly, "I used to be a stay-at-home mom, and I miss being with my daughter all day. Stretching in the playground helps me cope."

I'm baring more of myself here than I like . . . and it doesn't cut me one iota of slack with Jackson, as her eyes narrow.

"You make some of the other parents uncomfortable," she says.

"What?" I've misheard her. I must have.

"How would you feel, if you took your kid to the playground, and you kept seeing this woman there, hanging around, with no child in tow."

My cheeks blaze. "It's not like that. I stretch near the playground sometimes. That's all."

"And you watch the kids."

"I . . . I guess I do. While I stretch. I just . . . I enjoy seeing kids play."

"Do you know how often we hear that, Ms. Finch? Every time we question a pedophile for hanging around a playground."

My heart slams into my throat. "Wh-what? No. I have *never* —"

"No one's accusing you of that." Cooper glares at his young partner. "We're just pointing out how it could look."

"And that if you were a man, this would be a very different conversation," Jackson says. "Personally, I don't think gender should play a role in how we handle these complaints."

"There was a *complaint?*" My voice squeaks.

"No," Cooper says. "A couple of people mentioned it, but we all know parents can be overly cautious. You might want to run somewhere else, though, in future."

Humiliation swallows my voice, and it takes a moment for me to say, "Yes, of course."

Cooper continues, but I don't hear it over the blood pounding in my ears. I always figured I was invisible, just a jogger stretching at a bench. It never occurred to me that anyone would notice, let alone remember me from one day to the next.

I made other parents nervous.

They saw me as a threat.

Did they talk about me? Whisper warnings to each other?

Have you seen that woman with the dark

ponytail? She comes by every lunch and pretends to be stretching, but she's watching us. Eavesdropping on our conversations. Staring at our children.

I'll never be able to set foot in that park again.

"Ms. Finch?"

I struggle to refocus. This is about the boy, not me. Remember that.

"I know what I saw," I say. "And it wasn't an angry dad hauling his kid into a car."

Jackson gives Cooper a look, as if waiting for him to respond. When he doesn't, she opens her mouth, but he cuts in with, "Either way, we are taking it seriously, Ms. Finch. We put an alert out for the SUV."

"An AMBER Alert?"

"Without a parent reporting a child missing, we cannot do that. We need to know who we would be looking for."

"It's been five hours," Jackson says. "It's not as if Mom left the park by herself, forgetting she brought a kid."

"We *are* investigating, Ms. Finch," Cooper says. "We wouldn't ignore something like this." He pushes to his feet. "If a child is reported missing, we'll let you know."

FIVE

After they leave, I sink into the sofa, ignoring the broken spring that pokes back. Did I make a mistake? My gut insists that I know what I saw. And what I saw was a child being dragged, screaming, into an SUV. A young child who'd been wandering alone in the park. That isn't normal.

Not normal, yes. But maybe like Officer Cooper said, it was just bad parenting. Charlotte has had tantrums. She's three — it happens. Once, when she got overtired, she threw a fit in a restaurant, deciding the world was a cruel and unfair place if they didn't have sprinkles for her ice cream. I carried her to the car while Paul quickly paid the bill. I remember hurrying through the restaurant, dodging glares. Then I got outside and heard her gasp and discovered that in trying to quiet her, I'd been pressing her face into my shoulder. Forcibly silencing her.

When I realized what I'd done, I nearly threw up in the parking lot. It took everything I had to wait for Paul to reach the car before I blurted my confession.

He laughs softly and hugs me. "Charlie's fine. Everyone's just tired. And hey, it did make her stop crying, right?"

On top of the guilt came the shame. What if someone saw me and thought I was intentionally smothering my child to keep her quiet?

I remember another time, when Charlotte smacked a kid in the playroom at McDonald's. Horrified, I'd hauled her out while apologizing to the boy's grandfather. After we got home, I found a red circle around her wrist. Not only had I been hurting her as I marched her along, but she hadn't complained. Had it seemed as if I was dragging Charlotte from the playroom? Had that grandfather watched me, and shaken his head, thinking, *Well, I know where that poor child gets it from?*

What if *that* was all I saw this morning? A frustrated dad forcibly putting his protesting son into their vehicle.

That could be what I saw.

But it doesn't feel like it.

It just doesn't.

■ ■ ■ ■

An hour later, I get a call from Paul. He has a client emergency.

"Is there any way you can take Charlotte for the evening?"

"You don't ever have to ask," I say. "Even if I was working, I'd find a way to swing it."

"Thank you."

I tense hearing that. It's genuine gratitude, which is the problem. He knows I'm eager to take Charlotte any chance I get, but he still acts as if each extremely rare circumstance is some great favor. I want a casual "Thanks, Bree," perfunctory and off hand. I don't want to keep score.

"She can stay the night," I say. "I'll drop her off at daycare tomorrow."

Silence.

"Unless that's a problem . . ." I say.

"No, no. That would be great. Saves me worrying about how late I get back tonight."

I'm waiting downstairs when Paul arrives. He sees me out front and motions he'll pull into the lot. He insists on that, as if dropping her at the curb smacks of abandonment. Also, there is a clear NO STOPPING sign in front of the building, and Paul always obeys the law. Which is one reason I never told him about my past.

I don't wait indoors, because Paul has only ever seen my building from the outside, where it looks like a stately old apartment complex in the city core. Oxford began life as a small town before exploding into a bedroom community. What remains of that original town is well-preserved old buildings — like the library where I work — and shabbier ones like this. Paul grew up and works in Chicago, which means he doesn't know Oxford well enough to tell the good areas from the . . . less good. He parks his Mercedes across the lot from my decade-old Corolla. I think he does that on purpose, so no one will see the disparity and judge him for it. They shouldn't. The Mercedes used to be mine. He bought it when Charlotte was born, wanting a newer, safer car for us. When I left, I took his Corolla instead. That was fair. That was right. Which didn't keep him from acting like I'd thrown the keys in his face.

"I bought that car for you, Bree."

"You bought it for Charlie. Since you have her now, you keep the car."

He hung up on me after that. Didn't slam the phone down. Didn't curse. Just disconnected and never said another word about it.

I open the door to get Charlotte as quickly as I can, so I don't waste a moment of our time together. I remember when I used to fist-pump every time she went down for a nap, as giddy as a kid granted an unexpected recess. Now, when she naps, I sit in the room, reading with one eye, watching her with the other, waiting for her to wake up again.

As I open the door, Paul comes around the car. He looks . . . like Paul. Nothing new. Nothing different. Every time I see him, there's a moment when I forget we're separated, and I only see the face I woke up to every morning. Familiar and comfortable. Then I remember that I'm not his wife anymore. Not his wife, not his friend, not even an ally in raising our child.

I'm the woman who could take Charlotte from him.

I'm the enemy.

He looks tired. He always does these days, and guilt stabs me. Anger chases the guilt, though. I'm here, anytime he needs me, eager to take our daughter and give him a break.

I go to lift Charlotte out, but he waves me away. When he pulls her out of her seat, I see his expression, and I slingshot back to those times he came home from work a little irritable, a little distant, and my first thought had always been *He knows.*

He knows about me.

Which was ridiculous, of course. If my past ever did reach Paul, he wouldn't be coming home "a little irritable," and telling me, "It's nothing, just work." He'd be scooping up Charlotte and making a beeline for the nearest hotel.

Now, when I see that expression, there is only a split second of the old fear. Then I realize the far more likely truth.

Someone told him about the boy in the park.

Someone at the police department recognized my name and knew my husband was a defense attorney and contacted him. Told him that I reported a kidnapped child . . . where, evidently, no child has been kidnapped.

And I am okay with that. I see him, see the set of his mouth, and all I can think is *Good.* If Paul knows, he can help. He's a lawyer. He has contacts. I will explain what I saw, and even if he doesn't quite believe me, it'll be in his best interests to prove his ex isn't delusional.

"Is everything okay?" I ask carefully.

He spots something on the passenger seat and heaves a sigh of relief. It's Matt, Charlotte's beloved stuffed rat. I made the mistake of watching *The Princess Bride* with her last year, and she's obsessed, both with the movie and the ROUSes — rodents of unusual size. Other kids have teddy bears and puppies; mine has a stuffed rat.

"I thought I forgot him," Paul says. "That would have been a crisis."

He slides me a smile, and when he does . . . God, I hate that smile. I hate how it makes me feel. I hate *that* it makes me feel. The first time we met, I will fully admit that I dismissed Paul. He was just a very average guy, the sort I never really noticed. Then he smiled, and I saw more. I paid attention, and I never stopped paying attention; even now, when he smiles at me, I stop and I stare, and I feel.

I feel so much.

He hefts Charlotte and glances at me. "Are you sure this is okay? Dropping her off?"

"Absolutely. Go save the world. I've got this."

I find myself leaning forward to kiss his cheek. At the last second, I manage to divert and shut the car door instead, as if that's what I'd been leaning in to do. How long does it take for this to stop? For the neural pathways of my brain to reroute. To see Paul and hear his voice and smell his aftershave and not tumble back in time, ready to kiss his cheek or lean my head on his shoulder or tell him all my troubles.

Well, not all my troubles. Never all of them.

He lifts Charlotte and kisses her cheek before passing her to me. "What time do you work in the morning?"

"Nine. Like I said, I can get her to daycare."

He passes over Charlie's bag. "Why don't we meet up for breakfast first. Charlie would like that. And we can . . ." He shrugs. "Talk."

Does that mean he *has* heard about the incident today? Or does he really just want to talk? I would love that. I really would, and I should be able to look at his expression and tell whether this is a "we have a problem" talk or just an invitation to breakfast. But we never developed that bond, the kind where couples finish each other's sentences. I loved him. Still do. Yet there had been a surface quality to our marriage. My monsters lurk in the depths, so I swim in shallow waters, and if I insisted on staying there, I couldn't dive deeper *with* him.

48

I do want to talk to him about the boy. I want his advice so badly. Yet if he doesn't know, should I tell him? What if he uses it against me in the custody battle, as proof that I'm not quite stable?

I cannot take that chance. The boy is important, but my daughter is more important. I will not jeopardize my future with her to enlist Paul's help.

"I take it that's a no?" he says as his smile fades.

"I —"

His phone rings. He glances at it. "My client. Probably wondering where I am. I should go."

I open my mouth to say breakfast would be fine, and yes, let's do that. But he's already saying goodbye to Charlotte and then walking around the car, without another word to me.

Six

I circle the daycare lot, waiting for a spot. Two have cleared so far, only to have other drivers whip in while I was figuring out which of us had been there first. Evidently, not me.

I check the car clock. Five minutes to drop Charlotte off, twenty to drive to work, five to get at my post. Exactly enough time . . . if I find a parking spot in the next ten seconds.

"Mommy? I has cough. See?" Charlotte gives two quick — and obviously fake — hacks. "I stay home with you?"

I wish you could, baby. I really wish you could.

"Mommy works now, remember, Charlie?"

There! A spot. I start turning in . . . just as a toddler darts from between parked cars. I hit the brakes so hard I slam into the seat belt. The car stops twenty feet from the child, but I still squeeze my eyes shut, catching my breath as my heart pounds.

Careful. Always be careful.

It only takes a moment.

Another car ducks into the empty spot.

"Damn it," I mutter.

"Dammit," Charlotte chirps. "Dammit!"

"No, baby. That's not a good word. Mommy —"

Spot!

I snag it. Out of the car in two seconds. Two more, and Charlotte is on my hip as I sprint for the door.

An exiting father holds it open. I race through with thanks.

I couldn't sleep last night. I'd been stressed over the missing boy. After a night of tossing and turning, I'd woken early to go online, hoping for news that a child . . .

Hoping for news that a child was missing? That sounds horrible. Of course I hope to see he's been found. That's the ideal situation. A boy was temporarily missing, but now he's home. Yet if that wasn't the case, then yes, I hoped for proof that an investigation had been launched.

When I didn't find it, I kept searching, digging deeper, calling on skills I hadn't used in so many years, cursing my crappy computer as I hunted.

51

No, no, Paul, I don't need a fancy laptop. I can barely use email.

Liar, liar, pants on fire.

I searched online until the last possible moment before getting Charlotte up. I managed to get her outside with just enough time to drop her off and get to work. Then, as I buckled Charlotte into her gazillion-point car seat . . . I realized she'd dropped Matt in the apartment hall.

For one moment, I had wondered if I could just go grab it. Leave her locked in the car and run back inside. The impulse only lasted a second, shut down by a wave of horror, but the memory still shames me.

I jog down the daycare hallway, ignoring the looks from other parents. Someone has jacked up the building's heat. Sweat beads on my forehead, and the smell of a loaded diaper makes my stomach regret that wolfed-down breakfast muffin.

As I run, Charlotte giggles on my hip. When I plunk her onto the floor, though, her giggles evaporate.

"I has cough." Big brown eyes look up into mine. Two more fake hacks.

"You shouldn't bring her if she's sick," a mother says as she walks by.

"She's not really —"

The other woman is gone, judgment rendered.

Charlotte's hand reaches for mine. "No go, Mommy. Please."

A dart of frustration, quickly squelched. If I'm running late, that's on me.

I bend. "Charlie, if you really are sick, then I *will* stay home. But I'll have to cancel our princess tea tomorrow, and we'll do it another time, just to be safe."

She straightens. "All better."

I ruffle her hair. "Excellent. Then we shall have tea tomorrow. Mommy and Charlie in their new princess dresses."

I take her hand. Then I spin and say, "Oh, wait! You don't *have* a princess dress."

"Yes!" Charlotte squeals. "Blue like Princess Buttercup. We buy."

"Are you sure? I don't remember buying a blue dress. Now, there was a pink one . . ."

"Pink? Nooo." Her face screws up.

"Oh, I'm sure it was pink. Bright, bright pink."

I continue teasing Charlotte as I lead her inside. The distraction works right up to the moment where I hug her goodbye and her arms death-grip my neck, soft face pressed against my cheek.

I swallow. *Don't feel guilty. The moment you leave, she's fine. You know that.*

53

"Tomorrow," I say, as the daycare worker takes Charlotte's hand. "I'll pick you up tomorrow for the princess tea. Daddy said you can wear your dress all day."

Charlotte nods and lets the worker lead her away. With each step, she glances over her shoulder, puppy eyes finding me.

She *will* be fine. I remember the first time I brought her, when she clung and cried. I got as far as the door before guilt forced me back. I think that might have been the one thing that could have sent me back to Paul, begging for reconciliation. I'd wanted to be a stay-at-home mom until Charlotte was in school. If she suffered because I left, it'd have been a reason to go home.

No, let's be honest. It'd have been an *excuse.* A chance to say I made a mistake and beg Paul for another chance.

That first day, I'd run back into the daycare, ready to scoop her up and take her home . . . and instead found her happily playing with a little boy, already chattering away.

So I know now she will be fine. That doesn't mean I can turn and walk away while she's in sight. Every time I bring her, I stand here, and I suffer those sad eyes, and I remind myself that this was my choice.

I wait until she's gone. Then I hurry back into the hall.

SEVEN

I'm at work, in the central library, a gorgeous period building where every whisper echoes under the domed ceiling. When my phone vibrates with an incoming text, I swear people in the stacks jump and spin, as if a swarm of bees is launching an attack from the circulation desk.

The text is from Paul. I don't check it, just tuck the phone away. My supervisor, Ingrid, looks over, her long face drooping with disapproval.

"Sorry," I say, and continue checking in returned books.

With a sniff, she swoops from behind the library desk and trills, "Can I help you find something?" to a hovering patron.

I texted Ingrid to say I'd be a few minutes late. Texted from the first red light . . . and then glanced up to see a cruiser right beside me, the officer staring my way. I dropped the phone so fast it fell between the seats, and I spent three extra minutes in the library parking lot fishing it out.

I did not, however, get a ticket, thank God. That would have been the capper to my morning. Let's just say it wouldn't be my first traffic violation. That's actually how I met Paul. I'd worked in the ground-floor bookstore of his law firm's offices, and he'd seen me get a ticket out front. He'd suggested I fight it. It became a cute "how we met" story.

He's a lawyer . . . and I needed one. Ha-ha.

As it turned out, that's also the story of our marriage. The competent professional and his screwup bride.

My running-late text hasn't cut me any slack with Ingrid. Nothing does, ever since she found out I'm a noncustodial parent.

"How does a mother lose custody of her child?" I heard her whisper to Nancy, another librarian. "Everyone knows the courts favor the mom, no matter what."

There hasn't *been* a court hearing. I don't explain that to Ingrid. It would only lead to a bigger question: *What kind of mom voluntarily gives up her daughter?*

A good mother, I thought. Mature and fair.

Or stupid. Naive and unbelievably stupid.

My phone vibrates, reminding me of that

waiting text.

Ten feet away, Ingrid still hears it. Before I can apologize, she waves in annoyance.

"Take your break," she says. "And leave *that* in the staff room."

As I close the door to the tiny staff room, the smell of stale leftovers envelops me. I make a coffee to cover the stink as I check the text from Paul. It's nothing more than a check-in, making sure all went well this morning.

I send back a thumbs-up. Then I pause. Pause. Deep breath as I send another text.

Me: Breakfast would have been OK. Just caught me off guard. Sorry if it sounded like I was hesitating.

He sends his own thumbs-up, and I spend way too long staring at that, trying to interpret it. Paul is not an emoji guy. I'm actually surprised he knows where to find them on his phone. Is he saying it's fine, and he understands, or . . .

I rub my eyes. *Stop, Aubrey. It's an emoji, not the Enigma code. Just stop.*

I set a timer on my phone, so I won't linger past my break. Then I get to work on the old staff room computer, my fingers flying over the keyboard as I run a few lines of machine code to cover my virtual footprints.

I'm hacking the police department's internal email system.

I glance at my phone and imagine saying that to Paul. Imagine the look on his face. There would be, of course, a moment of horror that I'd suggest such a clearly criminal action. But that would last only a moment before he'd laugh, certain I was joking. Hacking? His *wife,* who had to ask him to install security updates on her laptop?

Liar, liar . . .

It hasn't been easy, pretending I barely know how to operate a computer. That's part of the price I pay, though, for my choices straight from the *How to Disappear* handbook. Distance yourself from all aspects of your former life, particularly those you excelled in.

The first thing I ever hacked was a radio. It started with my dad bringing home a couple of walkie-talkies. Surplus from base.

"They don't work that well, but I know a guy who can fix them up, give you and your friends something to play with."

Which was great, except that Dad wasn't always quick to fulfill promises. He got busy and remembering to get the radios fixed wasn't a high priority.

So I did it myself. I wrangled schematics from an indulgent engineer on base, and I opened up the radios. At first, Dad was as amused as that engineer. Sure, let the kid take a shot at it — curiosity is good. Then I not only fixed them, but made them as good as new. As for using them to hack into a secure military frequency, well, that came later.

Once Dad realized I had a talent for electronics, he brought me things to fix, things to take apart. And the guy who wouldn't stop working long enough to play cards with me would watch me tinker for hours. He'd give me a look, like he couldn't quite figure out where this little girl came from. For the first time in my life, I was a revelation to him. The more fascinated he was by my talent, the harder I worked to improve it.

I still remember the day he brought me my first computer. I came home from school, and it was there, and he waved at it, much like one might wave at a troll crouching in the corner.

"You know how to use these things?" he asks.

I laugh. "It's a computer, Dad. We have them in school."

Let's just say that my father is the reason I'm able to impersonate a technophobe so well.

Computers, as I discovered, were for much more than just typing up an assignment. I could control them. Bend them to my will in a way I couldn't — or wouldn't — with people. I could open them up, like a radio, and manipulate them there. Or I could go in through code and use them to achieve my goal that way. Which sometimes meant hacking.

When I was young, hacking was a challenge. Nothing more. I didn't do anything with my skills. Not until my world fell apart, and a tech career in the army was the absolute last thing I wanted, and I was angry, so damned angry, and it was just the right time in my life for someone to suggest I use those skills in a very different way.

I don't get access to the police email system over my lunch break. My skills are far too rusty for that. Instead, I accomplish step one: finding the server and poking at it a bit, seeing how hard it'll be to hack.

Hack in and find out what's going on with my case. What Officer Cooper really thinks of my story.

Find out whether that boy has a hope of ever being found.

And if the answer is no?

I'm not sure what I'll do about that. Not sure what I can do.

No, that's a lie. I know what I *can* do. I'm just not sure that I will.

EIGHT

I get an early start the next morning . . . and my car does not. It won't start at all. I open the hood to find a broken fan belt. An easy fix, and I mentally calculate the time it'll take me to jog to the hardware store.

No, I can't risk showing up at work late again. So I catch a cab. Not really in my budget, but if I lose my job, I won't have an income *to* budget.

I arrive at the library twenty minutes early. Not that it does any good — my coworker Nancy doesn't show up with the keys until mere seconds before her shift begins.

I put my things away, head straight to the book-return bin, and focus on my task. I'm still distracted, fretting about yesterday, and I cannot afford to make any mistakes.

I like my job. Being a librarian isn't just shelving and checking out books. There's so much else — from helping a senior citizen send an email to helping a student find research material. A combination of public service and problem-solving that I love.

I'd love it even more if I could throw my tech skills into the mix, but that would lead to questions I can't answer. Like how I got those skills when there's no postsecondary education or tech job on my résumé.

I do use those skills on my break. I try hacking into the police system. It's been thirty-six hours since Officer Cooper came to my apartment, and I haven't heard a peep from him since. Nor have I found any mention of the case online. So I'm determined to get into the departmental email and see what they're doing about it.

That takes both coffee breaks and my lunch hour, which would have been embarrassing five years ago. This isn't the Chicago Police Department. It's a suburban force with outdated cybersecurity. I've been out of the game so long, though, that even "outdated" means it's newer than most systems I've hacked. By the time I succeed, my last break is over. I'll need to postpone actually searching emails until tomorrow.

There's something bugging me, too — a growing sense that I'm forgetting something. I keep running through the scenario in the park, both when I first met the boy with his mom, and later, when I saw the

64

boy taken. Am I missing something?

The more I fret, the harder I need to concentrate on work. I count the minutes until my shift ends. Then Ingrid asks me to stay an extra hour — to make up for my double tardiness yesterday — and that sense that I'm forgetting something surges.

I finally get off work, and I'm walking to the parking lot when my phone buzzes. Thinking it's the police, I scramble to yank it from my pocket.

Bright Horizons Daycare.

I wince. There's only one reason they ever call me: if Charlotte is sick. Paul can't dash in from the city, obviously, so this is the one responsibility he allows me to take.

Maybe Charlotte *wasn't* faking her cough yesterday.

I answer quickly with, "Aubrey Finch."

"Ms. Finch? Your husband said you were picking Charlotte up today."

Today? Why would I pick Charlotte up on a Wednesday —

The princess tea. *That's* what I forgot.

"Yes, I'm getting her today," I say as calmly as I can. "Thank you for checking. I'll be there in a half hour."

A pause. "We closed five minutes ago, Ms. Finch."

What? No. I get off at five and . . .

I stayed an extra hour. It's past six.

"I'm so sorry," I say as I run for the parking lot. "I was asked to work late and totally lost track of time. I'll be there in . . ."

I look around the lot. Where is my — ?

Oh, no . . . I don't have my car.

"In a few minutes," I say as I race back to the road, frantically searching for a cab. "I'll pay the late fee myself. Please don't charge Paul. This is on me, and I'm so sorry. I'll be *right* there."

I jump out of the cab. As I run across the empty daycare lot, the side door opens, and Charlotte walks out . . . clutching the hand of a stranger.

For two seconds, reality snaps, and all I can think is *I'm losing my mind.*

That's the only explanation as I watch my daughter being led away by a stranger, two days after I saw a boy snatched. This is not possible.

"Mommy!" Charlotte shouts.

She breaks away from the stranger and starts to run. The woman hurries after her and catches her hand. Then they walk toward me.

"You must be Aubrey," the woman says.

She isn't a daycare worker. Not dressed like this — sensible but stylish, from her heels to her dress to her hairstyle, short and smart.

Sophisticated. That's the word that comes to mind. Stylish and sophisticated.

She's in her late thirties. Not beautiful, but striking and self-possessed. The kind of woman I visualize for my future, when I've overcome all the bumps and gotten my act together.

The woman extends her free hand, the other one still holding Charlotte's.

"Gayle Lansing," she says.

Gayle . . .

Oh, no.

I shake her hand and babble something about being pleased to meet her. It is, quite possibly, the biggest lie I've told in a long time, and that's saying something.

Gayle Lansing is Paul's new girlfriend.

When he told me a few weeks ago that he was seeing someone — doing the right thing and warning me that there was a new face in Charlotte's life — he said she worked in his office, and I thought, *Really? He's dating some cute young assistant? Figures.*

Except that it didn't figure at all, and deep down, I knew that. So I looked Gayle up . . . and promptly began wishing Paul really *were* dating a twenty-something assistant.

Gayle Lansing. Thirty-nine, the same age

as Paul. A lawyer at his firm. A new *partner* at his firm. As I've learned since, Gayle is divorced, with custody of her two children, who attend a private school, win tons of awards, and are shining examples of parenting perfection.

Naturally.

I look at her, and my memory kaleidoscopes through scenes from every social function I attended as Paul's wife. At first, they'd seemed endless — the firm dinners, the charity banquets. At every one, I'd looked at wives like Gayle, poised and professional, and it didn't matter how conservatively I dressed or intelligently I spoke, I felt like the stripper Paul met in Vegas and married after too many free drinks at the casino.

I tried to tell myself I was imagining it — being self-conscious again — but eventually we stopped going to those functions, and when I asked Paul, he shrugged it off and said he didn't need to do that, now that he'd made partner. Which was a lie. The truth was that having me at those functions hurt his career more than not attending.

Having someone like this woman on his arm, though? That would be an entirely different matter.

"I am so, so sorry," I say. "My supervisor

asked me to work late, and I completely forgot why I *couldn't.* I was just about to call the daycare when they phoned me. I guess I'm not the only number they dialed."

"They notified Paul, but he's in court, and I was already heading home, so he asked me to come by."

"Again, I'm sorry. I know this looks terrible."

She smiles. It isn't exactly a bright and friendly smile, but it's not fake either. Just restrained.

"Work emergencies happen," she says. "I tried daycare when mine were young. I had to switch to a nanny because they threatened to kick my kids out if I was late one more time."

I relax a little. "I *am* sorry they called Paul. I'll —"

"Mommy?" Charlotte cut in. "Where princess dress?"

I smile down at her. "Don't worry. It's —"

In my car. I'd put it in there last night, so I wouldn't forget it.

"It's in my car," I say. "Which broke down this morning, and I completely forgot to grab my outfit. We'll head there now. I'll call the princess tea shop and tell them we'll be a little late for our reservation."

"Late?" Charlotte's eyes widen.

"Or I could just go like this." I force a smile. "Ever heard of a librarian princess?"

She looks me up and down, and her lower lip quivers.

"Let's decide on the way," I say as I boost her up. "We don't want to be *too* late, and I'm sure Ms. Lansing has to get home to her kids." I turn to Gayle. "Thank you, and again, I cannot apologize enough."

I got two steps when Gayle says, "Aubrey?"

"Hmm?"

"Did you come by cab?"

I nod. "I have an app. I can get one here in a few minutes."

"And Charlotte?"

I pause.

"Her car seat?"

I only mouth a curse, but Gayle winces as if I shouted the word.

I look around. "The cab company might have . . ."

"Let me drive you," she says. "My youngest is seven, not quite out of a seat yet, so I have a booster in my car."

"I . . ."

I want to die. Right now. Just let the pavement open and swallow me.

"Mommy need dress," Charlotte says.

70

"Princess dress."

"I . . . I know."

"No be late." She shakes her head, curls bouncing.

"I could take her," Gayle says softly.

My head jerks up.

"I don't mean to interfere," she says. "I know you two had this planned for weeks, but you do have a reservation, and you're already . . ." She clears her throat. "A little late. You can rebook, and I'll take her today." She waves down at her outfit. "It's not exactly a princess dress, but . . ."

But it's a whole lot closer to it than my outfit: a blouse, dress pants, and flats.

I want to say no. Hell, no. You've been dating my husband for three weeks. That doesn't give you the right to take my daughter to tea. *Our* tea.

Step off, bitch.

As soon as I think that, I am ashamed. This isn't a smooth play to win my daughter's affections. It's a sensible woman offering a sensible solution.

I bend in front of Charlotte.

"Ms. Lansing is going to be your fellow princess today, okay, baby? I don't want you to miss tea. I know how much you were looking forward to it."

That lip quivers even more. "Mommy not come?"

"Mommy will come next time." I hug her as tight as I can. "Two princess teas with two princess friends. How lucky are you?"

She nods, saying nothing.

"You look so pretty in your dress," I say.

"Blue like Buttercup's," she whispered, gaze down, words almost too soft to hear.

"Blue like Buttercup's. And do you know what else is blue?" I take off my necklace, a turquoise pendant my dad gave me when I got accepted to MIT. "Mommy's special necklace." I fasten it around her neck.

"The perfect finishing touch," Gayle says.

I get a tiny smile from Charlotte.

"Be sure to get pictures for me, okay? Now hurry, you don't want to be late."

Gayle says, "At least let me drop you off somewhere, Aubrey."

I don't want her kindness. I want snide remarks and rolled eyes. Because this feels like pity, and it only makes the humiliation that much worse. Even my husband's new girlfriend doesn't feel threatened by me.

"I've got this," I say. "I'll probably . . . walk a bit and grab a coffee, steal a few minutes to do some work. Thank you again. I really do appreciate it."

I accompany them to Gayle's car. Like

her, it's nothing showy. A solid, dependable sedan . . . with a price tag triple my annual salary.

I put Charlotte into the booster. Secure it. Double-check. Kiss her cheek. Then I go around the car and fumble for my wallet so I can pay for the tea. Instead, I endure the fresh humiliation of Gayle's sympathetic smile and assurances that she has it covered.

Don't even think of paying, Aubrey. You very clearly need that money more than I do.

I thank Gayle again. As the car pulls away, I wave and smile. Then, the moment it turns the corner, I run.

I run as hard and as fast as I can.

NINE

I don't drink. That was my father's crutch, and after his death . . .

No, his *suicide.* Call it what it was. He got back from Iraq, and I was off at college, too caught up in my life to realize he was in trouble, and no one else gave a damn — suck it up, buttercup — and by the time I realized how bad it'd gotten . . .

Gun to head. Bullet through brain. A note left on the counter. *I love you, Bree.*

Didn't love me enough to hang on, did you?

I squeeze my eyes shut. That's how I felt then. I know better now. I understand that in his depression, he didn't see me, *couldn't* see me. And I didn't see him. I was busy, and the damned army certainly didn't help —

I don't blame him now. Don't even blame them as much as I used to. But at the time, God, I'd been furious. At myself mostly, but

74

I couldn't handle that so I blamed the world. Dropped out of MIT. Abandoned any thought of enlisting — vomited just thinking about it. And then . . .

Hey, Bree. Got a proposition for you. Use those magic fingers to put some cash in your pocket.

I shove that aside. The point was that no matter how bad life got, I didn't drink. I won't take meds for my shoulder either. I refuse to engage in any activity that could provide a false sense of relief.

But that day, after Gayle leaves with Charlotte, I walk into a grocery store and stare at the glittering rows of bottles.

Just this once. Please just this once.

I tear myself away and wander the aisles, looking for something to cheer me up. I stand in the ice cream aisle and gaze at the Ben & Jerry's. That's the cliché, isn't it? Drown your sorrows in ice cream?

If only I liked ice cream.

I walk to the cookie aisle. Again, not really my thing, but I select a small bag for Charlotte as a treat. She won't get the whole bag, obviously. One cookie, and maybe even a milky cup of decaffeinated tea. Our own princess tea, to hold her over until I can have a new reservation. I try not to think of the fact that it took me two months to get today's.

I've already left a message at the tea shop, and when my phone rings, I yank it out. It's a spam text, offering me work as a mystery shopper. At this point, if I thought it was legit, I might take it. God knows, I could use the money.

I console myself by opening my photo album to find the pictures of Charlotte trying on her princess dress. The first photograph I see is one I don't recognize. I'm not even sure what it is.

A mis-hit shutter button, it seems — the kind where you get a shot of your leg while taking out your phone. Except it isn't my leg. It's the back end of a vehicle.

The back of a dark SUV, its license plate smeared with mud.

It's *the* SUV. The one that took the boy. I had been lifting my phone, fumbling to set up the camera, and I must have snapped the shutter without realizing it.

It's a crappy shot. Off-center and blurred, the camera in motion. But the full plate is there, and I can make out enough of the vehicle emblem —

"*Excuse* me." A glowering senior waves me aside brusquely. "You are blocking the biscuits."

76

I pay for the cookies and hurry from the store. When I spot a coffee shop, I veer toward it. I'm tempted to bypass the counter. Sit and pretend I'm waiting for someone while I get a better look at the photo. But I squelch the urge, treat myself to a caramel latte and a blondie, and then take a seat buoyed by the righteousness of having paid to occupy it.

I import the photo into an app and refine it. I don't have proper graphics programs these days, but basic apps will do a decent job. The first thing I notice starts my heart pounding.

This isn't mud splatter from a dirt road. The dirt has been deliberately applied. I have a three-year-old; I know the pattern finger painting leaves. I can see the marks where fingers smeared on the mud. The rest of the car is spotless.

I reach for my phone. Then I stop.

A child is missing. And while I pray it's only a custody issue, it could be more. It could be worse. I need all the ammunition I can get before I place this call.

I can see part of the SUV emblem and the first two letters of the vehicle name. *TA.* I'm no good at recognizing car logos, so I search on my phone browser and get a page of images.

It's a Chevrolet. And while my mind immediately fills in the rest of the name as "Tahoe," I search for all Chevrolet SUV and crossover names. Three start with *T*: Tahoe, Trax, and Traverse. It's possible that the second letter is an *R* instead, but I'm definitely looking at a big SUV, not a crossover.

A Chevrolet Tahoe with a deliberately mud-smeared license plate. I can get access to better enhancement software and try making out the plate, but that takes time. The police need this information now.

I pick up my phone and dial Officer Cooper's number. Voice mail answers.

I call the station's main number instead and say I need to speak to Officer Cooper urgently, concerning a case.

I'm finished with my latte and my blondie before he phones back, and even then, when I answer, he greets me with a weary, "Yes, Ms. Finch," as if I've been calling him hourly.

"I have a photo. Of the vehicle."

A pause long enough that I wonder if he's hung up. Then a slow, "Photo?"

"I wanted to take one of the SUV, but it pulled away while I was getting my camera ready. Apparently, I still snapped a shot. It's not great, but I can identify the vehicle as a

Chevrolet Tahoe. A dark blue Chevy Tahoe."

A sigh vibrates along the line. "I appreciate you letting me know, Ms. Finch, but we still have no report of a missing child. Without any evidence of a crime, I can't chase down a vehicle based on a make, model, and color."

"The license plate was deliberately smeared with mud."

"What?"

I try to keep the lilt of satisfaction out of my voice. Calm and steady. "I have a shot of the plate, which you may be able to analyze for the actual number, but right now, I can tell you that it isn't accidentally splattered with mud. It's been smeared on. I can see finger marks."

Silence.

"There is no mud on the rest of the vehicle, sir," I say. "Just the plate, where the number has been disguised."

"You can tell that the plate has been deliberately smeared with mud."

"I have a three-year-old, sir. I know what smearing looks like. Paint, food, dirt, you name it, I've seen it smeared. The whorl pattern is there, and the lines —"

"I . . . appreciate your . . . diligence in this matter, Ms. Finch. You have gone . . . above and beyond."

That tone in his voice isn't admiration. I hear the hesitation, as if he's struggling not to tell me I'm crazy. I open my mouth, but he continues.

"There isn't a missing child," he says. "It comes down to that. Few crimes are reported as quickly as a snatched kid. Even then, kidnapped children are exceedingly rare. I know you've probably seen a hundred movies with children grabbed on the street, but I've been on the force thirty years and never worked a single stranger-grab case. It just doesn't happen."

"Because it's usually custody based. The noncustodial parent takes their child. There's no reason that isn't what we have here, sir."

"Yes, there is, Ms. Finch. There is the lack of a reported missing child. You're a single mom with a little girl. Imagine if your ex lost custody and grabbed her at the playground."

He wouldn't. First, Paul is too good a parent to ever lose custody altogether. Second, he'd never take her. He will fight like hell, but he would never resort to kidnapping.

Would I?

My gut seizes at the question. I don't want to consider it. I certainly don't want to answer it.

Cooper continues. "How long would it take you to report her missing, Ms. Finch? Not two days, I bet."

"Maybe the mom is trying to resolve this on her own. Maybe the father is threatening their son, and she's afraid to call the —"

"Again, you are falling into dangerous speculative territory, Ms. Finch."

"Okay, but —"

"It remains an open case. I am still investigating. I can assure you of that. Now, I'm afraid I'm going to have to let you go, but I do appreciate your diligence in this matter. Thank you."

He disconnects before I can say anything else.

Cooper has a point. Without a missing-child report, there isn't a case. The situation fully supports his theory — that I witnessed a parent-child dispute — and in light of that, I can see where my "I can tell the mud was smeared" revelation seemed like something from a civilian who watches too much *CSI*.

When my phone rings, I've been on the internet for hours, hunting for other cases that might explain why this disappearance wasn't reported.

I reach over and answer, engrossed in an article and not checking caller ID.

"You actually picked up," Paul says. "That's a first."

His tone tells me I shouldn't have.

"Hey," I say.

"So, it's almost eleven at night, and I've been telling myself you'll call. Of course you'll call. Well, no, you never call. You text. Sometimes email. But you will make contact and explain yourself."

"Explain myself?" I bristle. "If you're talking about Gayle and the princess tea —"

"Is there another fiasco I should know about?"

I grit my teeth and count to three.

"You're right," I say. "I should have told you. I got . . . caught up in something. I did ask Gayle to pass on my apologies to you."

"She shouldn't have to."

"Fair enough. I'm sorry, Paul. I really am. I'm sorry you got called when you were in court, and I'm even more sorry that Gayle had to clean up my mess."

Silence.

Not the calm response you were expecting? I have other things on my mind right now. More important things.

"I'd like to call Gayle," I say. "To apologize again. If you could give me her number —"

He snorts. "No, I'm not giving you her number. God only knows what you'd do with it."

"Excuse me? I would use it to apologize and thank her. If you think I have any issue with you dating again, I don't. I'm glad you are. She seems —"

"This isn't about Gayle. It's about our daughter, who has been looking forward to this for weeks. To having tea with her mother. Her mother who *forgot.* Completely forgot, and then made up some story about working late and car trouble and —"

"Made up?" My calm teeters, ready to shatter. "Seriously, Paul? When I make mistakes, I *own* them. This is no one's fault but mine. Yes, there was a moment where I forgot, because I have a lot on my mind. But I *did* work late, and my car belt *is* broken." I head for the apartment door. "Here, let me send you a photo of the engine."

"You don't have to do that, Aubrey." His voice lowers. "You're right. That was un-called for. I'm sure your car —"

"Oh, hell, no. I'm sending you the proof. Just like I'll send you a photo of my time card. You aren't going to question me and then not give me the chance to defend myself, Counselor."

"Don't pull that. I am not a lawyer here, Aubrey. I'm your — the father of your child, who is calling about that child."

I keep walking, stocking-footed, into the building hall. "And I disappointed her. Do you think I don't realize that? Do you think I'm not completely ashamed and humiliated?"

"You don't need to be. It was . . ." He sighs. "It was a mistake. I understand that. If you need money to fix your car —"

"No."

I swear he inhales, as if fighting an argument, before he says, calmly, "You are entitled to alimony, Aubrey. You took three years off to raise our child while I worked. My income was *our* income."

"I'm fine."

"No, you're stubborn. Stubborn and impulsive and absolutely impossible to deal —" He bites off the rest. A moment's silence as I walk into the parking lot. Then he says, his voice softer, "What's going on, Bree?"

"I'm having a really crappy week."

"Maybe, but it's more than that. Something has that busy brain of yours whirring."

"Just . . . work. And I meant it about conveying my thanks again to Gayle."

"I will. She has photos for me to send. And she got you reservations for tea a week from Sunday. Does that work?"

It does. I originally wanted a Sunday

reservation, and was told they were booked up for the next six months. So how did Gayle manage it?

Because she's the kind of woman who knows how to do things like that, skills I will never possess.

"That's perfect. Thank you. And yes" — I pop the hood — "I'm sending you a photo of my engine, Paul, because I *am* stubborn, and if you call me on it, I have to defend myself."

"You realize I wouldn't know a broken fan belt from a loose wire, right?" He pauses. "And since when do you know how to fix a car?"

Damn it. I really am distracted.

"I don't," I say. "But I can Google the symptoms and narrow down the issue, and apparently, it's a broken belt. I know Charlie's in bed, but tomorrow, please give her a kiss for me, and we'll Skype after dinner."

"All right. Good night, Aubrey."

Back in the apartment, I find an online florist and send a small thank-you arrangement to Gayle, at the law firm.

I do appreciate what she's done, even if it makes me uncomfortable. I should be happy Paul's new girlfriend isn't an evil bitch, but somehow, it might have been easier if she were. When he first told me he was seeing someone, I was genuinely happy for him. What I hadn't realized was that it raised the potential of a scenario I never considered.

A stepmom for Charlotte.

If there ever is such a thing — and there will be, Paul isn't going to leave that void unfilled — then I want her to be everything Gayle seems to be. Kind, intelligent, and responsible. The perfect partner for Paul. The ideal role model for our daughter.

But where does that leave me?

TEN

I've turned off my alarm — I don't work Thursdays. My internal drill instructor still wakes me at seven and berates me for sleeping the day away.

While I lie in bed for another twenty minutes, it's obvious sleep isn't an option. I decide to make sure my floral delivery for Gayle went through okay. Leaving Paul also meant leaving our joint credit cards. That had turned into a weird game of Mastercard hot potato.

I'd left my card on my nightstand after we had "the talk." Then two weeks passed, and maybe that was how long it took him to realize I wasn't coming back. After those two weeks, he mailed the card to me. No note. Just the card.

I returned it, also by mail. He put it into Charlotte's weekend bag. I *left* it in Charlotte's weekend bag. He put it on my passenger seat while I was strapping Charlotte in. I gave up and shredded it. The whole time, we didn't exchange a single word about the card — just kept silently passing it back and forth.

I have my own card now, but with my lack of credit history, the limit is embarrassingly low, and even a small arrangement of flowers isn't cheap, so I'm worried the charge might not have gone through. I check, and then I pay off enough to buy a fan belt and try not to reminisce about the days of a platinum Mastercard with a limit that would have paid for a whole new car.

Even back then, though, I only used the card for necessities. Paul used to fret about that. He'd get the statement and say, "You can spend more, Bree."

"I don't need to."

"The card isn't just for household expenses. We're sharing a salary. You can buy things you'd like."

"I'm good."

His lips would tighten at that, and I'd tease that he should be *glad* I wasn't blowing up the card at Lululemon. He'd mutter and walk away, and I never figured out what I'd done wrong.

That had been in our last few months together, when it seemed like nothing I did made him happy. When I felt like an intruder in his house, in his life.

I inhale and flip to the local news. Today's top headline?

UNIDENTIFIED WOMAN'S BODY FOUND IN PARK.

I scroll past that to see if there's any more useful news . . . like a missing child. Yet I can't help skim-reading the article as I scroll. A woman in her early twenties. Found in Harris Park. Shot in the head, execution style. No ID, but CCTV cameras picked her up just outside the park on Tuesday morning —

I stop scrolling.

I turn up the brightness on my phone and enlarge the CCTV photo. It's been en-hanced, but it's still blurry around the edges. At the moment of the freeze frame, though, she was turned toward the camera, giving a near-perfect head shot of a young woman with a blond ponytail.

It's the woman from Sunday. The one with the boy.

I stare at the photo. She's grim-faced, but I remember her smiles — the hesitant one for me and the joyful one for her son.

Her son.

I scramble up and start hitting 911. Then I stop and go into my recent calls and redial Cooper's number instead.

When I get his voice mail, I hang up and try the main line I used yesterday.

"I'm calling about the murdered woman," I say. "The one you're trying to identify."

"Do you recognize her?"

"Yes, I —"

"Let me connect you."

A click. Another click. Two rings. Then a message, telling me that the line is in use, but my call is important and please hold.

Please hold.

Yep, keep holding.

As I wait, I look back at the photo.

Do you recognize the woman?

Yes, I met her.

You know her then?

Well, no, I mean, I don't know her name or . . . anything about her actually, but I spoke to her briefly in the park.

The park where she was killed?

No, two blocks over, in Grant Park.

You saw her in Grant Park the day of her murder?

No, I saw her two days before. On the day of her murder, I saw her son being kidnapped . . .

Yeah, that conversation is not going to end well. I need to speak to someone who knows about my initial report.

I need to speak to Officer Cooper.

ELEVEN

I catch a cab to the police station, well aware that I'm now spending more on taxi fares than I would on a damned fan belt. This, however, is urgent.

I get into the station and ask to speak to Officer Cooper. He's out. I explain that it's about the murdered woman, and that just gets confusing. Cooper isn't involved with that case, and the woman on the desk isn't aware of any kidnapping.

I'm about to try explaining better when an officer crosses behind the desk. She's about my age, with dark skin, close-cropped curls, and high cheekbones. She wears a tailored blouse with a pencil skirt, but I recognize her even out of uniform.

Officer Jackson.

I hesitate. She's not exactly my biggest cheerleader, but I brush off the misgivings — when she hears what I have to say, her opinion will change. It has to.

I leave the desk and take off after her, catching up near the entrance.

"Officer Jackson," I say. "Aubrey Finch. I'm not sure if you remember me —"

"Yes, ma'am, I do." Her lips tighten, and I swear her gaze shunts toward the door, as if measuring the distance.

"It's about the murdered woman, the one whose body was found in the park. She's connected to the kidnapping."

"There is no kidnapping, Ms. Finch." She speaks slowly — clearly I'm having trouble processing this concept. "No child has been reported missing."

"Because his mother is dead. That's the woman you found. I recognized her the moment I saw her photo."

"I see . . ." Another glance toward the entrance, now filled with people coming in, talking fast among themselves. "If you believe you have information, I suggest you speak to the front desk. I really need to —"

"I'm telling you why that boy hasn't been reported missing. His mother is *dead.* She was murdered only two blocks from where I saw him taken. That's why he was in the park. That's why she didn't report his disappearance. She's *dead.*"

Her gaze rises over my shoulder. "Ms. Finch, why don't you —"

"Are you listening to me? Look at my report. The woman in that photo matches my description. She was murdered two blocks from where I saw her child kidnapped — on the *day* she was murdered. Her son was wandering around the park alone, and then he was grabbed into an SUV, probably by the guy who just shot his mom."

"Excuse me," a voice says behind me. "Ms. . . . Finch you said?"

"Aubrey Finch," I say as I turn to see a man in a suit and overcoat. A detective. Thank God.

"You said you saw the dead woman?" he continues. "With a child?"

"Yes, a little boy who was kidnapped by a man in an SUV —"

That's when I spot the camera. Right over the shoulder of the man in the overcoat. A video camera with the local news call letters emblazoned on the side.

I see that camera with the recording light on, and I see myself reflected in the lens, my eyes wide, my hair shoved into a ponytail, my collar half tucked under.

I flip out my collar as I turn away from the man and the camera.

"The press conference is being held in room 1-B," Jackson says as she shuttles me

93

off down a side hall. She opens a door and bustles me inside.

"I'm sorry," I say. "I thought that was a detective."

"I don't know what your deal is, Ms. Finch —"

"My *deal* is that I witnessed a kidnapping, and I understand that without a reported disappearance, there's no case. But this woman's death explains it. She was murdered, and her son ran to the playground. Her killer came for him. He knew the boy's name and when he called it, the boy ran over. Then he saw a stranger and freaked out. Her killer took him."

"There is *no* sign of a child with the woman on that CCTV footage. Which was taken two blocks away . . . and almost an hour *after* you reported the supposed kidnapping."

"Then . . ." I struggle for an explanation. "Then they grabbed the boy first."

She crosses her arms. "So why wasn't he with his mom? Why wasn't she in the park with him?"

"I . . . I don't know, but there must be an explanation. What I do know is that this is, beyond any doubt, the woman I saw Sunday afternoon."

"Sure, okay, this woman matches the

description you provided. The very, very vague description."

"I can give you more. On Sunday, she wore no makeup except thick black eyeliner. She had what looked like track marks on her arms. Old ones."

Her brows shoot up. "You know what track marks look like, Ms. Finch?"

"I have seen them before. Now, when I was talking to her on Sunday, she took a call. She sounded very upset. She was speaking in another language. I don't know exactly, but I'm guessing Slavic."

"And your linguistic experience comes from . . . ?"

I walk farther into the room, taking a moment to relax. Don't get my temper up. Don't take offense.

"I'm not claiming any expertise, Officer. They may have been pockmarks, not track marks. She may have been speaking Portuguese. I'm taking wild guesses, the upshot being that this woman has marks on her arms and speaks a second language."

"You may say you're not positioning yourself as an expert, Ms. Finch, but there is a name for what you *are* doing. It's called attention seeking. Officer Cooper believes you did see a boy pulled into an SUV. I'm not so sure, and I think this proves I'm right. You invented a kidnapping story, and when that failed, you jumped on this tragedy to insinuate yourself into a real investigation."

"I don't want to insinuate myself into anything. I just want you to take my information and do your damned job."

Her eyes flash. "We are *trying* to do our job, Ms. Finch. That job right now is solving a murder. Please do not make that any more difficult than it already is."

She opens the door for me to leave.

"I'd like to speak to Officer Cooper, please," I say, with as much dignity as I can muster.

"You've wasted enough of his time."

I straighten and walk out, head high. I get three steps when a woman says, "Ms. Finch?"

I turn too eagerly, as if in the last three seconds Jackson has realized her mistake. Instead, I'm facing a woman with a microphone, a cameraman behind her.

"Ms. Finch? Aubrey Finch? Is that right?"

I look at the camera. I see that recording light on again. I see the call letters again, too, with two words I'd missed: Live News.

LIVE.

The reporter continues, "Did you say you know the woman whose body was found in

96

Harris Park this morning?"

Live. I am on live TV.

My face. My name. On the news.

I back away slowly. "No, I'm sorry. I need to —"

"You said her son was kidnapped? You saw him taken the same day she was murdered?"

My face is on live television.

That's all I can process, her words barely penetrating.

"N-no. I'm sorry. It — it was a mistake."

I try to stop the babbling denials. I should not retract my words. I *know* the dead woman is the young mom. I know her son was taken.

I want to say yes. State my case. If the police aren't paying attention, well, maybe they will when I explain the situation on live television, and they're flooded with calls demanding that they investigate.

That is what I want to do. The heroic thing.

Instead I babble something unintelligible, and then hurry off down the hall. I take the coward's path, but it is already too late.

My name is in the news. My face is on television, connected to a major crime case.

What have I done?

TWELVE

I spend the rest of the morning obsessively watching the footage of me on the local news channel. It's there before I get back to my apartment. I stand at my laptop, newly bought fan belt abandoned on the counter as I watch and rewatch the video.

I could remove the segment. I know how. But that's as pointless as pulling a risqué photo uploaded by a pissed-off ex. Believe me — I know *that* from experience. The guy has the original, and by removing the copy, you only show him that it's upsetting you, which is the point. If I remove this, the news station will just replace the video and then wonder what made it hack-worthy.

My footage is short. Mercifully so. I tell myself I don't look that bad in it. Yes, I appear to have just rolled out of bed, but I don't look crazy.

Is that what it's come to? I don't look *crazy*?

I don't *sound* crazy either. That's even more important. On the way home, I kept replaying those moments, and with each iteration, I imagined myself falling deeper into raving-maniac territory. But what I see is just a harried-looking woman explaining an admittedly wild theory.

My five seconds of infamy is buried in a longer clip of raw footage shot as they'd been coming into the station and caught me trying to talk to Officer Jackson. There's already a polished version of the live broadcast, which I have been left out of. Discarded on the editing room floor.

I should be grateful for that. This raw footage will be removed soon, and I will disappear. That's what I want. Let me fade back into anonymity again. My fear is not that the police will come after me. The statute of limitations has already run out on my crimes. But if my past catches up, it'll give Paul so much ammunition that I might as well sign Charlotte over to him now.

I'm glad that I've been cut from the official news clip. The problem is it means my claim is being ignored. There's even a brief note under the raw footage, reassuring the viewer that no child is missing.

No child is missing.

Not even "no child has been *reported*

missing." My claim has been red-stamped with the absolute certainty of a veto.

Please ignore this woman. No child was harmed in the making of this murder.

I don't need to hack into the police department email server now. I know what they've decided. No child has been reported missing, and so my claim is being ignored. Understandably ignored. I must admit that. This isn't a case of incompetent policing. Officer Cooper, at least, has been fair and patient with me. The fact remains, though, that three days have passed with no evidence of a missing child.

Because his mother is dead.

That makes perfect sense to me, but I can see how it sounded to Officer Jackson, considering that she already thought I was attention-seeking. There's nothing to tie this boy to the dead woman.

Over and over, I refresh the news page and pray that I will see more. An update. That the woman has been identified, and the police have discovered she *did* have a child, who is now missing. Once that's out, the authorities will throw all their resources into the hunt, and the child will be found, frightened but safe, the killer caught, the young mother avenged.

And they all lived happily ever after.

Except they don't, do they?

His mother is still dead. And her son will live with that forever.

I know what that will be like. I know exactly what it will be like.

I tell people my mother died when I was "just a baby." I'm parroting the words I heard growing up. People often presume that means she died in childbirth, and I don't correct them. The truth . . .

The truth is the sickening crunch of metal. The world spinning, flipping upside down. Me, screaming, wordlessly screaming in absolute terror. Then my mother's voice, weak and whispery.

"Bree?"

Her fingers finding my arm. Clutching it. Her hand wet and sticky.

"It's going to be okay, Bree. Someone will come."

Someone will come.

Night fell, and the car went dark. My mother told me she loved me. Over and over, she told me. And then, after a while, everything went quiet.

Once I admitted to my father what I remember.

"Stop that."

"But I —"

"You couldn't remember that. You were just a baby."

Except I *wasn't* a baby, not in any more than the colloquial sense. I'd been two years old, and I do remember. I remember waiting for someone to come and save us. I remember hearing cars passing on the country highway. I remember that no one stopped, not until the next day, morning sun glinting off the car, and by then it was too late.

People saw the car. They must have. Whoever hit us knew what they did, and they just kept going, driving away as fast as they could. Then others passed, and they saw a damaged vehicle in the field, and they told themselves there was no one in it. Just a crashed car waiting for a tow truck. Or kids abandoning a wreck after a joy ride.

I'm sure no one's in it, and really, I don't have time to stop and check.

My mom died when I was a baby.

I was not a baby. I was old enough to have toddled to that road and gotten help.

"Stop that, Bree. You were trapped in a car seat."

"Maybe if —"

"You were a baby."

I was not a baby.

My phone rings. I jump. It isn't a number

102

I recognize, so I wait to see if they'll leave a message. When they don't, I stare at my list of received calls, and see Paul's number, from yesterday.

I've thought of calling him. Twice, I've gotten as far as pulling up his number, my finger hovering over the Call icon.

Hey, Paul. Sorry to bother you at work, but I, uh, need to tell you something. So there's this news clip . . .

Is that really necessary?

This is the question that stops me. The video clip will probably be removed. My name doesn't appear in the article. Paul is the kind of guy who flips through his headline feed once a day and assimilates the data based on that. UNIDENTIFIED WOMAN MURDERED IN GRANT PARK. Check. CITY HALL ARGUING OVER INFRASTRUCTURE BUDGET. Check. TENSIONS RISE IN MIDDLE EAST. Check.

There, I have a basic idea of what's going on in the world, now let's get back to work.

When we were dating, I learned that if I mentioned current events I'd get a long pause followed by him saying, "Tell me more about that." He was happy to get the information; he just felt no need to seek it out on his own. If I wanted that kind of conversation with Paul, I was far better off delving into the background of the news. Let's talk about the issues surrounding murdered women. Let's talk about the city's infrastructure problems. Let's talk about the history of the conflict in the Middle East. *That's* what interested him, and I remember how exciting it was to be able to talk to someone who wanted a conversation deeper than news bites, a guy who knew the history *behind* those news bites, who actually enjoyed talking about it, having a *real* conversation.

Except, for us, that's what passed for real conversation. An in-depth discussion of Middle Eastern politics.

Paul, I need to talk to you. There are things I need to explain. Things about me . . .

I put my phone aside. I'm going to roll these dice and play the odds and wager on Paul never seeing the video clip. If he does, I can explain it.

As for who else might view it, I won't worry about that either. It's five seconds in an unedited segment from a suburban news station. No one outside of Oxford will see it, and very few inside will.

I'm safe.

Which is more than I can say for that little boy.

■ ■ ■ ■

It's six o'clock Thursday evening. I've been out for a couple of hours, getting groceries after replacing the fan belt in my car. It doesn't take me that long to shop for myself, but before I go, I always check on a few less-mobile neighbors to "see if they need anything from the store."

In truth, I didn't need *anything* myself today. I was conducting a test. If I go out in public, will anyone recognize me? While I caught a few looks, no one said anything, and I suspect I was just being paranoid about those looks. I will presume that if anyone saw me on the news this morning, they didn't recognize me. Given how I looked in that video, I'd hope they wouldn't recognize me.

I return to my building, drop off bags for my neighbors, and bask in a few moments of Zen calm. There's been no fallout from the video clip, and now I have done good deeds. I have made people smile. I feel good about myself.

Then I climb the stairs to my floor and hear someone banging at a door. I pause, groceries in hand, and I consider withdrawing.

I consider fleeing.

Because I hear someone knocking at a door? It's probably not even mine.

I glance around the corner to see someone standing in front of my door, hand rising to knock again.

Paul.

I pull back and ponder sneaking down the stairs, tossing the groceries in my car, and going for coffee. Wait it out.

That would be cowardly. Also, pointless. If Paul wants to talk to me, he's going to find a way, even if it involves skywriting "Pick up the damned phone, Bree."

I step from the stairwell. He turns, and I expect he'll wait there, not saying a word until we're safely ensconced in the privacy of my apartment.

Instead, he bears down on me, and on his face there's an expression I don't think I've ever seen. Barely contained rage.

"What the hell is this?" He waves around the hall. "I didn't even have to ring up. There's no damned lock on the front door."

"There is. It's broken."

And has been since I moved in.

"This place reeks of pot," he says.

I stare at him. "Are you accusing me of smoking pot, Paul?"

"Well, that might explain a few things."

He knows about the news clip.

I fix him with a level stare. "You know I don't drink. I certainly don't do drugs. If you are accusing me of that, I will take a test. Just say the word."

"I'm not accusing you of anything, Aubrey. I'm saying people here are smoking pot."

I sputter a laugh. "If you think you can find any building — uptown or downtown — that doesn't have at least one resident smoking pot, you need a reality check, Counselor."

"Don't —" He bites it off and advances on me, voice lowering. "This is about embarrassing me, isn't it? I keep offering you money, but you've made it clear that you're fine. And then I see this."

I pass him to open my door. I step inside and hold it open. He follows.

"My apartment isn't fancy —" I begin.

"It's a dump."

"The fact that you can even say that proves you need to get out of midtown Chicago a little more often. Go see how people live when they aren't born with an Ivy League education fund. This isn't skid row. It's working-class America, and I'm fine with it, and I think it's fine for our daughter to see a little bit of it, too. Broaden her horizons."

"My daughter's horizons don't include walking past that junkie parked on the front step."

I wheel on him. "That is a military veteran who lost his damned leg. Show a little respect."

He steps back. Rubs his hands over his face. "All right. I'm sorry. That was uncalled for. But I don't understand what you're doing here, Aubrey."

"Not trying to embarrass you or punish you."

"Punish yourself, then." He meets my gaze. "That's it. This is about punishing yourself. You had an affair, didn't you?"

"What?"

He walks into the apartment, still talking, his back to me. "That was the first thing I thought when you left. You'd met someone. I expected you'd wait a few weeks after leaving and then drop the bomb. When you didn't, I thought that must not be the answer. But it was, wasn't it? Not that you left me for another man. That you met someone and had an affair. A fling. Then you left out of guilt, and now you won't take anything from me because you're punishing yourself."

I laugh. I can't help it. The sound startles

him, and he turns.

"Seriously, Paul? I was home with a toddler. How the hell would I find time to meet someone, let alone have an affair?" I walk into the kitchen. "Now, if you'd like coffee —"

"I saw the video clips," he says. "Someone spotted you on the news and told me. I watched it and . . . and I don't know what to say."

I stop. Then I turn to face him. "I'm sorry. I should have warned you. If this causes you any embarrassment —"

"Christ, Bree. No. I'm worried about *you*. You saw something in the park."

"I didn't see 'something.' I saw a boy get taken. Kidnapped."

"Putting aside what you think you saw —"

"What I *think* I saw? A boy was taken, and now his mother is dead, and the police are ignoring me."

He goes quiet. Then he says, carefully, "I know you wanted more children —"

"What?"

He runs a hand through his hair. "You said that had nothing to do with you leaving, but you left shortly after I told you I wanted to wait."

"What does this have to do with me seeing a child abducted?"

"You want more kids, so when you thought you saw a child in danger —"

"You think I'm hallucinating a kidnapped kid because, what? I feel like my future babies have been stolen from me? That is the most messed-up amateur psychobabble I have ever heard."

His lips compress. "Don't mock me, Aubrey. I'm trying to help."

"You know what help sounds like, Paul? 'Aubrey, I saw that clip on the news, and I can't believe the police are brushing you off. Let me see what I can do — I have contacts in the department.' "

He opens his mouth.

"No," I say. "Those aren't the words coming out of your mouth, so I don't want to hear the ones that are. Get out."

"I just want —"

"And I don't give a damn. You want to know the real reason why I don't take money from you? Because paying for this place means it's mine. All mine. So if I tell you to get your ass out, you are going to turn around and do it. *Now.*"

He hesitates. Then he stalks out, the door slapping shut behind him.

Now I'm angry. No, I am furious, in a way I haven't been for years. A way I haven't allowed myself to be. At last, I have a target for my bottled-up rage.

Paul.

He didn't give me hell for being on the news. Didn't storm over here to accuse me of publicly humiliating him. I think that might be better. Then I could have snarled back that this wasn't about him.

What he did is worse. It's condescending crap. It's Paul thinking his wife has lost her mind. Poor, poor Aubrey. She's hallucinating missing children because she's sad that she doesn't have another baby yet.

Screw you, Paul. I saw a boy kidnapped. Any doubt I had evaporated the moment I saw his mother's photo. That is the woman. He was the boy. He was taken.

And I'm going to prove it.

THIRTEEN

I have the photo. The one the police are very clearly not interested in. So it's time to show them what I can do with it. I'm going to get numbers on that plate, and then I'm going to find that SUV, if it means hacking into the damned DMV to do it.

Yeah . . .

That doesn't turn out quite as well as I hope. I can't get any characters from the plate even when I download an illegal copy of the best enhancement software I know. Whoever obscured that plate knew what they were doing, and the mud is caked on thick enough that all I can make out is a few straight lines.

It's a setback, but not a dead end. I'm too pissed off to let it be a dead end.

I met the dead woman. However shallow our conversation might have been, there is a clue there. I'm sure of it. So I meditate, clearing my mind to focus on our conversation, tugging wispy threads from memory and writing them down. Then I return to meditating and teasing out more threads.

It takes two hours to recall our brief chat, one that wasn't even a conversation, but simply a series of exchanges punctuating a lesson on cartwheels.

"A librarian," she laughs when I tell her what I do for a living. "I did not picture you as a librarian. But I suppose that proves it's been a long time since I set foot in a library. I really should take my son sometime."

"You should. We have great early-reader programs."

"That'd be good. I've been reading with him at night."

My son. Him. She never gave me a name. Not for the boy, not for herself.

"Do they have morning programs?" she asks. "I work at a pizza place. We don't open until noon so I never work mornings."

A pizza place. That's all I have. She works at a pizza place that opens at noon.

There are thirteen pizza parlors in Oxford. Only five open at noon, and two are chains. If she worked at one of those, I'd think she'd say, "I work at Domino's."

I'll start with non-chain pizza parlors.

I rise from my laptop . . . and see the clock on the microwave. It's after eleven at night, and I won't get far questioning sleepy employees.

This can wait until tomorrow.

It has to.

I wake the next morning to a voice mail from Paul.

"Aubrey, it's, uh, me."

As if I couldn't tell by the phone number.

"I realize how my remarks yesterday could have been misconstrued."

Yeah, pretty sure you knew exactly what you were saying.

"I don't doubt that you saw a child pulled into a van."

You just think, like Officer Cooper, that I overreacted to a frustrated parent hauling their kid from the playground.

"I'd like to discuss this. If there's any possibility that the police are in error here, I will help you get through to them."

Sure, you'll help . . . if I'm actually right, which you seriously doubt. Let's talk, and you can convince me that I've made a mistake.

"Call me, Bree. Please."

I hit Delete and get ready for work.

Ingrid knows about the video clip. So does Nancy, the other librarian on duty. One of them saw the live coverage and told the

114

other. They don't say a word about it to me. Which means I'm robbed of the opportunity to explain. They just keep sneaking looks my way.

Those looks aren't disapproving. Again, like with Paul, I almost wish that they were. I can deal with disapproval. Instead, their looks ooze trepidation. Like Paul, they question my mental stability.

By eleven, I'm ready to confront Ingrid. March her into the staff room and have it out.

I know you saw that news clip. Let me give my side of the story.

Let me show you I am fine.

I'm considering how to do that without being confrontational, when a voice says, "Aubrey?"

I turn with my "How may I help you?" smile. I don't recognize the guy. He's about my age, good-looking in a ten-years-post-frat way. Really not my taste in men, but he fixes me with a blazing smile that says he's pretty damned sure he's *every* woman's taste in men.

"Hey there," he says.

"May I help you?"

Another toothy grin. "I certainly hope so."

Not today, asshole. Come back tomorrow, and maybe I'll be ready for your crap, with an empty smile and then, "Oh, I think you want to speak to Nancy about that."

Nancy is nearing retirement age, and on my first day, she said that if I ever had a customer being too friendly, I could pass him off to her. I'd laughed at the time, certain that no one hits on librarians. I'd been wrong. I have appreciated Nancy's kindness and help in the past, which makes her wary looks today so much harder to handle.

Right now, though, I am in no mood for this. The old Aubrey rises as I stand, stone-faced, waiting for the guy to say something productive.

"Has anyone ever told you that you don't look like a librarian?" he says.

"I'm sure every librarian has been told — repeatedly — that she does not look like a librarian. Or, at least, not like the image of a librarian held by people who don't frequent libraries."

His smile falters at that. He opens his mouth. Shuts it. Straightens. And I think he's actually going to abort course. But after a moment, he leans over the counter.

"You're the girl from the news, right?"

"I stopped being a 'girl' about ten years ago. But if you're asking whether I was briefly on the news yesterday, yes, I was. I

116

didn't realize I was talking to a reporter. I was just there to make a statement."

"You don't like reporters?"

He smiles when he says it, casual, overly charming, gaze never leaving mine. But the problem with trying to flirt while holding eye contact? You give yourself away in little things. Eyelids lowering or rising. Pupils dilating or contracting, just for a second.

"I like reporters just fine," I say. "Except when they're trying to get a story by pretending they aren't reporters." I lean in to whisper, "Don't you *hate* that?"

He blinks.

"Go away," I say. "There's no story here."

I walk toward the other side of the circulation desk. The guy skirts the exterior, following me.

"Can't blame a guy for trying, right?" He winks, sliding back into frat-boy mode. "You said you were trying to give a statement. The police weren't listening. That doesn't seem fair. You're obviously a smart woman. Look where you work." He waves around the library. "And you saw right through my patter. I don't think anyone has ever —"

"Cut the crap," I say.

Ingrid looks over fast enough to inflict whiplash.

"I made my statement to the police," I

say. "I trust that they will handle it. I don't want to impede their investigation, so I have nothing more to say on the matter."

"They're ignoring you. You do know that, right?"

"Their priority is identifying a murdered woman. As soon as they do, they'll discover she has a child, who is missing."

"Can I quote you on that?"

"No, but you can quote me on this."

I start to raise my middle finger. I stop myself, but Ingrid still lets out a chirp of alarm and scampers over.

"I am so sorry, sir. Ms. Finch has been under a great deal of stress."

"He's a reporter," I say. "One who doesn't understand that I am at work."

"What time do you get off?" he says. "We can grab coffee. Maybe a drink."

I snort.

Aubrey," Ingrid whispers. To the reporter, she warbles something about stress again as she shunts me off to the staff room.

"You cannot speak like that in front of patrons," she says as she closes the door.

"I'm sorry," I say.

She hovers, as if waiting for an argument.

When I don't give it, she nods slowly and says, "I'm concerned. That's not like you, Aubrey."

Actually, it's totally like me. It's the me I abandoned when I met Paul. I'm not saying I miss that girl. In some ways, I feel like her older sister, rolling her eyes and saying, "Seriously?" Yet the other part of that girl, the part that had no problem telling a reporter where to shove his shtick? Yeah, I kinda miss her.

"You're right," I say. "I'm under a lot of stress. About the news clip, I'd like to explain —"

"No need."

"I'd really like —"

"Why don't you take the rest of the day off? It's slow today." She pats my shoulder, but there's a hesitancy to it, like patting a Rottweiler.

"I'm fine," I say. "I —"

"Really. I insist. Take the day off and rest. We'll see you tomorrow."

I have an unexpected half day off. I'm trying not to freak out about that. In fact, I'm trying to tell myself it's exactly what I need. The more time I have to investigate, the faster I can vindicate myself.

Of course, the first thing I do is go online, in hopes I've already been vindicated. But there's no update on the case, nothing to indicate the murdered woman has been

119

identified.

Time to get to work. When I left this morning, I took care with my outfit. Dress pants, a white blouse, a dark blazer. Hair pulled back in a sleek ponytail. Minimal makeup. I leave my contacts out and wear my black-rimmed glasses.

Does the mirror show a woman who could pass for a police detective or federal agent? Yes, and that's no accident. I won't tell anyone I'm a cop, but if they draw that conclusion, it isn't my fault. Or so I tell myself. The truth is that I'm no longer the pissed-at-the-world twenty-year-old who pulls crap like that and doesn't give a damn. I know better.

It's 12:10 when I reach the first pizza place on my list. No one there has seen the woman in the photo. On to the next one. I hesitate in the parking lot. Pop's Pizzeria is a hole-in-the-wall. A tiny take-out parlor in a tiny strip mall. The sign actually reads POPS PIZZERIA. It's that kind of sign, the sort you get done by a friend who has a buzz saw and a few cans of paint and a C in grade school English. It's either going to have the most amazing pizza ever . . . or the worst. From the lack of cars out front, I'm betting the latter.

I go inside. The counter area is empty, of

both customers and staff. When I call "Hello?" I hear voices in the back, speaking Italian. I call again. A door opens and a woman emerges, wiping flour-covered hands on an apron. A mix of yeast and tomato and oregano wafts out, and it smells amazing.

"Five minutes," she says in heavily accented English. "It is ready in five minutes."

"I'm not picking up an order," I say.

"You make order?"

I smile. "I wasn't planning to, but judging from that smell, I might." I extend my hand. "Bree Minor. I'm trying to find a missing woman."

I'm straddling a line, using my maiden name and not calling myself a police officer. I'm still nervous. Still not sure I can pull this off. But for the missing woman and her son, I'm going to try.

I continue. "We have reason to believe she worked at a pizza —"

"Kim." Before I can speak, she opens the door into the back room and calls out in urgent, rapid-fire Italian.

A man walks out. He's younger, maybe my age.

"Is Kim okay?" he asks.

I hesitate. I have no idea what police protocol would be in an actual murder investigation. But these people aren't going

121

to know either, and I'll have better luck getting details if I admit there's been a crime.

"I'm sorry," I say. "I'm investigating a murder."

I pause a moment, respect for the dead; then I open a manila folder and hold out the printed photo.

The man takes it, and his eyes shut for a second before he nods. "Yes, that's Kim. She didn't come in to work yesterday, and I've been calling. That isn't like her. Mamma was worried. I said I'd stop by her place later."

He bends in front of his mother and talks to her in Italian. She crosses herself and then folds her hands in her lap, her gaze down.

"I'm very sorry," I say. "But I do thank you for identifying her. I also need to ask about her son."

The man frowns. "Kim had a son?"

My heart thuds. "Evidently."

"She never mentioned any kids. Did he live with his father?"

No. Please, no.

"I only know she had a little boy," I say. "Four or five years old."

The man frowns, turns to his mother, and says something. Her eyes widen, and she shakes her head vehemently.

122

"Kim did not have any children," the woman says in English. "I would always tease her, saying she needed to find a nice young man and have babies. Perhaps this woman is not her."

"That's Kim, Mamma," her son says softly.

"When was her last shift?" I ask.

"Monday. She works Fridays, Saturdays, and Mondays. Can I ask when she . . . ?"

"Tuesday."

"And it was in the news?" He curses under his breath, and his mother berates him in Italian. He apologizes for the profanity and says, "I haven't been paying attention to the news lately." He gestures at the shop. "We only opened a few months ago, and Kim is — was — our only employee. I've been putting in twelve-hour shifts every day."

"I understand. Would I be able to see her employment record? I need her current address."

"Sure." He starts heading for the back and then slows. When he turns, he stammers. "I-I'm not sure I have her record. Here, I mean. Like I said, we're new, and we haven't quite caught up on paperwork."

"I'm not with the IRS, sir. Whatever arrangement you had with Kim, I'm sure she planned to pay her income taxes."

He nods. "Right. Yes. It was just . . . informal."

"While a Social Security number would be useful, I'll take anything. My only interest is in catching her killer."

"Give the girl whatever you have, Francis," the woman says.

"Of course, Mamma."

FOURTEEN

Kim *must* be the dead woman. Her employers both ID'd the photo, and they haven't heard from her since before the murder. But Kim doesn't have a child.

So how can she be the young mother I met in the park?

Is there a chance the dead woman isn't the person I met?

No. The young woman I met said she worked in a pizza parlor that opened at noon. Two people just identified the murdered woman as an employee in their pizza parlor, which opens at noon.

I must pursue this until either I solve this puzzle or I am somehow proven wrong. Even thinking that last part sets my heart racing, my breath coming short.

If I am wrong . . .

If I am wrong, I've given Paul what he needs to paint me as an unstable mother. First, I start hallucinating kidnapped kids.

Now, I'm pursuing my delusion even after I've learned that the dead woman didn't seem to *have* a child.

I am risking the one thing that is most important to me — custody of my daughter — and for what? Even if I am right, is it worth the risk to help a stranger?

I should have stopped as soon as Cooper told me there was no missing child. That's what other people would do. Normal people. If they even took the time to *report* what looked like an abduction, they'd have dropped it there. Duty done, let the police handle the rest. It's none of their business.

I did report the kidnapping. I reported that the dead woman was the boy's mother. Now I've learned that the dead woman wasn't *anyone's* mother. So drop it. Drop it and step away before I get into more trouble.

I should do that. But I can't. I will always be that little girl trapped in a car with her dying mother, the girl who grew up knowing she might still have a mother if someone had stopped, if someone had even taken a moment to report seeing a wrecked car. I will always be the eighteen-year-old rushing home to help her father when no one else would, arriving too late to stop him from taking his life.

126

No one helped my mother. No one helped my father. No one wanted to get involved. I cannot be that person. Ever. If there is any chance that a boy is out there, in trouble, and no one is searching for him, then I must *be* that one person. The person who cares. The person who gets involved.

Whatever the cost.

Kim's employers gave me her address. Before I check it out, I place a call to the police station tip line.

"Hi, I'm phoning about the young woman found in the park. I'm sure I've seen her working at Pop's Pizzeria over on the west side. I think her name's Kimberly."

It's not perfect, but at this point, calling in under my own name is a surefire way to make sure no one follows up.

The address leads to an apartment building. A nicer one than mine, though hardly upscale. At least it has a controlled entry. That would work better if I didn't just need to stand outside fumbling in my purse for my "key" until a resident came out. He even held the door for me.

I head straight up. Kim's apartment is at the end of the hall, which is perfect. I slip out through the stairwell, make sure no one's around, and walk to her door.

I should just go get the super. Make up a story, like I did with the pizza places. That *should* be my only option here, confronted with a locked door.

It is not my only option.

Hacking isn't the extent of my skills. It isn't the extent of my crimes.

I bend to check the lock. Old building; simple security. I can open it.

I'll get inside and find evidence of a child. That's all I need. Just the reassurance that a child exists, and then I will back off and wait for the police to ID Kim and figure it out for themselves.

I'm about to start on the lock when I hear a noise inside. I put my ear to the door and pick up a radio or TV.

Maybe she left it on when she went out.

That's reasonable, but still . . .

I rap on the door. Ten seconds later, it swings open. A woman stands there, late twenties, tiny build, brown skin, her hair swept into the kind of style I know well: grab an elastic at 5 A.M. when the baby wakes, shove your hair up, and leave it like that until you collapse in bed at night and maybe, just maybe, remember to take it out. Sure enough, bright-colored wooden blocks litter the hall floor, and through the open door I spot a high chair in the kitchen.

128

The woman stage-whispers, "Yes?"

"Baby napping?"

A tired smile and a nod. "She just went down."

I gesture to ask if she'd rather speak in the hall. She nods again and steps out, while keeping the door cracked open.

"I'm looking for Kim Mason," I say.

Her brows knit. "Kim . . ."

"Mason. Her employer gave me this address."

The frown deepens. I tell her the address, and she says, "That's this apartment, but I don't know a Kim."

"How long have you lived here?"

"My husband and I moved in after we got married. Two . . . no, two and a half years ago."

Long before the pizza place even opened, meaning Kim didn't move recently and forget to update her address with her employer.

I take out the photo. "Have you seen this woman before?"

Her eyes widen. "That's the girl on the news. The one who was murdered."

"Have you ever seen her anywhere else?"

She shakes her head. "If I had, I'd have called it in." She looks up at me. "You're with the police."

"I'm helping with the investigation." *True enough.*

Her gaze returns to the photo. Then she looks at me. "This is exactly why we left the city. My parents said that since my husband had a good job, we should move someplace safe to raise our babies."

No place is safe. Because every place has people, and the threat isn't always the gangbanger on the corner. It can be the woman next door. Or the guy lying in bed beside you.

Which isn't what she wants to hear.

I remember Paul last night, giving me crap about my building's broken front door. When we picked our house, he'd looked around and declared it a good neighborhood. A "safe" one. The sort of place he felt comfortable leaving his new wife and raising his future kids, and I wanted to gape at him and say, "You're a *lawyer*. You should know better."

It was like mistaking our white picket fence for ten feet of electrical barbed wire. But he couldn't see that. Which I suppose explains how he ended up with me. He saw what he wanted. He accepted the image I presented, of a woman who had never done anything worse than rack up traffic tickets. A bit scattered and quirky but totally harmless. That's the package he bought. What he got . . .

What he got was very different. He'd finally sensed that and backed away.

I ask the young woman a few more questions. It's clear, though, that she'd never seen Kim before her photo appeared on the news.

Outside, I walk around. There's only one other apartment building on this street, and it's five stories tall. Kim gave a seventh-floor address.

Which means she gave a *false* one.

FIFTEEN

I am at home, tracking down Kim Mason. Or the woman pretending to be Kim Mason. It's a fake identity, too, as I quickly discover. Working under the table. Giving her employer a false address. Hiding the fact she has a child. Those are not the actions of a young woman who's just a little cagey with her personal info.

A fake ID takes this to a whole other level, especially if she had documentation to back it up. There was a time when I toyed with that option. It didn't last long, but I learned what building a false identity entails, and despite what we see on television, there isn't some guy in the shady part of town who'll set you up with an ironclad birth certificate for ten grand.

What you *can* get from that dude in the shady neighborhood, though, is fake ID cards, and for a whole lot less than ten grand. Those cards will get you into a bar before you hit twenty-one. They will not get you past a police check.

If Kim Mason was working under the table, that suggests she's only using fake ID, not an actual false identity complete with Social Security number. She's living under a false name the cheap way.

Why would she do that? Tons of reasons, as I well know, most of them involving mistakes made, a fresh start needed. But her situation adds a wrinkle. A hidden son.

But I need to prove there *was* a son. That a child has been taken. And I am no closer to accomplishing that goal than I was when the police first turned me away.

So I am home, utilizing skills left rusty for years. I'm hacking my way to Kim Mason.

I know that's a fake name. Her address, and likely 99 percent of everything she gave her employer, is also fake. But there will be that 1 percent. The single piece of information she provided that needed to be genuine.

A phone number.

Her boss said that he'd used that number in the past, and she answered. So it is correct.

I quickly establish that it's a prepaid. Which is what I expect. Someone like this won't have a legitimate credit card, much less be paying a monthly cell phone bill with it.

What I need are her call lists. That could take serious work. Tech companies update their security constantly. Or they do . . . if they're not selling cheap prepaids, which is ironic really. People buy prepaids because they provide anonymity, and yet hacking into those records isn't nearly as tough as it would be with a regular phone.

I download an encrypted version of her call records for my laptop and run it through a simple decryption program. Then I write out the last dozen numbers of calls made and received and dial her last call placed. That number goes to a take-out place. The next is her work. The third just rings, no voice mail. The fourth tells me the number is no longer in service, which means I put a big red circle around it for later. It's the fifth-oldest call that actually gives me a response. When a man answers, I say, "Hi, I just found this phone on the sidewalk, and I'm trying to track down the owner. All I have is a first name. Do you know anyone named Kim?"

"Kim Lyons?"

"Maybe?"

"I've got a girl, rents a place of mine, named Kim Lyons."

"Is her phone number . . . ?" I read it out.

He checks and says, "Yeah, that's Kim."

"Great! I'll drop this off for her. Where does she live?"

I don't expect him to actually tell me, but I guess that just goes to prove that the world is full of people far more trusting than me. People who hear a friendly female voice on the phone, a Good Samaritan trying to return a lost phone, and they don't even consider nefarious possibilities.

He rattles off an address and then says, "That's really nice of you, you know that? Most people would just walk right past a phone on the ground. Or swipe it. Kim's a good kid. She'll appreciate that."

"It's the least I can do. I know how tough it is, being a single mom."

He pauses. "Single mom?"

"Bad guess?" I laugh. "Sorry. Apparently, I suck at this amateur detective stuff. I was trying to figure out whose phone it was, and I saw a photo of a little boy. I thought it might be hers."

"Nah, Kim's just a kid herself. No little ones yet. But she'll be thrilled to get her phone back. So thanks for doing that."

"Happy to help."

Kim Mason — or whoever she is — has

rented a house on the outskirts of Oxford. It's no country manor. There *are* no country manors in that area, too close to the city's waste disposal, too close to the railroad tracks. The house is much bigger than any apartment, but in a secluded area, away from public transport and city amenities.

A secluded place.

A private place.

That's the first word that comes to mind when I see the property: "privacy." It's on a dirt road, and the house itself is surrounded by trees and set a couple hundred feet back. There's a rear yard where a child would never be spotted. The nearest neighbors are a half mile away. A child could play unseen *and* unheard, even at preschooler decibels.

Could I hide Charlotte in a place like this? Yes. Room for the two of us to walk and play, and a driveway that loops around the rear, so I could get her out into a waiting vehicle and take her into the city, where I'd be just another woman with a child.

I break in the back door. It's easy work — simple locks and no chance of a passerby spotting me behind the house. Once I get the door open, though, I see that it shouldn't have been so easy to break in. There are two dead bolts. *Good* dead bolts, plus a basic security system. But the dead bolts weren't fastened and the security system isn't on.

I head straight for the kitchen. This is where I'll find evidence of the boy. When Charlotte isn't staying over, I put away her toys and store her booster seat, and take her special pillow from the bed we share, and she disappears . . . until you open my fridge.

I am not a mass consumer of juice boxes or string cheese or tiny yogurt containers covered in cartoon animals. Even without that, you'll find signs of Charlotte in my cutlery drawer, two child-size sets with plastic handles. There's more plastic in the china cupboard — cups and plates and bowls. A five-year-old might have graduated to silver cutlery, but I know there will be signs of him in that kitchen.

There are not.

I check every cupboard, and all I find is glassware and china. There's food in the fridge and the pantry, but nothing particularly child-friendly. Not even a box of Cheerios.

I open every drawer and door, and I see only what I'd expect in the house of a twenty-three-year-old. The basics. That's it.

He is here.

He must be here.

And what if he's not?

I won't think of that. I can't. There is a

child, and I will find evidence of him in this house, proof I can take to the police.

The living room is empty. Yes, there's furniture, but only the sort that comes with a rented house — not so much as a magazine or a blanket added. In the bathroom, I find only women's toiletries. No tear-free shampoo. No superhero-shaped bottle of bubble bath. No tiny toothbrush alongside hers.

I grip the counter, looking at myself in the mirror.

Have I made a mistake?

What have I done? What have I risked?

Keep looking.

I head into the bedrooms. There are three. Two have nothing but bare beds and empty dressers. The third is Kim's room. There's not much, but it's clearly occupied, and again, it's all hers. Women's clothing. Women's shoes. Women's accessories. Nothing more.

I walk into the bedroom right beside Kim's. That's the one I'd pick for Charlotte, keeping her close. But then I hear a truck rattle past and realize the window overlooks the front yard. While I can't see the road through the trees, if I was being paranoid, I wouldn't want light visible from more than one bedroom at night.

I search the third bedroom, with a rear-facing window. I open every drawer. I pull them all the way out and check underneath. I open the closet, pat the shelves and then bring in a kitchen chair to examine them closer. I don't even find a piece of LEGO.

It is only when I peer beneath the bed that I spot something. I crawl under it, and my hand closes around the familiar shape of a juice box.

Gripping it, I start backing out, and my other hand brushes something smooth and slick. When I pull that out with me, I find myself holding a book.

Where the Wild Things Are.

I smile, as I crack open the cover. I know every word of this book. It's one of Charlotte's favorites. I flip through, and I remember the woman's words.

"I've been reading with him."

I hold the book up to the light. There's no dust on the cover, meaning it hasn't been under there since the last tenants.

I flip through again, and there, written on the inside cover in shaky block letters . . .

BRANDON.

I examine the empty drink box. It's a child-sized one, grape juice, with a purple mouse on the front. Also no sign of dust. When I turn the box upside down, a drop of purple liquid falls.

As I watch that drop fall, a thought forms. I toss the book and box onto the bed and race around the house, checking the garbage cans.

Every one is empty.

Completely empty.

There is not one item of trash inside. And no bags outside.

You erased him. You knew something was coming — someone was coming — and you erased every trace of him.

I go back into the bedroom, and I pick up the box and the book.

Found you, Brandon.

No, I've found proof of him. Proof that I cannot take to the police, because it'll be like when I told Officer Cooper about the mud-smeared license plate.

"See this juice box? This book? Here's the proof."

"A . . . juice box. And a . . . book. Left under a bed."

"Right, but —"

"Tell me again how you happened to find these things, Ms. Finch?"

I would admit to breaking in — even to hacking — if it would convince the police that a child is missing. It will not.

140

I found *evidence* of you, Brandon.
And now I need to find *you.*

SIXTEEN

When I leave Kim's rental, I head to Chicago, for a rental locker I have not visited since the day I married Paul. No, that isn't true. I did come here three years ago. To the locker I rent under a fake name, from the kind of company that doesn't ask questions if you pay in cash.

The last time I visited was a week after Charlotte was born. And I removed a gun. For six months, I kept that between the mattress and box spring of our bed, until Charlotte started to crawl, and the day she did I brought it back to this locker.

Paul never knew about the gun. Aubrey Finch isn't the kind of woman who'd even know how to hold one. She certainly wouldn't want one in the house. Not with a child. I agree, yet when Charlotte was born, all my old fears ignited.

They are irrational fears. I know that. It isn't as if I have a million bucks, stolen from my partners, stashed in this locker. No one is going to come after me. When I first left home, I'd slept with a gun under my pillow for a year before realizing I was safe. After Charlotte, though, nightmares plagued every bit of post-baby sleep I got — nightmares of someone coming for her, taking her, hurting her. Those, too, eventually died down, and I was fine returning the gun.

Now, though, I am again worried. I'm digging into something dangerous. Kim is dead. Her son is missing. It is my earliest fears with Charlotte come to life. Someone from Kim's past came for her. I'm certain of it. If that person finds out I'm digging into Brandon's disappearance? Into Kim's death?

Time to visit the storage locker.

The space is barely closet sized. My possessions would actually fit into a box. But I can't exactly stick a box in a sketchy storage locker without the risk of someone prying open the door and knowing they've hit the jackpot.

I've scattered my treasures among thrift store furniture. Taped under each drawer of a dresser is twenty thousand dollars. None of it is stolen. When Ruben first came to me with his hacking offer, it'd been a get-rich-quick scheme. Such things always are, aren't they? The problem is that most thieves don't funnel their ill-gotten gains into a 401k. They stuff it into a needle or spend it on a blackjack table. Not me. Of the money I made, I kept one-third to live on. One-third I donated to charity for veterans suffering from PTSD. The final third I gifted, anonymously, to people in need. That doesn't make me Robin Hood. I *did* keep the one-third, and I enjoyed "sticking it to the man" a little too much.

This hidden money, though, comes from my father. It is my inheritance. When I walked away from my criminal life and reinvented myself, I knew better than to throw around money, even if it was legally mine. I lived the life I'd created for myself — a girl with a high-school education, working sales jobs. Then I met Paul, and I couldn't exactly produce a hundred grand in cash without raising questions. So the money stays here until I have a condo and joint custody of Charlotte. Then I can begin slipping it out to pay off my mortgage.

I'm storing memories here, too. My mother's photo album. Her rings. My father's medals. His watch. A locket he gave me when I turned sixteen. Thumb drives, too, of digital documents and photos. My past takes up so little space. Less even than the money.

The gun is taped under a nightstand. As I pull it out, I remember the first time I held one. On my twelfth birthday, I asked my father to take me to the range. He refused. Continued to refuse until he caught me in a field, target shooting with friends.

At the time, I thought he refused because I was a girl. I know now that he didn't want me following him down his path into service. He never said that, but I see proof in my memories, of every time I raised the subject and he'd start talking about good civilian tech jobs and I'd get so angry, certain he just didn't think I could handle army life.

I'd been determined to prove him wrong. I practiced shooting until my shoulder ached. I ran until I collapsed from exhaustion. I lifted weights until I tore muscles. And still he talked about that damned desk job, tossing around visions of Silicon Valley like it was Disney World. Which it had been, to him — the dream of a safe and successful life for his daughter.

I'm sorry, Dad. I didn't understand.

I heft the gun — a Glock 19 — and I remember the day Ruben tried to hand me a Ruger LC9. Until then, I'd worked from my laptop, hacking security systems so his group could break in. That day, two members were out sick, right before a massive job.

"We just need eyes on the ground," Ruben said. "The same thing you do from your computer, except IRL."

He actually said "IRL" as if we "tech geeks" spoke in text acronyms.

"You'll get your cut, plus one of theirs," he said.

"I want both of theirs."

He laughed. "You can't do the job of two —"

"If I can, you'll pay me both their shares?"

He agreed . . . and he paid out. After that, I was no longer sitting on my laptop. I learned how to wield a set of lock picks. I learned how to case a property. I learned how to steal . . . IRL, as he'd put it.

Yet when he'd tried to hand me the Ruger, I refused.

He rolled his eyes. "Let me guess. Army Girl needs a bigger gun."

"No, 'Army Girl' doesn't carry a gun. That escalates a situation."

"That's the idea, kid."

We argued. I won, and never once did I regret being unarmed. Not even after the last job, when the guy who was playing "eyes on the ground" screwed up, and the returning homeowner shot me in the shoulder. Afterward, Ruben said, "I bet you wish you'd had a gun for that."

No, I was glad I hadn't, or I might have returned fire, and a guy defending his property did not deserve that. I *did* deserve what I got, and that awareness proved I was no longer the angry kid who signed on with Ruben.

It was the proverbial wake-up call, not even the shot itself so much as what followed — the realization that I couldn't check into a hospital. Not with a gunshot wound. Ruben knew people. Doctors, or those who passed for doctors, because honestly, someone who takes cash for off-the-books medical care has probably lost his license, and not through a tragic miscarriage of justice. So I pay the price, with the pain in my shoulder as a constant reminder of a choice I made.

I put the gun into my purse, and my phone rings, making me jump. I look to see an unfamiliar number. I answer.

"Aubrey?" a woman's voice asks.

"Yes?"

"It's Gayle. Gayle Lansing. I wanted to thank you for the flowers."

It takes a minute to realize what she's talk-

147

ing about. Hell, it takes a minute to remember who she is. Standing here with a gun, among the ghosts of my storage locker, I am someone else. I am the Aubrey who's never had a husband, never imagined she would have one, certainly not a woman who envisioned she'd someday have an ex-husband with a girlfriend.

I cover my hesitation with a babble of "Oh, you're welcome" and "Thank you again for taking Charlie." That goes on for a few exchanges — her with "I was happy to" and me thanking her again and her assuring me it's all good.

Then she says, "I wanted to ask you a favor. About this weekend. Is there any chance Paul can keep Charlie for Saturday?"

"Keep her?"

"I know he brings her over first thing Saturday morning, but it's my daughter's birthday, and we were going horseback riding. Charlie would love it."

My hackles rise. I force them down. Gayle isn't inventing special treats to woo my daughter. She's taking her daughter for her birthday and asking Charlotte to join.

Still, I can't resist saying, "I don't think she's old enough for horses."

Gayle laughs. "Oh, of course, she isn't going to ride by herself. She'll be with Paul.

And I haven't mentioned it to her, so if you would rather not, I completely understand. Libby would *love* to have her along, though, and we could bring Charlie to you first thing Sunday morning."

"Why not Saturday night?"

There's a pause. Then, "The horseback riding is in Wisconsin, so it's a bit of a drive. I know you had Charlie this week for an extra night, so I thought you might like the evening to yourself. We'll bring her first thing."

She's being reasonable. Perfectly reasonable. Which only makes some childish part of me dig in her heels and want to be *unreasonable.* That extra night had been a bonus, not a chore, and I will take every one with my daughter that I can. Also why the hell didn't she ask this sooner? It's Friday night, for God's sake. I might have had our weekend planned.

Except I didn't, and the reason she's asking now is because she's met me. We have exchanged our peace offerings — she got me the princess tea reservation and I sent flowers. She has to have been worried about me, what kind of person I'd be, how I'd treat her, and now all is fine, so she's taking a chance on asking for Charlotte to come to her daughter's party.

Yet even as I calm myself down, there's a part of me that cannot help but wonder whether I'm misreading this entirely.

Could this be Paul's idea? He thinks I'm a wee bit unstable right now. Did he confess his fears to Gayle?

"I . . . just don't want Charlie going over this weekend."

"Wait. I have an idea, Paul."

Have they conspired to undermine my parental rights?

Or am I being a paranoid bitch even considering that?

I shift my weight, and as I do, I feel the extra heft of the gun in my purse.

Charlotte.

I forgot about Charlotte.

I didn't forget she was coming for the weekend, of course, but I failed to put the pieces together. I was retrieving a gun to take home . . . when Charlotte will be there.

If I am so concerned about safety that I'm getting a gun, should I even have Charlotte over?

No, I'm overreacting on the threat. Charlotte is not in danger. I do not *need* a gun. I could put it back and insist on taking Charlotte tomorrow. Still . . .

I make it clear to Gayle that I don't require an extra night off and that I'm more than happy to take Charlotte anytime Paul needs it. However, I don't want to interfere with their plans. Bringing her Sunday morning is fine.

We make arrangements. After I sign off, I tuck the gun back into its hiding place. If I need it, I'll come back — after Charlotte's gone.

SEVENTEEN

Gayle's call caught me off guard. The more I think about it, though, the more suspicious I become. The drive home from Chicago, in Friday-night traffic, gives me plenty of time to think. Too much time.

After that call, part of my brain whirls in a cyclone of paranoia. A little homunculus inside my head runs in circles shouting "Doom! Doom! Doom!" like a cartoon character. That is the worst side of me. The most childlike side. The most guilty side. The part that is somehow convinced I have gotten off far too easy in life, considering my crimes, and the hammer of karma hangs over my head, waiting for the absolute worst way to punish me.

You are a thief, Aubrey. You stole from people, and you were not caught, and that ache in your shoulder doesn't repay your crimes.

You think you can run from all that? Fall in

love and marry a great guy and have an amazing child and a perfect life? You think that a marriage breakup is the worst thing that can happen? Think again.

The worst thing that can happen is that I lose my daughter. Not through a court of law, but through a foe I cannot fight. Through Charlotte herself. She lives in the only home she's known. Sleeps in the only bedroom she's known. She lives there with her perfect daddy, and the only thing missing is her mommy. But what if another mommy comes along? A mommy who'll take her to princess teas when her own mother forgets. A mommy who'll whisk her off on surprise horseback rides and birthday parties. A mommy who brings a cool older sister and brother. A mommy who could slide into that house and take her mother's place, and everything will be the way it was. No, everything will be *better.*

I want to scream at that version of Gayle, the one who knows exactly what she's doing, the one who wants to steal my daughter, steal my place. Steal my husband? I can say I'm happy for Paul, but is there a tiny part that hoped for some fantasy reunion? Yes. Yes, there is. And it *isn't* tiny. Not at all.

Yet Gayle isn't that monster. She's just a woman who's gone through her own divorce and has now met a wonderful guy . . . a guy I gave up. While part of me wishes she would move a little slower — *does Charlotte really need to go to your daughter's party already?* — that might just be my own fears speaking. The fears that know this is one step along a road I don't want to see them take.

Whatever Gayle's intent, Paul is up to something. It's too coincidental otherwise. We parted on bad terms yesterday. Could this be his revenge? That's not the man I know, but I *have* hurt him — I know that — and maybe he's finally lashing out.

Whatever the answer, he should have been the one to call me. That's what I realize during that drive home, what I'd missed earlier, in my confusion. Paul wanted a day of my time with our daughter. Time that we had agreed upon. We allow for exceptions, of course. We were determined never to put our own needs above our child's. We've negotiated these exceptions with no actual negotiation required. The one who said "I'd like her for *x*" was the one who also said "I know that isn't our arrangement, so here's how I suggest making up for it."

His requests are always reasonable, and so I am reasonable in return. Even this one — for Gayle's daughter — is logical. So he should have called me.

Having Gayle phone only makes me more suspicious. Makes me wonder whether adding Charlotte to the outing seems last minute because it *is* last minute.

"I . . . just don't want Charlie going over to Aubrey's this weekend."

"Wait. I have an idea, Paul. Why don't we invite Charlie to Libby's party?"

"I would love that. I'm just . . . I'm not sure Aubrey will go for it. She knows I'm upset. She might see through this."

"Here, let me handle it."

I'm in Oxford when my phone rings. I go to grab it. I'd never talk on my cell with Charlotte in the car, but she's not here, and I'm certain it's Gayle calling again or maybe Paul this time.

"On second thought, I think we should keep Charlie for the whole weekend. She'll be so tired Sunday."

I snatch up the phone, only to see a private number. I pull over and let it ring to voice mail. Then I retrieve the message.

"Ms. Finch? It's Laila Jackson from the Oxford PD. Please call me back." She rhymes off a number.

I sit there, holding the phone. If it were Officer Cooper, I'd be hitting those digits as fast as I could, certain he was calling to

155

say they'd finally realized I was right — their dead woman had a son, who is now missing.

But it's his partner, the woman who really doesn't like me, which means this almost certainly isn't a you-were-right call. Still, I cling to that hope and replay it a couple of times, as I listen to her tone. It's crisp, sharp even. Laila Jackson does not sound like a woman calling to tell me she's made a horrible mistake.

She knows I'm the one who left that anonymous tip about Kim. I'm sure of it. I was careful. I found a pay phone, which isn't easy to do these days. I made sure it wasn't near my home or work. I left nothing that could identify me. I even pitched my voice lower, and there'd been enough traffic in the background to add to the distortion.

It doesn't matter. A woman called in that tip, and Jackson is convinced I'm an attention-seeker. She'll know it was me.

Does that mean they're ignoring the tip? Has she said "Oh, I know who that is" and told the department she'll handle it?

Just ignore her. She's a bit of a nutjob.

My fingers hover over the keys. I need to set her straight. I need to make sure the police investigate. Finding this boy isn't my job, damn it. I'm not that person anymore. Not someone who puts her own safety in danger, breaking laws to help strangers. Certainly not someone who'll endanger her daughter to do that.

I need the police to pay attention.

Which means I need more evidence. If Jackson has convinced the police to ignore me, I have to dig deeper. I need Kim's real identity, and then I need to send it to someone they'll listen to.

Paul.

My gut rejects that the moment I think of it. Paul isn't exactly my ally here. Yet as angry as I am with him, I still trust him to do the right thing.

Without Charlotte coming over, I have all of tomorrow to track Kim down online. Find her name. Talk to Paul Sunday morning. Prove that I'm not losing my mind and ask him to take my information to the police.

"Here's her real name. The dead woman's. The boy's mother."

"Her real . . . ? The police don't even have this, Bree. How did you find it?"

Cross that bridge when I come to it. For now, I have a goal.

Paul phones at eight the next morning. He

157

leaves a message not unlike Jackson's — call me back. Nothing more. I consider doing that, just as I considered answering when I saw his number. What if he's changed his mind, and he wants to bring Charlotte over?

Then he'd say so in his message. He doesn't, which means I cannot afford to place that call. I'm afraid he's found an excuse to keep Charlotte all weekend. He won't leave that on a message. And if I don't return his call, then he has to carry through on his promise to drop her off in the morning.

Last night, before I left the storage locker, I'd taken some money. This morning, I drive back to Chicago and pay cash for a better laptop. Then I plot out a map of coffee shops, all within walking distance of each other. Each of these shops offers free Wi-Fi, and that's the attraction, far more than the fancy drinks.

I still get one of those drinks at each shop. An overpriced coffee and a pastry, which buys me ninety minutes in a Saturday-busy café. That's how long I figure it'll take before anyone realizes I'm camped out in the corner. I could probably go longer — I'm a thirty-year-old white woman on a new Apple laptop, hardly attention-getting — but I want to play it safe.

158

Step one: analyze the call logs from Kim's phone. There's the number that's no longer in service. That's important. I know it is. Same as the one that goes unanswered. Judging from the time stamp, that's the call that came in while we were in the park. I don't start there, though. I need more data.

I pull the call logs for the past month. One entry stands out. Every week, like clockwork, Kim calls a number with an area code I don't recognize. I look it up. South Dakota. It's a landline number, and when I do a reverse check, it's registered to a Thom Milano. I consider my options, and as tempted as I am to go deep, I know I don't have to here. With an uncommon name like that, hacking probably isn't required.

I head over to Facebook. I have a name. I have a vicinity. Two minutes later, I have a personal page. Thom Milano, thirty-five, married, two kids. Owns a construction company, which sets off alarm bells — construction is a good cover for illegitimate business interests. But a quick search reveals that it's just a small, local company. Milano and his crew build homes in Sioux Falls, South Dakota.

He's posted a few photo updates this week — his daughter at her softball game, his men working on a house, a candid shot of

159

his wife laughing at home. That's where I stop. I'm looking for signs that Milano is Brandon's father, and instead I get a picture of Ellie Milano . . . who is the spitting image of Kim Lyons.

On closer inspection, I realize that's not actually true. Ellie is older, close to my age, and she's heavier than Kim, but in a healthy way, with no sign of a hard-spent youth. In this picture, I see Kim a decade from now. If she kept her life on track. If she'd settled into the kind of life I had once. Healthy, happy, and carefree.

This is the person Kim has been calling. Not Thom Milano, but his wife. A relative of Kim's. A *close* relative. I would guess sister, but I won't jump to that conclusion.

I find Ellie's profile easily — Thom's links to it. Neither has theirs set to private. They aren't that sort of people. A very average middle-class couple, raising their family in a flyover state, posting pics of softball games. Maybe that should make them boring. It doesn't. I read their profiles and skim their pages, and envy stabs so sharp it physically hurts.

This isn't just a couple putting their best face forward on social media — there is such genuineness in their smiles, in their posts, that I do not for one moment doubt their happiness. When I envy them, I feel guilty, too. Guilty for thinking of myself, how once upon a time, I had this. Had it. Lost it. The guilt comes because I should be thinking of Kim. This is about her, and if I feel anything, it should be sorrow for this reflection of a life *she* might have had.

Forget all that. Focus on Ellie.

Thirty years old. Married since she was twenty-one. Two kids quickly followed. Ellie grew up in Cedar Rapids, Iowa. Maiden name: Mikhailov. I search on the name. It's Russian. I remember Kim on the phone. I remember telling Officer Jackson about it.

"She sounded very upset. She was speaking in another language. I don't know exactly, but I'm guessing Slavic."

Russian had actually been my guess, but I'd been wary of saying that. I didn't want to sound too certain.

Had Kim been talking to her sister?

I jump to Ellie's profile section for languages spoken. "English. Some Russian, but really only enough to curse out people who cut me off in traffic :)"

Kim hadn't been talking to Ellie on the phone then. It was, however, a family mother tongue. So maybe they were cousins rather than sisters — Kim coming from a branch of the family that maintained their native language more.

That's when I get to the section for family. Ellie lists a sister. Seven years younger. And her name? Kimmy.

I mine Ellie's profile for every mention of this younger sister. There's no link to a Facebook profile for her. There are photos, though untagged. Ellie has posted old photos of herself and sometimes she's with her little sister. In those photos, Kim grows from a baby to a fifteen-year-old. There's a final picture, for Kim's fifteenth birthday. And then she's gone.

Fifteen.

Is that when Kim had Brandon? Ejected from her family for a teen pregnancy? No. I'm sure Brandon was no older than five, and according to this timeline, Kim would have been twenty-three when she died, meaning she'd had Brandon when she was closer to seventeen.

While I don't find more recent photos of Kim on Ellie's page, I do find references to her. Old friends periodically ask how Kim's doing, and Ellie replies that she's fine, living her own life, but they're in contact and she's doing great. Sometimes she'll say she visited with "Kimmy" last month or that she just talked to her.

Still, there are no recent photos of them

together. No updates saying that Ellie was going to visit her sister or that Kim was coming over. If I hadn't seen those phone records, I might think these claims of contact were fake. But they did talk, weekly, often for an hour or more. That isn't two sisters who've drifted apart and only exchange cards at Christmas.

There are a couple of instances where someone asks "Where's Kimmy living these days?" . . . and Ellie doesn't reply, as if she missed the question. In another one, a guy from Cedar Rapids asks if he can get in touch with Kimmy, and Ellie answers that her sister isn't on Facebook. When he asks for an email address, she pretends not to see the question.

There are also no mentions of Brandon. No suggestion that Kim has a child. And that, I am sure, is not accidental.

Ellie is guarding her sister's privacy. Because her sister is in hiding. Using a fake name. Concealing her child from the world. Staying in close contact with her sister, but otherwise cutting all ties with her former life.

I imagine a world where I had someone I could keep in touch with. A sister or a brother or even a cousin I couldn't bear to cut from my life when I went on the run. I tell myself it's better this way — beholden to no one, endangering no one — but that's a lie. I envy Kim for having Ellie in her life.

That's when I realize Ellie is out there, going about her Saturday in South Dakota, with no idea what's happened to her sister. No idea her sister is dead.

I have Ellie's phone number. I could call. But that'd be wrong. As hard as it will be to hear this news from the police, it wouldn't be any easier from a stranger. Let Ellie continue her weekend unaware. Let her enjoy it. The news will come soon enough now that I have Kim's real name.

EIGHTEEN

I do not stop with that name. I can't. I feel like I'm catching snippets of Kim's life, just enough that my analytical brain cannot help filling in the gaps and making educated guesses. It's like catching a glimpse of an elegant security system and think *I wonder if I can hack that.*

I can't walk away now. I need to know, to satisfy my curiosity. What I'm doing here is perfectly safe and legal. I'm sitting in coffee shop number three, drinking a decaf latte, and browsing the Web, like half the other people here. I expected to spend the day with Charlotte, so I have no other plans. I can continue working this puzzle.

Girl from Cedar Rapids seems to drop out of family life at fifteen. She has a child two years later. A child she hides from the world, as she lives in a Chicago suburb under an assumed name. Yet she maintains contact with her older sister, who keeps her secrets for her.

There are patterns in life. Old stories, often told. Personal tragedies rendered almost banal by their very commonness. I see one of those in Kim's story, and I want to chide myself for being so unimaginative. The truth is, though, that I am very good at recognizing patterns, at predicting cause and effect. I remember in high school, we'd done some aptitude test measuring our intellectual strengths. Mine was logical reasoning, and when my guidance counselor saw the results, she actually double-checked to be sure she was reading them right. This is what makes me so good with computers. I can analyze, and I can foresee outcomes, and it's hard for me to understand why others cannot.

When I took that bullet to my shoulder, I didn't for one moment think *Why me?* I wasn't shocked. Not even surprised. This was one of the potential outcomes. So was jail. Or betrayal. Or death. The others had been outraged on my behalf. I'd laughed at them.

After I split with Paul, I'd gone to a group for newly separated women. I could say I was seeking support, but really, I just wanted information. I wanted to learn from their experiences. I remember one woman who'd been shell-shocked by her separation . . . which she instigated. She'd given her husband an ultimatum, and he chose divorce. Somehow, that surprised her. She'd only wanted him to know she was serious, and threatening divorce seemed the way to do it.

That baffled me. When I told Paul our marriage didn't seem to be working, of course I wanted it to be the wake-up call that would save us. But I knew it might also be the excuse he needed to jump in and say "I agree." Which is exactly what he did, and as much as that hurt, I would rather know how he felt and set him free to be happy. I love him. I'm not going to trap him in an empty marriage.

So in Kim's story, I see a pattern. There's more to it. I have noticed that while Ellie talks about going home to see her mother, there's no mention of her father. According to condolences in her timeline, he died three years ago, yet she never mentioned the death, responding to those messages with a simple "Thank you."

My dad and I had our differences — blow-out fights, the front door slammed, me spending the night at friends' — but I loved him like I loved no one else before Paul came along. When my father died, I was inconsolable with grief and rage. The chill I see on Ellie's page speaks to more than a strained relationship. Death heals those wounds. This one did not.

I study the last photos of Kim. At her fifteenth birthday celebration, it is obvious she's putting on a good face for her big sister — home from South Dakota and very pregnant — but I do not miss the look in Kim's eyes, the one that says she has already, in her mind, hit the road, putting as much distance as she can between her and a bad home life.

I know I might be wrong. I might be carelessly stuffing Kim into a convenient box. Girl with harsh home life flees and ends up in an even worse place, addicted to drugs, hooking up with the wrong guy, pregnant at seventeen. Then she has a maternal-instinct wake-up call, takes the kid, and flees, living under a false name with a child hidden from his daddy.

Old story, often told.

So I take Kim's real name and what few details I can glean, and I set about trying to prove myself wrong. Find the piece of evidence that says I'm full of crap, seen too many movies, read too many novels.

There are traces of Kim Mikhailov online.

Nothing since she was fifteen, but I expect that. I skim through those bits and pieces — high school website archives, abandoned social media footprints — and put them aside for later. I'm looking for . . .

I find what I'm looking for in a newspaper article dated two months after Kim turned fifteen. LOCAL TEEN MISSING. The article has been written with obvious reluctance by a journalist who's convinced he's dealing with a teen runaway, but has been persuaded to mention it briefly and make the family happy.

Kimberly Mikhailov disappeared one night after an argument with her father. Her mother admitted this wasn't the first time she'd left but said she always returned the next day. This time, she didn't. After two weeks, the family was desperate for any word from her. Mom and sister, Ellie, pleaded for news, any news.

I see no mention of her dad.

I find another scrap online, dated two years later. The passing mention of a divorce case, nothing newsworthy, just a tidbit in a list of court proceedings. The dissolution of a marriage between Kim and Ellie's parents. I find her father's obituary, too, asking for donations to be made to the American Liver

Foundation and AL-ANON. An alcoholic's death.

Old story. Often told.

After that I begin to reconstruct Kim's missing past. Which sounds like I'm some kind of detective prodigy. *Give me an hour on the Web, and I'll give you the bio of a woman who's been in hiding for ten years!* It's not like that. I'm chasing threads, vapors really, of the trail she's left. A comment here. A mention there. Spot the faintest whorl of smoke and follow it for miles, only to find a long-dead campfire at the end, the stories told around it evaporated. I am running through the internet pathways for hours, popping pain meds when my shoulder screams for mercy, setting timers on my watch so I don't overstay my welcome, moving from shop to shop.

I know how to use this piece of metal to my advantage, how to stalk the Web for my prey with every tool at my disposal. Image recognition is my best friend today. Here is this picture of a fifteen-year-old girl. Find me more like it.

The tool I'm using isn't a free Web service either. A couple of years ago, I saw a news piece about a "suburban housewife" who'd been exposed as a former drug mule by a partner in crime stumbling over her photo online. That sparked a fresh wave of my paranoia, and I'd gone through a period of obsessively checking for my photo online, untagging it on Facebook and so on. I found the best photo-recognition software available, and I still have access to it.

Even that entails wading through photos of blond girls until I have to make a pit stop at a pharmacy for eye drops. There is something about Kim's face that sets it apart, though, things I hadn't fully processed when I first met her. Wide-spaced eyes. A widow's peak. A nose that's just a little crooked, as if it's been reset. A tooth chipped and never repaired.

I excavate the mountain of near hits and find Kim Mikhailov at the bottom, in an advertisement for "barely-legal exotic dancers" in LA. At the time, she'd been sixteen, wearing enough makeup that men could tell themselves she was older, but they'd know better.

I then find her in another photo, dated six months later, when she'd have just turned seventeen. She's under the arm of a guy who looks about twenty. She's dressed in a sheath dress that barely covers her top or bottom, and the photo catches her tugging down the back. I see marks on her arm now, but there's no drugged-out vacancy behind those eyes. Instead, there's a wide-eyed . . . Not innocence. I didn't see that in her even at sixteen.

This look is one that's staring wide-eyed at the world, feeling it stare back and not enjoying the sensation. She's ducked down into the man's arm, taking shelter there. He's well-dressed, sleek-haired, looking very pleased with himself.

The photo appears on an old Facebook page for a defunct club. There's no name attached to either Kim or her date. It's just part of a series of photos taken at the opening celebrations. But when I search on the guy's face, I get an exact copy of this photo on a personal Facebook page, a private one that I have to hack to access. There the same photo has a caption: "The boss & his girl, looking fine."

Dig, dig, dig. Find the connection. Endlessly chase those connections.

The guy who owns this page once worked for the young man with Kim, and the fact that he called her the boss's "girl" suggests she was more than a casual date.

I find the answer with less work than I would have expected . . . because the guy who owns the Facebook profile once worked for the club where Kim danced. That club had been owned by two guys. One of them died years ago of a drug overdose. The other's name is Denis Zima. He's the one in the photo with Kim.

It doesn't take much research to learn that Zima wasn't just an entrepreneurial nineteen-year-old with the cash to open a strip club. He's the son of a guy with links to the Russian mob. He started the club with a friend from high school — the one who died of an overdose. That club, where Kim worked, closed a year later, and Zima started a chain of nightclubs without the strippers and underage girls.

I'm not sure this gets me anywhere new. Yes, Denis Zima seems to have been Kim's boyfriend at the right time to make him a candidate for Brandon's daddy. And he's definitely a shady character. But that's for the police to investigate.

I'm about to close my browser when I see the results of my last search, looking for more information on Denis Zima and his clubs. My gaze catches on the third listing from the top, the search engine picking up my current location and highlighting results that might interest me most.

It's an advertisement announcing the opening of Zima's fifth club, Zodiac Five. Right here in Chicago. While it's been operating for the past week, it hasn't had an official grand opening. That's tonight.

I do not make plans to go to the Zodiac Five grand opening. That would be crazy. I am not — I am *rarely* crazy.

The point is that, according to the article, Zima is in town for the opening. Coincidence that he's here around the same time his ex was murdered? I have no idea. I'll leave that to the police. I'll let them know about Zima when I give them Kim's name. That doesn't stop me from periodically pausing my searches to look for any progress on the murder case, hoping that I'll see something new. That I'll find proof the police have followed my lead and identified the murdered woman, at least as Kim Mason. When I don't, I'm frustrated, and it only furthers my fear that Officer Jackson blocked my tip.

It doesn't help that Jackson has left two more increasingly terse "Call me back" messages. Before I leave Chicago, though, I make a call of my own, after hunting down a pay phone. I dial the Oxford Police Department tip line. This time, I don't bother with the preamble.

"Your dead woman is Kimberly Mikhailov," I say. "She's been living here as Kim Mason. She's originally from Cedar

174

Rapids, and she has a son named —"

"Please hold."

"What? No. You don't understand. I know the identity of the woman shot in Harris Park this week. Her name —"

The phone is ringing, my words unheard. I wait, seething. I understand Oxford is a small city, but putting a tipster on hold is unbelievably —

"Laila Jackson," a woman's voice says.

I freeze.

"You have the identity of the woman murdered in Harris Park?" she prompts.

"Yes . . ." I say, dropping my voice an octave.

"Is this Aubrey Finch?"

I hang up. Then I stand and stare at the pay phone.

This can't be happening. It's like something out of a B-grade thriller, the kind I'd watch and roll my eyes at, saying, "Real cops wouldn't do that."

Or would they? Yes, from my point of view, I'm being blocked from giving the police a vital clue toward solving a crime. To Officer Jackson, though, I'm an attention-seeking nutjob, and she is not going to let me waste one moment of the department's time.

There *are* people like the ones she's pegged me for. People who fixate on the

175

police and fancy themselves thwarted law officers. Or those who want their fifteen minutes of fame.

How do I convince Jackson that isn't me? I keep thinking I have the evidence to do that . . . only to be stopped from delivering it.

Paul.

There's no pretending anymore. I really need Paul's help.

Except that asking for his help risks exposing my secrets. If he found out about my past, that would endanger my chances of joint custody.

I won't give up my daughter. I'm sorry, Kim. I'm sorry, Brandon. I just won't.

I will, however, keep trying to solve this dilemma. I spend the ride home coming up with scenarios. My best bet is Officer Cooper. I must find a way to get to him . . . circumventing his pit bull partner, Laila Jackson.

Email. That's the answer. Find Cooper's personal email and send him everything. Include photos and screenshots. Send him evidence that, once seen, he cannot unsee, cannot deny.

I return to my apartment. It's after eight, and I need dinner — my stomach is complaining from the nonstop coffee and pastries. I'll pop in here and then go hang out in a local coffee shop, buy something relatively healthy and send that email.

There, that's my night sorted. Afterward maybe I'll even rent a movie and try to distract —

I'm stepping out of the stairwell when I spot a figure at my apartment door. I flash back to Thursday and think it's Paul again.

It's not.

It's Officer Jackson.

She's in civilian clothes — jeans, heeled ankle boots, and a stylish leather jacket — and she's standing outside my door, browsing on her phone. Killing time. Waiting for her quarry to return.

I back up fast, ease open the stairwell door, and retreat as quietly as I can. I go straight for my car, and I don't pause to think until I'm a few blocks from home. Then I pull into a strip mall, park, and sit there, hands on the steering wheel as I stare out the windshield.

I can't make an end run around Jackson to get to Cooper. She won't let me. For whatever reason, Laila Jackson has made "stop Aubrey Finch" her mission, and she's locked fast to it until I back off.

I will not back off.

So what do I do now? Check into a hotel

for the night to avoid her? Paul will be bringing Charlotte to my apartment in the morning.

That's fine — she won't still be there come morning. I just need to find something to do for a few hours, something that will help bolster my case.

Like what? I have Kim's *name.* I have her bio details. I even know who might be the father of her child. What more can I get?

I keep thinking of the club's grand opening tonight. Which is, again, crazy. What do I hope to gain there? Get a look at Denis Zima and confirm he's Brandon's father? A visual scan is hardly a DNA test. So what would I gain from going to that club tonight? I have no idea. I just know that I'm frustrated and restless, and there's a police officer staking outside my apartment door, and I have time to kill and . . .

And I know none of that is a reason. Excuses, that's all I have. The truth, I suspect, is that I've been fighting this urge ever since I saw that ad. I have no idea what I expect to accomplish at Zima's club, but I'm going.

Which is crazy.

And, right now, I don't care.

NINETEEN

Being unable to get into my apartment means I can't get ready there. Not that it matters much. Nothing in my closet these days is clubworthy. I did have a few dresses, back when I met Paul, and my coworkers could occasionally drag me to a club. That isn't Paul's scene, though.

I remember a couple of weeks after we'd begun dating, he suggested a club, which shocked the hell out of me. I'd pulled on my little black dress, and we spent exactly twenty awkward minutes in the club, before I confessed it really wasn't my thing, and I swear he melted in relief. Instead, we'd bought a bottle of champagne and checked into a hotel, and he showed me that, while clubs themselves weren't for him, he *did* appreciate my clubwear.

Even if I had those dresses, they wouldn't fit anymore. I put on fifteen pounds with Charlotte, and I decided to keep most of it.

I was in good shape, and I kind of liked the extra weight — it made me feel more like my image of a mother, whatever that might be. So I needed to do some shopping.

Fortunately, I'd taken out more money than I needed for the laptop. I bought a dress, heels, undergarments . . . I left my fancier underthings behind when I split with Paul — not much use for them in my current celibate life. While I won't be showing off my panties tonight — definitely *not* on my agenda — the new ones make me *feel* like a single girl going to a club.

Buy clothing. Buy makeup. Buy pins and styling products for my hair. Find a mall restroom and transform from suburban mommy into . . . well, suburban-mommy-goes-clubbing. That's still what I see when I look in the mirror. At least all the component parts are there — the hair, makeup, short dress, and heels — and if I look like a young single mommy on the make, oh well. I'm sure I won't be the only one there tonight.

I arrive at the club just after eleven, which I seem to recall is a good time, not too early but not hard-partier late. What I've forgotten after three years of stay-at-home-mommy life is that you don't just show up to a club and walk in. There's a line. A massive one that isn't moving because, duh, it's the grand opening.

I also realize, as I'm getting out of the cab, that I'm alone. Of course I am — I'm on a mission. But I have enough ego to be very aware of how I look, a thirty-year-old going to a club by herself. So as I'm trying to figure out my next move, I stand at the head of the line, pretending to scan it for my friends.

"Hey, Blue Dress," someone behind me says.

I keep searching the line, wondering what my chances are of sneaking in a back entrance, when the guy calls again, and I realize *I'm* wearing a blue dress.

I turn to see one of the bouncers waving me over. He's mid-forties, bald, steroid-pumped. I wonder what I'm doing wrong, maybe breaking some rule about hanging out too close to the doors.

"You look like you know your way around a gym," he says, as I walk over.

"Uh . . . yes . . ."

"You should try Bart's."

"I . . . don't think I know that one."

"It's very exclusive. Here." He takes a Sharpie from his co-bouncer's pocket and motions for my hand. I give it to him. He writes "Bart," and then what I think is an

181

address, but when I look, I realize it's a phone number. It actually takes about five seconds for me to realize *he's* Bart, and this is his cell, and there is no gym.

Yes, I've been married for a while.

"I might . . . check that out," I manage to say, as my brain struggles to ignite my rusty flirting skills and use them to get into this bar. "Thank you."

"No problem. And your friends? They're inside. They said to watch for you." He winks. "Hot brunette with a blue dress and biceps. That's gotta be you, right?"

"Yes . . . Yes, it is. Thank you."

He opens the door. Again, it takes a few seconds for me to realize I don't coincidentally fit the description of an actual "friend" someone's waiting for. He's letting me in ahead of the line, in hopes I might actually call his number. If not, well, a party can always use more single women. Maybe I *don't* look as mom-ish as I feel. Or maybe the bouncer just decided to shake things up for variety.

Inside, the club is packed, as one might expect from that line. If I felt old walking up, I feel ancient now. It's loud. So freaking loud. And it stinks — perfume and after-shave and BO mingling together. Then there are the lights, colored strobes and mirror balls.

I stare at the mirror balls before remembering that's the theme of Zima's clubs: faux seventies. Mirror balls. Caged go-go dancers. Disco songs that have been remixed because the illusion of the seventies is all well and fine, but please don't make us listen to the music.

Outside, I'd been worried about how I'd fit in without friends. Now I laugh at that. Even if I had friends in here, I'd lose them in three seconds. No one's going to notice that I'm alone.

I make my way to the bar. When I get past the mob hanging out there, I lean over the bar and say, "Dark and stormy, please."

The bartender hesitates.

"It's rum and —" I begin.

"Oh, believe me, I know how to make it. I've made so many that I'm out of ginger beer."

I must look surprised, because he chuckles, "Haven't been clubbing in a while, huh?"

"Evidently not. I guess it was just a matter of time before my drink actually became popular. Now I'll have to find a new one."

"Hipster," he says, and I laugh at that, and he promises to make me "something special."

We chat a bit. Nothing flirtatious. He's wearing a wedding band and seems happy to spend a few moments talking to someone who isn't checking him out.

When I go to pay, a guy behind me leans over and says, "I'll pay . . ."

He stops as he gets a look at me. Apparently, I look younger from the back. Or hotter. When he sees me, he withdraws the twenty in his hand and mumbles something as he turns to talk to his friends.

"Asshole," the bartender says. "This one's on me."

I shake my head and give him a twenty and a "keep the change." Then I slide away, smiling to myself. I'll admit to an ego bump when the bouncer let me in, and apparently the universe decided that needed straightening out, with the put-down at the bar. The thought puts me in a better mood than it should, and I'm wandering, sipping my drink, lost in my thoughts when I spot Denis Zima.

That's no coincidence. Zima is there to be seen, as much as those caged go-go dancers. Along one side of the room there are box seats, like those you find in old theaters, except these are raised just enough that the plebes on the dance floor can't stumble into them. In the biggest box seat, Zima sits in an oversized throne-like chair, surveying his club while others in his box try — and fail — to catch his attention.

According to my research, Zima is only twenty-seven. He looks older, though. There's no uncertainty in his gaze, no hesitation. He's the king of his pride, surveying the watering hole while his lionesses and hyenas all jockey for his attention.

Seeing him up close does not answer the question of whether or not he's Brandon's father. Brandon takes after his mother, and Zima looks like the photo I saw — good-looking white guy with dark blond hair and blue eyes. Brandon is also white, blond, and blue-eyed. So is — was — Kim.

But this is still Denis Zima. The reason I'm here. Now what?

I have no idea. I don't know what I was hoping for — that I'd see him and notice some secret mark that proved he was Brandon's father? Hell, I hadn't seen such a mark on the boy, so how would I find the same one on Zima?

I didn't know why I came here. Now I don't know why I'm staying here. Desperation, I guess. Desperation and frustration, and the sense that this was the next logical step and that if I showed up here tonight, all would be revealed to me.

Forget what I hoped to find. What *can* I find, now that I'm here? What am I looking for?

Brandon.

I am following a trail to Brandon. To a lost boy that no one else knows is lost.

Kim Mikhailov is dead. After years of hiding her son from the world, she has been murdered, her son gone. And the boy's potential father just happens to be in Chicago at the same time. That must mean something.

I slip into a back hall. I'm looking for an office. Looking for a computer. There's bound to be one, and there's unlikely to be anyone working on it at this time of night.

Find an office computer and search it for anything useful. I'd love to find emails or documents telling me where Zima is staying — and might be keeping Brandon — but I'll settle for any useful tidbits. A computer always has those.

I establish the layout of the building quickly. That's one thing Ruben taught me. When breaking into a place, don't go straight for the goods, even if you know where they are. Look around and get a mental map. Note exits. Note hiding spots. Note areas that might contain unexpected

186

treasure . . . or dangers.

The first floor is the club itself. There's also a small kitchen. Nothing huge — this is a place that serves food because it doesn't want you leaving if you get peckish, not because it wants you coming for dinner. There's a basement. I'm going to guess that's storage. There's also a second story, with stairs around the back. That's the most likely spot to find an office.

I don't just walk around opening doors. There are people here, staff zipping up and down the corridors. Staff who will be quick to point me back to the dance floor. Still, I do know how to do this. These skills don't come from Ruben. We only ever broke into empty houses. I learned this part from, well, from playing video games.

I've always been fond of first-person shooters, and I'm not the kind of player who blasts her way through to a goal. I approach the task with care, favoring stealth over force. Games like that offer an endless array of almost-empty buildings with the quest target hidden in the middle, requiring the player to pass umpteen guards who are, apparently, assigned to patrol one hall and only one hall. Which means that I'm very good at scoping out an area, finding every hiding spot, and then leapfrogging from one to the next while avoiding that gun-toting commando . . . or eagle-eyed server.

I make it upstairs without being spotted. It's not a full level — the club takes up part with its high ceiling. From the top of the stairs, it's dark, and I see and hear nothing.

I check doors as I walk. There's a lounge area. An empty room with construction equipment. And then a locked door. It's a simple lock, intended to keep people from accidentally wandering in. I open it with a credit card.

Right inside the door, a dead bolt waits on the floor, along with a cordless screwdriver. That makes me chuckle. It seems that someone did foresee the need for more security . . . they just haven't quite gotten to it yet.

This is indeed the office. Filing cabinets. Two desks. One desktop computer. I check the cabinets first. Empty. Then I flip through a stack of papers on the desk. Purchase orders and work orders. On to the computer.

It's password-protected, which would take time to crack, if I didn't check under the keyboard and find the password there. Hey, it's a new office, new computer . . . it's easy to forget these things. To their credit, they've used a complex password, one of random letters and numbers. Good for security; lousy for remembering.

I enter the password. The desktop opens, and I go straight to the contact list. I find an entry for Zima. I make note of his cell phone number and email address. That's when I remember the two unidentified numbers on Kim's phone record, the one with no answer and the one out of service. I pull those up on my cell and punch them into the desktop computer for full file-system search. No match.

I zip through email, but the computer belongs to whoever is playing office manager, and it's clean. Clean in the sense that there's nothing incriminating. It's all business.

I type in Kim's names, real and fake. A global document search brings up nothing.

I try "Brandon." I do get matches, but only because that's the surname of a contractor.

Next I go into the trash — the computer's trash bin, that is. Nothing.

If the office manager plays any role in Zima's less-than-legal business, it's not here. I don't even know that Zima *has* less-than-legal business. I'm —

Footsteps sound on the stairs. I dart into the supply closet. I pull the door shut behind me and duck behind a stack of boxes.

The footsteps echo through the empty upper floor. Then the office door opens and the footsteps enter.

"What do you mean we don't have the security cameras up and running?" a man's voice asks.

There's a pause, as if he's on the phone. Then, "Dummy cameras? Well, guess who's telling Denis that. Hint? It's not me."

A creak, as if the guy sat on the edge of the desk. "Right now, he's busy looking for the chick from the news. He thinks she's here tonight."

I freeze in a moment of sheer panic before I almost laugh aloud. Chick from the news? At a grand opening? Obviously, he means that Zima is hoping he's spotted media coverage.

The man continues. "Yeah, well, if those cameras aren't working, I'd suggest you get all eyes on the floor. You saw her in the news?"

A moment of silence. Then a frustrated growl. "Pay attention, asshole. Didn't you get the memo?"

Pause.

"No, it wasn't an *actual* memo. No wonder you're a security guard. You aren't even

190

bright enough to be a beat cop, and that's saying something. Yeah, yeah, stop sputtering. The chick's about my age. Dark hair. Bright blue dress. That's the clincher — the dress."

I look down at my dress.

It's bright blue.

He means me? Zima saw *me* on the news? Saw me downstairs?

The man continues, "Between you and me, I think Denis is seeing things. He's all worked up about the kid."

The kid. My heart slams into my ribs.

Stop panicking and get your phone out. Start recording this conversation.

I'm fumbling in my purse as the guy says, "Yeah, I don't know why she'd be here. She's some chick from the suburbs, says she met Kimmy in the park. And now she's clubbing in the city? Doesn't make sense. But you know Denis. We've got to make it look good. Find every dark-haired chick in a blue dress, and tell her she's . . . won free drinks or something. Specially selected to come speak to the boss."

I finally find my phone.

"Yeah, I know it's a pain in the ass. But it's your goddamned job."

Where's the app to record? I've never used it before.

191

Damn it!

The guy's talking again. "Hey, asshole, watch your mouth. I might think Denis is wrong about the chick, but I don't blame him. Not one bit. Put yourself in his place."

There. Found the app. I open it and click Record as the man continues.

"Imagine your girl takes off. Disappears from the face of the earth. Then, five years later, you see this chick on the news, talking about your girl having a little boy. A little boy who's *five years old.* Suddenly you know why your girl left. Not only did she leave, but she took something of yours, something you never realized you had. A son."

My head shoots up.

Did he say Zima didn't know about Brandon?

No. I've misheard. Please let me have misheard.

"Yeah, that's what I thought," the guy says. "Denis might be hallucinating this chick being at the club tonight, but he's not hallucinating the fact he's got a little boy. A kid who's disappeared."

A pause.

"No, dumbass. The boy didn't randomly get kidnapped the same day Kimmy dies. Someone has him. Someone's taking care

192

of him. Someone who is not his daddy. That's a problem. One Denis is going to fix."

TWENTY

of him. Someone who is not his daddy.
That's a problem. One Denise is going to
[...]

TWENTY

The guy has been gone for at least three
minutes, and I'm still in that closet, para-
lyzed, barely able to gasp breath.

What have I done?

Oh God, what have I done?

Zima never knew he had a son . . . until
he saw me on the television, telling the
world I'd seen his dead ex with a five-year-
old child.

Kim must have run from Zima before he
knew she was pregnant. She hid Brandon
so Zima would never find out he had a
child. When she realized she was in danger
she must have made arrangements for
Brandon. That's what this guy obviously
thinks, and from the way he's talking, he
knew Kim.

She found a safe place for Brandon, put
him in that park and told him to wait for
someone to come get him. His rescuer
comes. Brandon hears his name, and he

runs over. He sees a stranger. He's confused. He panics. The man quickly bundles him into the SUV and spirits him off to safety.

Kim has protected her son again. Her final *act* was protecting him. She got him to safety before Zima found out he exists.

And then I came along and ruined everything.

As I make my way down the hall, I focus on how I will fix this. Get my audio recording to the police. Let them stop Zima. I've made a terrible mistake, but I can still fix it. I *will* fix it.

That resolve lets me concentrate on my escape. There's no one upstairs again, so I get to the first level easily. I leapfrog from hiding place to hiding place. I remember an exit door partway down the back hall. I'll use that.

I get to the door and find it emblazoned with a huge sign warning that opening it will set off an alarm.

I do not want an alarm. But the alternative is to go back through the club, while every employee is looking for a dark-haired woman in a bright blue dress.

I remember the conversation between Zima's employee/ friend and the head of security. If the cameras aren't operating yet, and the dead bolt isn't on the office door, that suggests the security team wasn't fully prepared for tonight's opening. Is it possible, then, that this door *isn't* armed?

Even if an alarm does sound, I can run. It's not like I have to worry about security cameras.

I tug off my heels. Then I press down on the bar handle and carefully push the door . . .

It doesn't budge. I depress the handle harder. Still nothing.

They've locked the damn emergency exit.

Shoes slap the concrete. I duck into a hiding spot. A guy hurries past. Once he's gone, I make my way toward the club. The entrance to the dance floor is just up ahead. I'll cut a beeline through it to the exit, sticking to groups of people and avoiding that box where Zima sits. I'll just —

There's a security guard outside the women's restroom. He's stationed there, and he's watching every woman who walks in.

I dart back to my last hiding spot and duck in. As I do, I hear footfalls. It's the employee who passed me earlier. He's returning with a crate of bottles.

Once he passes, I retrace his steps to the basement door. It's unlocked. I open it and use my phone flashlight to guide me down the dark steps. At the bottom, I see closed doors. The ones at the end have key locks. At this end are two doors with regular knobs marked with makeshift stick figures of a man and a woman. I push open the door with the skirted figure and find the women's staff room.

I quickly open lockers. Most have jeans or sweats. A couple, though, contain dresses. I check tags. There's a black one in my size. I quickly change and wad up the blue dress into my purse. Then I take out a hundred bucks and slide it into the employee's bag.

Out the staff room. Listen for footsteps. Scamper up the stairs. Down the hall and . . .

I still need to pass that security guard, who'll notice I've come from the wrong direction.

I'm tucked into a side hall, considering my options, when I hear him talking. I poke my head out to see a dark-haired girl in a blue dress.

He's turned away, talking to her. I slip off my heels again and creep into the restroom behind his back. A moment later, as I'm putting my shoes on, the girl comes in. The guard must have dismissed her, realizing her dress isn't *bright* blue and she's barely drinking age.

I walk right past him. I make my way through the club. I'm trying not to rush — I don't want to call attention to myself. I'm weaving toward the exit when I catch a glimpse of what looks like a familiar face. A face that stops me short.

It's Laila Jackson.

No, that isn't possible. I'm seeing another thirty-year-old, short-haired black woman and making a horribly stereotyped mistake. Except I'm not. At my apartment, she was dressed in skinny jeans, high-heeled boots, and a cropped leather jacket. This woman is wearing skinny jeans, high-heeled boots, and a cropped leather jacket.

Laila Jackson followed me to the club.

What is wrong with this woman? What have I done to piss her off so much that she's trailing me in her off time?

No, I shouldn't think of it that way. Not "What have I done to this woman?" but "What have I done to this police officer?" I haven't personally pissed her off. This is business.

Something is up here. There's no way she's tracked me to a club to warn me, yet again, to back off.

I feel the weight of my cell phone in my purse. The cell phone with that recording,

198

proving Kim had a child. Whatever Jackson's beef, I could end it here by triumphantly presenting her with proof that Aubrey Finch is not a crazed attention-seeker.

But do I trust her?

No. Her behavior is suspicious, and I must be extra cautious here. A child's life is at stake.

I'm turning toward the exit when Jackson's head swivels my way. She spots me. I pick up speed, weaving through the few people between me and the exit. I hurry outside, past the bouncers, and the one from earlier thankfully doesn't notice me in the black dress.

I move at a fast walk to the alley beside the club. Then I dart in, tug off my heels, and break into a run.

"Aubrey!" Jackson's voice shouts behind me.

I keep going. There are trash bins ahead, and I race around them like an obstacle course. A wooden fence blocks the alley. I grab the top and swing my legs up, ignoring the pain stabbing through my shoulder. I crouch on top to get a quick look at where I'll be jumping down. Onto trash bins. Great.

"Aubrey Finch!"

I grip the edge, ready to leap, hoping I

can clear the bins —

"Aubrey Stapleton!"

I stop.

Run, just run.

That's what I want to do. What my gut screams for me to do. But my head knows better. My head analyzes the scenario and calculates possible outcomes in an eyeblink.

The chance that I can swing down, escape, and then pretend it was never me . . . and Jackson will buy it? Next to zero.

The chance that I'll only make things worse by running? Next to perfect.

I turn. Jackson walks toward me. She says nothing until she's right below. Then she looks up at me, crouched on the fence, and she shakes her head.

"You really need to work on your suburban-mommy librarian routine, you know that?"

"It's not a routine. I am a librarian. I am a mother. I live in the suburbs."

Another shake of her head. "Get down. Put your shoes on. We need to talk."

"If you're arresting me —"

"This isn't how I arrest people, Aubrey. We're going for coffee. Now come on."

TWENTY-ONE

We're in the coffee shop. Jackson pulls out her chair and sits. "So, Aubrey Stapleton . . ."

I say nothing. This hammer has been poised over my head for ten years now. The laws of probability say it will fall at some point.

The statute of limitations has passed on my crimes. That no longer matters. The problem is that I have a daughter, and if I am discovered, I will lose her. That is a fate worse than jail.

It's also a fate I've earned.

I can argue the whole "robbed from the rich and gave to the poor" thing, but I'm not Robin Hood. I can say I was only a kid. But I knew what I was doing.

Now my past has caught me. If I'm calm about it, that isn't indifference. I'm dying inside, numb and exhausted. Officer Jackson sits there, smiling like the proverbial cat that caught the canary, and I feel no urge to wipe that smirk off her face. This isn't about her.

"Aubrey Stapleton," she repeats. "Mother died in an accident when you were two. Dad when you were eighteen. PTSD."

She doesn't say suicide, and I'll grant her a point for that. PTSD is what killed my father. A life spent in service without the resources to help him deal with that. Without the resources to let him know it was okay to *need* to deal with that.

"You dropped out of college when he died. Dropped out of *MIT,* where you were in the top ten percent of your computer engineering class."

She's done her homework, and she's proud of it. Fine. Let her show off and get this over with.

She continues, "You rattled around for a bit after that with part-time jobs. Then you disappeared. Took off and dropped out. Stopped using your name."

"I used Minor. That's my mother's maiden name, and it's my second middle name. As long as I paid my taxes, I wasn't breaking any laws."

"By paying your taxes under a false name? I think the IRS would have something to say about that."

Yes, what I did isn't exactly legal, but I suspect the IRS's biggest concern is that they got their money, and I was meticulous about that.

"You married under a false —" she begins.

"No, I didn't. On the marriage license, I'm Aubrey Rose Minor. On my birth certificate, I'm Aubrey Rose Minor Stapleton."

She gives me a hard look, and my gut flip-flops. I've always told myself that what I did wouldn't negate my marriage. But did I ever investigate that to be one hundred percent sure? No, I didn't.

"I'm not asking for alimony or even an equal distribution of marital assets," I say. "I didn't deceive my husband."

Liar, liar, pants on fire.

I realize then that she's skipped something. Something vital. The part that I expected to be at the heart of her accusation.

My criminal past.

She's saving it for last. The sucker punch. *Go on, Officer Jackson. Just get it over with.*

"I saw you on that fence," she says. "You're no suburban-mommy librarian."

I tense but force a calm response. "Yes, I am. That's who I've chosen to be, like you've chosen to be a police officer. I may have been faking a few things, but not my job, not my daughter. And there'd be a lot of suburbanites and mothers and librarians who wouldn't appreciate you suggesting that they can't climb a fence."

"*Vault* onto a fence. In a dress and heels."

"In heels? That'd be crazy. I took those off."

She leans over the table. "You can leap that fence because your dad was a career soldier. You planned to join the army. You stay in shape as if you're *still* planning to."

"I stay in shape because I need to keep up with a three-year-old."

I get a small smile for that, and she eases back in her seat.

"The point is that you're in excellent shape, with skills that the average suburb — *person* doesn't have. Then there's the tech. You have a gift. One most people would take full advantage of. And you don't."

"That's my choice."

"Is it? I don't know what happened after your dad died. I can understand you deciding not to go into the army after that. As for the tech stuff, maybe you quit out of misplaced guilt, because you were in college when he died. I'm not going to play amateur shrink here. You have physical and technological skills that you choose not to use, having reinvented yourself for whatever reason, which is none of my business. *My* business is how you're using those skills now."

My mouth opens. Then it shuts, as I realize what she's said. That she doesn't know why I cut ties with my old life. She suspects it's my father's suicide, and that's good enough for her.

She has no idea what I did after his death. And she doesn't seem to care.

She continues, "Just because you have some special skills, Aubrey, does not make you a detective."

"You're right, and I have no desire to become one." I meet her gaze. "I'm stuck doing this because the police are not. And you aren't a detective either."

She flinches at that. I didn't mean it as an insult, but she clearly takes it as one.

"I only joined the force three years ago, and I have every intention of becoming a detective."

"That wasn't a challenge," I say.

"Then don't make it sound like one."

"Then stop talking to me like I'm the scatterbrained suburbanite you thought I was last week."

I wait for the rejoinder. Instead, she pulls back. Considers. Then she nods. "Fair enough. My mistake. My stereotyping. So I apologize. But you are doing a job you are not qualified to do. A job you are not allowed to do."

"Yes, actually, I am allowed to do it. As long as I don't break any laws or misrepresent myself —"

"The owners of that pizza parlor seem to think you were a police officer."

"I said nothing of the sort. If they inferred that?" I shrug. "Clearly a misunderstanding because I never said it."

She allows a small smile. Before she can speak, I say, "So you've been to that pizza parlor. Did they tell you about Kim?"

"Kim Mason. Also known as Kim Lyons. That's our dead woman."

I must look surprised, because she says, "I *have* been listening to you, Aubrey. I've been getting those messages, and I've been passing them on to the detectives-in-charge, and we've been investigating. That's what I've been trying to tell you. Thank you for the information, but stop. Please stop. Let us do our jobs."

"I haven't seen anything in the paper saying she's been identified."

"Because she *hasn't* been. We're still tracking down her real identity."

"Kim Mikhailov," I say. "Born in Cedar Rapids. Ran away at the age of fifteen.

Dancing in a strip club by the time she was sixteen. A strip club owned by a guy she ended up dating. Denis Zima. Who also owns —"

"Zodiac Five. The club you just left." She shakes her head. "I wondered what you were doing there. Okay, so you suspect Kim Mason is this Kim Mikhailov."

"Not suspect. *Know.* Kim was calling a woman named Ellie Milano weekly. Ellie's Facebook page mentions a younger sister, Kim. It includes photos of Kim as a teen. She is undeniably your dead woman."

"How the hell did you figure out all that?"

"I'm good with computers."

"Okay, you *would* make a good detective. But you're not one. I want to be one, and I'm using your tips, Aubrey, because they'll help me get my shield. So thank you. However, I truly need you to stop. For your own safety."

"Yes."

She eyes me. "I mean that. Don't blow me off —"

"You're not the one who's been blown off. I never wanted to play detective. Trying to get you to listen cost me a weekend with my daughter. All I want — all I *ever* wanted — was for you to take me seriously."

"Well, I am. I appreciate the ID on our

207

dead woman *and* the link to Denis Zima. With him involved, though, you definitely don't want to be chasing this lead."

"Because his dad is a Russian mobster."

She makes a face. "That sounds very Hollywood. Let's just say his family has been under investigation for years, which is public record. I have no idea how Denis fits in, but I'll dig for more."

"He doesn't have the boy."

She looks up sharply.

"Brandon," I say. "That's Kim's son. The boy I saw taken."

She sighs. Deeply.

"You still don't believe I saw a child taken?" I say. "You just said you misjudged me."

"You saw a kid get pulled into a car. I do not doubt that. You didn't intentionally misreport —"

"I didn't misreport *anything*. Kim had a son named Brandon. She was hiding him from Zima, who now realizes he has a son, thanks to me. I have the proof right here." I pull out my phone. As I flip to the recorder, I say, "I taped one of his men talking about it."

I hit Play. The man's voice is muffled. Too muffled to make out.

"No, no, no." I jack up the volume, but it

208

only increases the sound of my breathing. "Damn it, no. I was in a closet. You can enhance the quality, though."

"You taped one of Zima's men from a closet? You were *hiding* in a closet?"

"I was checking the office computer when he came upstairs."

She gives another of those deep sighs. "Aubrey . . ."

"Forget the tape for now." I put my phone down. "You can enhance the recording, and you'll hear the guy say that Denis is looking for his son. For Kim's boy. He thinks Brandon is someplace safe — that Kim got him to safety. He's not safe now, though, because Denis is after him."

"This guy randomly started talking about all this while you were in the closet?"

"Well, no. He was telling the head of security that Denis thought he spotted me at the club."

"What?"

"Denis saw me on TV the other day. That's how he knew he had a son."

Jackson closes her eyes and shakes her head.

"Yes," I say. "This is my fault. I accept that. If it wasn't for me, Denis wouldn't know about Brandon. He'd be safe with whoever Kim trusted to care for him."

209

"That's not why I'm shaking my head, Aubrey. First, having Denis Zima looking for you is like painting a target on your back. Do you even realize that?"

"He thinks he saw me in the club. Even his people believe he was imagining it. The security cameras aren't functional, and I changed my dress to sneak out. The only reason he'd be concerned about me is if he has proof I came snooping around. Otherwise, I'm just the crazy lady on the television."

"Fair enough. But I was also shaking my head because this doesn't prove there's a child. Denis believes there's a child because *you* said so. That's all he's going on."

"I found the house where she'd been staying. There was a drink box and a children's book there. A book with the name Brandon in it."

"You broke in —"

"I went in through an open window. Kim was in a hurry to leave and forgot to close it. That's still trespassing, but I was desperate. She'd cleared away every sign of a child being there. I found the drink box and book, though."

"That's . . . No. Just no, Aubrey. That isn't proof, and you know it, which is why you didn't report it."

"You *still* don't believe me?" I straighten. "Fine. It doesn't matter anymore. Talk to Kim's sister. She'll know there was a child. Just ask her."

"I will."

TWENTY-TWO

I don't know how much I trust Laila Jackson. I'm too eager for an ally, and she was clearly not one a few days ago. Yet I do believe, once she knows Brandon exists, she'll want to find him. She's also aiming for detective, and if she can use my information to get there, that's fine by me. Because she's right about one thing: I'm not a private investigator. I don't want to be. I just want justice for Kim and safety for Brandon. We seem to be on that track now.

I go home and get some sleep. Laila has promised to call as soon as she's made contact with Ellie. Yes, I think of her as "Laila" now. "Officer Jackson" seems oddly formal. Thinking of her as more than a cop also, ironically, *keeps* me from jumping to claim her as an ally. She's not an unbiased representative of the law. She's a fully rounded person, with her own agenda and her own ambitions.

I'm up at eight thirty, expecting Charlotte at nine. At 8:55, a knock sounds at my door. I throw it open to see Paul standing there . . . alone.

"Charlie's not with me," he says.

"Is everything okay?" My heart pounds. My first thought is that he's keeping her from me, that he's here to challenge me on custody. My second is that something's happened to her, that she fell off the horse or —

"She's fine," he says. "Gayle has her while I speak to you."

I step back to let him in. "It's . . . awfully early for her to be at Gayle's, Paul. It's none of my business if you're spending the night, but if Charlie's going to be there, too, I think we need to discuss that."

"What?" He seems confused. "No. Of course not. I dropped her off. I just . . . I want to talk, and I'd rather not do that with Charlie here."

"Okay. Can I get you a coffee?"

I expect him to say no, and I'm relieved when he nods, but it's an absent one, as if he's barely listening.

I go in the kitchen and pour a cup. "Just brewed, so it's still fresh."

"I'm sorry about keeping Charlie yesterday," he says.

It honestly takes a moment to realize what

he's talking about. When I do, I answer with care. My fury from Friday night has blown over, and I don't want to fight about this. Nor, however, do I want to brush it aside.

"I completely understand Gayle's daughter wanting Charlie at her party," I say. "I'd have liked more notice, but I know it was a last-minute decision. Next time, I would really appreciate it if *you* called. I don't have an issue talking to Gayle. This isn't me versus her."

He seems to flinch at that, and I'm not sure why. This should be what he wants to hear, right?

I hand him his coffee. "I don't know how serious you two are —"

He opens his mouth, as if to answer, and then shuts it.

"Even if you're serious," I say, "I just met her. A call to change our arrangement should come from you."

"I didn't know." He blurts the words and then hesitates, as if ready to pull them back. Instead, he sits at my tiny dinette table. "Gayle called you without asking me."

I pour a cup of coffee for myself and sit across from him.

"Her daughter asked, and Gayle . . . She wants . . ." He rubs his chin and shakes his head.

"She wants . . . ?" I prompt.

Another shake of his head, gaze down. "She's just . . . moving faster than . . ." He straightens and shrugs it off with a roll of his shoulders. "She overstepped her boundaries, and I've said so, as nicely as possible. She didn't see the harm in calling you herself. She thought, that way, it'd be clear it was her idea, and you wouldn't be upset with me."

"I wouldn't ever be —"

"I've told her that. You and I don't have that kind of . . ." Another roll of his shoulders, and he makes a face. "She didn't mean any harm. I've been clear — clear*er* — that you and I have a very cordial relationship."

Cordial.

That hurts. Cordial is the relationship you have with a cousin you don't share anything in common with beyond blood. It's the ex you don't share anything in common with beyond a child.

It used to be more.

So much more.

And now it's just "cordial" and I almost wonder if "hostile" wouldn't be better, if it wouldn't be easier.

For me, maybe. But not easier for our daughter, and that's what counts.

"Okay," I say. "Thank you for explaining.

I thought you didn't call yourself because you were still upset with me after Thursday night."

"No, not at all." He pauses. "About that. You said you could use my help. I want to offer it. If you're having trouble getting the police to listen . . ."

"They're listening," I say. "Well, they aren't convinced there's a missing child, but I helped them ID the murdered woman, so they know I'm not a complete nutjob."

As I say that, I realize that I'm taking this conversation in a direction it shouldn't go. The one that will have him furrowing his brow and asking *how* I helped ID a dead woman. Instead, he just nods and says, "Well, that's good."

He's still distracted, obviously. I should drop it here. Don't go filling in any blanks that can stay blank. Just hope Paul doesn't look back on this conversation later, when he's less distracted, and say, "Wait a second . . ."

But as I think that, I realize I can't drop it. Laila Jackson knows I'm not who I claim to be. She wields that power over me, and I don't know her well enough to entrust her with that secret.

"Paul . . ."

216

"Hmm?" He sips his coffee, his gaze distant.

"I . . . I need to talk to you about something," I say. "Something that came up with the police."

He puts the mug down. "All right."

"I . . ." My heart thuds so hard I can barely form words. "Before I met you . . ."

His gaze lifts to mine and the words dry up.

I swallow. "Before I met you . . . things happened, and I . . . I haven't been entirely" — *entirely?* — "honest with you about my past and . . ."

"And now you want to be, not because you've had an epiphany, but because you're in trouble."

His voice is cold. Colder than I've ever heard it, and those blue eyes turn just as icy. My insides freeze, and I'm seized by this overwhelming urge to hide, just hide.

"Do not ask me to get you out of this, Aubrey," he says.

"I-I'd never —"

"Good. I think I've done enough. My only advice is not to let the police bully you into a confession. The statute of limitations for theft in California is three years. You are well past that."

I stare at him. I just stare. Then my mouth

opens, and all I can manage is a strangled noise.

His hands tighten on his mug. "Nine months before you left, I received a call from a man named Ruben Dubrand. He tried to extort money from me, threatening to expose you."

"Ruben extorted *money* —"

"Tried." Paul gives me a hard look. "I'm a defense attorney. I know the law. I set him straight, uncovered his own identity and threatened to use that against him if he ever came at my family again."

I can't speak. I just can't even process this. I must still be asleep, caught in a nightmare where Paul tells me he knows what I've done. That he's known for . . .

Nine months before we split.

That would be our last Christmas together. Exactly the time when I started noticing rifts in our marriage. It'd been the holidays, and he'd found excuses to skip parties, given me a perfunctory gift, taken Charlotte to his mother's alone "because I know you two don't get along, and you can use a post-holiday break."

That's when he decided we should stop trying for a second child.

I always presumed that I first noticed the trouble at Christmas only because holidays are stressful, and so that's when the schism became obvious. That isn't true. The schism started there. After Ruben contacted him.

I have spent the last year trying to figure out where our marriage went wrong, how we drifted apart, how I failed him.

Now I know.

"I-I . . ." It's all I can say, all I can manage.

"You were someone else before you met me. I haven't dug into your past. I don't want to know. All Dubrand told me was that you'd committed robberies — break-and-enters — as part of a group. At first, I didn't believe him. Then he told me about your shoulder. On your last job, the homeowner shot you there, and you didn't get proper medical attention for it."

"Yes," I say, and when the word comes, it's an exhale of something like relief. "It's . . . it's a long story but —"

"I don't want to hear it."

My head jerks up, eyes meeting his. I hadn't been about to explain. I didn't want to hide behind excuses. But that cold rejection makes my hackles rise. I force them down again before I speak.

"I was about to say that it's a long story, but I'm not going to make excuses. Yes, I broke into homes and robbed them. I got shot. I got out. I started using my mother's maiden name and eventually wound up in Chicago, where you met me."

"Convenient, wasn't it?"

I frown. "Convenient?"

He pushes back his chair. "Before I met you, I was in serious danger of becoming one of those men who whines about how nice guys always finish last, how women don't want a nice guy. I had a couple of women break it off with the 'you're such a great guy, but you're just not for me' crap. The kiss-off that tells me I'm boring as hell. I stopped dating and started complaining. My friends sat me down for an intervention. They challenged me to try again. To take a real chance. Was there a woman I'd love to ask out, but was sure she'd turn me down? I said yes: you."

"Me?"

"I saw you when I'd go into the bookstore café. I'd hear you laughing. I'd see you goofing around with coworkers. I'd see you being kind to patrons. I noticed you, and I knew I was not the kind of guy you'd ever go out with. But that night with my friends, I'd had a few drinks, and they convinced me to go for it. Two days later, as I was trying to work up the nerve . . ."

"You saw me get a traffic ticket right

outside the building. You said I should fight it."

"Perfect timing, wasn't it?" he says.

I think he means the ticket. I've forgotten he's angry, and I'm about to smile and say, yes, that ticket came at the perfect time. Then I see his expression.

"A boring, ordinary guy," he says. "Who fell so hard for you he never once questioned what you saw in him."

I blink. "What?"

"Plus he's a criminal defense attorney," he says. "It didn't get any better than that."

"What are you talking about?"

"You used me, Bree. I realize that now. When Dubrand first contacted me and I began to have doubts about our marriage, I tried to tell myself I was wrong. Okay, not *wrong.* I understood that you were on the run, and you needed to hide, and I was your cover."

"*What?* No, I *never* —"

"I pursued you. So it wasn't as if you targeted me. But you saw an opportunity."

"*No.*"

"Maybe it wasn't that Machiavellian. I don't actually think it was. You just . . . settled. It was an arranged marriage of sorts. I just didn't realize it."

"Paul, *no.* I did not —"

"That's why I never confronted you. I loved you. Forget *why* you were with me. You were with me. By choice. Maybe I'd even won you over, however it started. And then you said it wasn't working, and I knew what that meant. I'd served my purpose."

"That was *not* —"

"At first, I thought you found someone. Eventually I realized that wasn't the case. Maybe you got tired of me. Maybe you just got tired of the lies. I go back and forth, Aubrey. When I'm feeling sorry for myself, I'm certain you used me. Used me and left me. Then I see you with Charlotte, and I must give you the benefit of the doubt. There was a time when I even wondered if you had Charlotte to trap me. Something to threaten me with, if I tried to expose you. Or if I wouldn't pay you off."

"I have not taken one red *dime* —"

"I know." His hands fold around his mug again. "You can stop pretending now, though. Bring out your money. I presume that's why you didn't take mine. You still have the money you stole."

"I gave that away."

His gaze lifts to mine. "What?"

"But I *do* have money. An inheritance, which means, yes, I don't need yours. I did not use you, Paul. I swear I did not. But I did lie to you. I misled you. Which is why I don't want any of our marital estate. All I care about is joint custody of Charlotte."

He looks at me. For at least a minute, he looks at me. Then he says, slowly, "Would a half-million dollars convince you to give up that claim?"

I stiffen. "I will *never* —"

"You can still see her. Still be part of her life."

I speak slowly, enunciating each word. "I would give you every penny I have for joint custody. Not full custody, because I would never take Charlie away from you. I don't have a half million. Maybe a fifth of that. But it's yours if you agree to joint custody."

He shakes his head. "I'd never take your money. And I'd never try to take her from you, either. I was just . . ."

"Checking. In case I'm faking maternal affection."

"I'm sorry."

"I did not do what you think, Paul. I fell for you. I fell in love —"

"Don't."

"I'm —"

"Don't. Please." He gets to his feet. "You need to say that. I know your secret, so you'll never risk hurting my feelings by admitting that you married me to be safe. I

223

understand that you love Charlotte. I understand that you aren't going to take anything from me, including her. I want . . ." He exhales. "I want a civil relationship, for her sake." A pause. "I'll go get her."

I shake my head. "I can't . . . Not today. If you had plans, if you need me to take her . . ."

"I don't."

"Then I'll wait until next weekend."

He nods, and he leaves. That's it. He just leaves.

TWENTY-THREE

I spend the rest of the morning in bed. Laila calls at ten, and I don't answer. Right now, I don't care about anyone else's problems.

Paul knew about my past. He's known for months, and that is what ended our marriage. My lies.

This was a possibility I never foresaw, and now that I do, I realize what a monumental mistake I made in not telling him from the start. If I'd done that, he'd know that marrying him wasn't about hiding or seeking sanctuary. But he's right that nothing I say now will matter. I never stopped to see it from his point of view. Even if I had, I'm not sure I could have anticipated how he'd feel.

Yes, he wasn't the sort of guy I usually dated. Yes, we didn't seem to have a lot in common. And, yes, God help me, I never noticed him coming into the bookstore café, because he wasn't the kind of man I noticed.

Guys like Paul didn't usually end up with girls like me, and that's no insult to him. We move in different spheres, and there was no point noticing a guy like him because he wasn't going to notice me back. He'd look for a woman like Gayle. A stable, competent fellow professional. Maybe, if I'd finished college and found a career in tech, it'd be different, but I'd been a twenty-five-year-old with a high school education, working in a bookstore. I had not been wife material for a man like Paul. And yet he married me, had a child with me, and I'd felt blessed.

I have hurt a man I loved. A man I still love.

I've deeply hurt him. Dealt a blow to his pride and his self-confidence but worse, I betrayed him. Betrayed his trust.

Whenever I've grieved over the loss of my marriage, I've fortified myself with the knowledge that Paul had been unhappy, so ending it was the right and noble thing for me to do. He had indeed been unhappy . . . because he thought his wife married him as a safe haven, a security blanket. When I suggested it wasn't working, his quick agreement had stung to the core. Surprised me, too, because I didn't honestly believe he was divorce-level miserable. Just less happy than I wanted him to be. To him, though, my leaving only proved his point. He'd done the same thing I had — he set me free.

I spend the first two hours that afternoon writing him letters. Write. Rewrite. Rewrite again. I cannot find the words to prove that he's wrong. I don't know how, and when I try to put my feelings on paper, it sounds like the worst kind of fakery, over-the-top sentimentality worthy of a cheap greeting card.

I try to tell him my past, but that sounds like excuses. He's a defense attorney — he's heard truly tragic life stories, and mine seems weak in comparison.

Your mommy died when you were little. Your daddy killed himself when you were eighteen. Boo-hoo. It happens. They raised you well, with everything you needed for a decent life. If you threw that away, Aubrey, then you're not a tragic heroine — you're a spoiled little brat.

My father dies, and I fly into a tantrum, turning to crime to repay the world for its unkindness? That's worse than a cheap greeting card sentiment. It's the lamest villain backstory ever.

I write. I rewrite. I send nothing.

Midafternoon, I pull on sweats to go for a jog. I'm swinging out the front door and nearly bash into a woman coming in. I murmur an apology and start past her.

"Aubrey?" the woman says.

I look, and it's Laila Jackson. She's dressed in a uniform, but not a police one. It's a softball uniform, one that used to be white, but it's faded to gray with use, the knees brown from slides into base. There's dirt on her cheek, and any makeup she'd worn has sweated away. Her eyes gleam with a look I know well — the afterglow of adrenaline from a good workout.

"Did you win?" I say.

"I did," she says. "Two home runs, and three runs batted in. Problem is the rest of my damned team."

I laugh softly. "Come on up, and I'll get you a soda."

She shakes her head. "Better keep me outside. Showers weren't working at the field. I was heading home, and then realized I was driving through downtown, and maybe I should stop and see why you aren't taking my calls. In case you got yourself into trouble and were lying in a pool of blood somewhere. Crazy thought, I know. You're such a nice, quiet librarian."

"You aren't going to let up on the librarian thing, are you?"

"Nope." She waves to the road. "Let's walk."

I glance over at her as we move onto the sidewalk. "What position do you play?"

"Right field. You got a team?"

I shake my head. "Organized sports aren't really my thing. Sports in general aren't my thing these days, not with my schedule. I'm trying to fit something in. Maybe a class."

"Let me guess. Hot yoga or SoulCycle?"

"Sword fighting."

Her perfectly sculpted brows shoot up. "Fencing?"

"No, swords. Real swords. I saw this notice come through on the interlibrary system for classes at a branch in Chicago. All-women sword fighting."

"That sounds . . ." She purses her lips. "I'm torn between weird and cool."

"Weirdly cool. Totally up my alley."

She chuckles. "I'm shocked, really. So, sword-fighting classes for women, at a library. That's just odd enough that I might actually ask you to send me a link."

"I'll do that."

We go three more steps before she says, "Ellie Milano says Kim didn't have a son."

I stop walking. My jaw works. I look at her. "What?"

She says it again, slower. I can't read her expression, and that only pisses me off more. Ten seconds ago, we're chatting about

229

sword fighting, and I'm finally relaxing, feeling like I've made a connection, and now I get this impenetrable stare, these words, spoken with no preamble, no buffer.

"All right," I say. "Clearly I have made a horrible mistake, and I hallucinated the fact that I spoke to this woman and her son in Grant Park last week. My daughter hallucinated it, too. It must be hereditary."

"I don't doubt that you spoke to someone who looked like Kim Mikhailov."

"Yep, wasn't her, though. Which is weird. I mean, this woman and I talked about her job, and she said she worked at a pizza place, and that's how I found Kim. Oh, and I heard that woman talking Russian on the phone, and both Kim and Denis come from Russian families, but hey, just a coincidence."

"You got the pizza parlor lead from the woman in the park?"

"No, I pulled it out of my ass. How else would I have known the dead woman worked at a pizza place?"

No change in her expression, as if my sarcasm bounces right off her. She just looks at me. After a moment she says, "Then you did speak to Kim."

"Kinda said that."

"Which means the boy who was with her

must not have been her son."

"He called her mama. Why the hell is it so difficult for you people to believe she had a son? A son she was hiding — which is why no one knows about him. You just keep explaining away everything I say —" I cut myself short. "No, never mind. I don't care. There's a boy, and he's safe, and that's all that matters. Now if you guys can stop Denis Zima, my imaginary boy will stay safe. I have more important things to do than bash my head against this wall."

I turn and stalk back to my apartment building. Laila Jackson doesn't follow.

I try to forget about Brandon and Kim. I really do. But thinking about them has temporarily distracted me from the crash-and-burn of my life. When I try to return to composing that letter for Paul, I keep feeling Brandon's tug.

There *is* a child. I can entertain doubt, when I get pushback from Laila Jackson, but it only takes a hard reality check to realize there is no other explanation for what I've seen and experienced. So why is Laila pushing back?

Is she lying about Ellie Milano?

Why would she?

She would if she's covering something up.

If she's complicit in all this. If she's on the payroll of Denis Zima or his father.

Oh my God. Did I really just think that? I sound like exactly what the police have accused me of being: a lady who watches way too much crime TV. I don't, actually. Sure, I can enjoy a classic or modern mystery novel, but I know that fiction isn't reality. Ruben didn't run an international ring of superthieves, able to break through the highest security to steal world-class art. The fact that he employed a hacker meant he was, for his field, very high-tech. Yet we were still breaking into houses with cheap security systems, stealing valuables left lying in drawers and closets. Easy pickings. Ruben selected his targets with care, too, and most times they never even called the cops, because if they did that, they'd invite more scrutiny into their income than they wanted.

When I suspect Laila of being in the Zima family's pocket, I feel like that layperson who watches too many police dramas. I also know, from living with Paul, that corruption happens. Police, politicians, lawyers . . . Most are good people, but if there's a way to make a little extra in *any* profession, someone will.

I want to call Ellie Milano myself and be sure she told Laila she doesn't have a nephew. I know I shouldn't. If Ellie calls the Oxford PD to complain, Laila will know it was me. Since there is no missing child, though, I can't be interfering with the investigation into a missing child, right?

It's not just idle curiosity that compels me to call. If Ellie is hiding Brandon for Kim, then she needs to know about Zima.

I have Ellie's number from Kim's phone records. She answers on the third ring.

"I'm a friend of Kim's," I say. "I'm calling about Brandon."

There's a pause. Such a long pause. Then a cautious "Brandon?"

"Her son."

No response. I swear I hear her breathing across the line. Swear I hear that breathing pick up speed.

She says nothing. She just waits, and this tells me what I need to know. There is a Brandon.

An oddly muffled voice speaks in the background. I hear other sounds, too, as if she's in a busy place.

"I met Kim in Oxford," I say. "I know she was hiding her son —"

"My sister didn't have a son."

"I met Brandon. He's about five. Blond hair —"

"I'm sorry, but you're mistaken. I understand there was a woman on the news who said she saw my sister with a son. She was wrong. Kim didn't have a child."

"I'm that woman. I know Kim had —"

"Stop. Please. I just lost my sister. I'm going to hang up now."

"Denis Zima," I blurt.

Silence. Then, "I don't know that name."

"He's Brandon's father. Or he thinks he is."

"I'm hanging up and phoning the police."

"Denis knows about Brandon. He's looking for him. He thinks Kim put Brandon someplace safe. I realize now that I saw a rescue, not a kidnapping. If you have any way to warn the people who have Brandon, please do. Denis Zima is looking for his son. If Kim didn't want Denis finding him, then I know you don't either."

The line disconnects. But she heard me. I know she did.

I'm finishing dinner when Paul texts.

Charlie would like to Skype with you.

She wants to tell you about yesterday.

I stare at the texts and draw a blank. Yesterday? What . . .

The party. The horseback riding. The fact that my daughter was supposed to be here with me today, and I canceled, and I never

234

even said, "Hey, I'd like to talk to her."

I text back quickly and ask him to have Charlotte call whenever she wants. I'll have my laptop ready.

I've barely got Skype open when she connects, and guilt churns my stomach. My daughter has been waiting, eager to talk to me, and I've been caught up in my own concerns.

I forgot her last week for the princess tea. Now I've done it again.

"Hey, baby," I say when she appears. She's someplace I don't recognize, with people passing behind her. "Where are you?"

"Train house," she says.

An announcement sounds in the background. She's in the Chicago train station. My gut goes cold with a sudden image flashing of Paul bustling her onto a train, out of my life forever.

I push back the panic. Paul would never do that. Even if he tried, seized by a sudden fit of madness, he would hardly have Charlotte call me from the station.

"What are you doing there?" I ask, as casually as I can.

Paul's voice comes from the background. He doesn't lean in to the camera, as he usually does. He remains a disembodied voice.

"Gayle's daughter is going on a school

trip," he says. "We were dropping her off."

"Ah, did she catch her train okay?"

He doesn't answer. I'm asking a polite but meaningless question, and he's not going to bother responding. This is where we stand.

"How Mummy tummy?" Charlotte asks.

"My . . . ?"

"Daddy say Mommy sick."

I exhale. *Thank you, Paul.* I'd wondered what excuse he'd given. The easy one would be to say I was busy, and I'd really hoped he hadn't — I'd never want Charlotte to think I was too busy for her. But he did the right thing, as always. No matter how upset he was with me, he rose above it.

I assure her that I feel much better — probably something I ate — and then I ask about the party. As she regales me with her day of excitement, another announcement blares, and it pokes at my brain. Then I remember the background noise on my call with Ellie. That muffled voice had been an announcement.

She'd been in a train station. Or an airline terminal.

Was she traveling to see Brandon? To take him back from whoever had him?

"Mommy?"

I scramble to remember what Charlotte said. I'm replaying her words when Paul leans down, just for a second, to be sure I'm still there.

"Sorry," I say. "It's a bad connection. What did you say, sweetheart?"

She repeats it, and I respond appropriately. I push aside thoughts of Ellie.

Repeat after me, Bree. This is what matters — your daughter. Let Ellie take care of Brandon. If she's going to fetch him, that's a good thing.

Charlotte keeps talking, and I corral my thoughts. It's a struggle, and that gnaws at me. I lost my weekend with Charlotte, and now I can't afford fifteen minutes to listen to her talk about her day?

I focus until Paul says it's time to go. This is the point where, normally, he'd come on for a quick exchange of parental information, like telling me she has a dental appointment or that she's really enjoying a certain book. Today, Charlotte says goodbye . . . and he disconnects the line.

I text him: I can have her next weekend, right?

He replies: Of course.

And that's it. Conversation over.

TWENTY-FOUR

I need to get Kim and Brandon out of my head. They aren't my concern, and they're interfering with things that are. After that Skype call, I plan my next weekend with Charlotte. We have tea reservations for Sunday. I'll get her a new dress. We'll do that on Saturday. Maybe I'll ask Paul if I can have her Friday to make up for my last weekend.

No, not maybe. I will. In fact, I'm going to do that right now. At the very least, it'll help me gauge how dire this situation with him is.

I send the text. Then I spend the next twenty minutes freaking out because he's not replying.

Things *have* changed. He might have found out the truth over a year ago, but this has brought it all back. Maybe he was holding out hope that I had another explanation.

Robbery? Is that what Ruben said? Not at all. He's a guy I knew back home. Yes, that shoulder injury is a bullet. It was a stupid thing — me and some friends — and I didn't want you to get the wrong idea, think you married a redneck. Ruben's just being a jerk.

He hoped for an explanation. I didn't give one. So now he must accept that he married a thief. A woman who robbed homes and got shot and went on the run and hooked up with him to reinvent herself.

He's going to take Charlotte away.

I'm not the person he wants raising his daughter.

He hasn't quite decided that yet, but the idea is forming. He has the ammunition he needs to take her. As for depriving her of a mother, well, Gayle is a much better role model.

Stop that, Bree. Just stop.

He's slow in responding because he's considering my request. I had Charlotte for an extra night this week, and it was my choice not to have her today, so he's thinking he doesn't owe me Friday. He just doesn't want to refuse and sound pissy.

I need to tell him that I have something planned. That ups the ante. If he still refuses me then, I'll know something's wrong.

As I pull up the calendar of local events, I

remember there's a pizza party at the library.

Pizza. Maybe Kim's employers know —

I thrust the thought aside and compose the text to Paul.

Me: My library is having a pizza-and-jammies evening Friday. I'd love to sign Charlie up, if that's okay with you.

Hit Send. Wait five minutes, counting it on the clock. Then I send another.

Me: I could give up Sunday night if it's a problem. I'd drop her off after our princess tea.

Giving her up early Sunday defeats the purpose of having extra time with her. This is another test, though. Is he not answering because I'm asking for extra time? Or is he going to start blocking me when I request off-schedule hours with Charlotte, even for something special?

Five more minutes. Send another text.

Me: I understand if you already have plans.

Two minutes. I'm going to call at the five-minute mark. I'll —

My phone buzzes as a text comes in.

Paul: Just got back from city.

Paul: Let me put Charlie to bed and check the calendar.

I curse myself. Of course it'd taken him a while to text back. He'd been at the train station in Chicago when I talked to Charlotte.

I make myself a tea and try not to obsessively watch the clock. It takes about fifteen minutes to settle Charlotte in. More if he gives her a bath, but it's almost nine, so he'll probably skip —

The text comes in at fourteen minutes.

Paul: Friday's fine.

Paul: Sunday is your call.

I send back that I'd love to keep her until Monday, dropping her at daycare as we usually do. I just didn't want to cut into his time. He replies that Friday through Monday is fine — he had her this weekend.

I want to say more. I want to tell him that I spent the afternoon composing letters. I want to tell him he's wrong, so wrong. I want to tell him my version of the day we met, that yes, I might not have noticed him before, but when he smiled at me, I noticed, and I never stopped noticing. When he asked me out, I did think it was a mistake, but only because guys like him never asked girls like me, and if they did, maybe it's because they were expecting something he wasn't going to get from me on a first date. When he continued asking me out, I kept waiting for the other shoe to fall, kept looking for *his* angle.

241

I want to tell him all that.

I start composing texts, and I don't get past a few words.

Finally, before he can put his phone away, conversation over, I text.

Me: I'm sorry.

He doesn't reply. He's already gone.

He's been gone for a very long time.

I go for a run after that. Laila Jackson's visit had aborted my earlier attempt, and I *really* want that jog now. I need to clear my head, run until my legs wobble and my lungs burn and I can no longer think about Paul or Charlotte or Kim or Brandon. Run until it takes every ounce of mental energy just to drag myself back to my apartment and collapse into dreamless sleep.

I've barely gone a couple of blocks when a voice at my shoulder says, "Where's the fire?"

I give a start and look over to see that another jogger has joined me. His voice sounds familiar, and I think immediately of the guy in the park, the fellow jogger who pestered me the day Brandon disappeared. It's not him, though — this guy is about my age. But that reminds me that I never did try to find that guy, get him to corroborate my story about Brandon.

242

Stop that.

No new evidence will make the police believe me now, and what difference would it make if they did? Brandon is safe unless Zima catches up with him. Zima, though, is going to be the police's top suspect in Kim's murder, so he won't have time to look for his son.

Brandon is safe. The only thing to be gained by proving he existed is repairing my public reputation.

See, I was right. I'm not a delusional attention-seeker.

Clear my name . . . and put Brandon in more danger. As it stands right now, Zima only thinks Brandon exists because I said so. If everyone believes I'm wrong, then while that hurts my pride, it's better for the child.

"I asked, where's the fire," the guy says, and it takes me a moment to mentally snap back to him.

He's smiling at me, friendly. A little too friendly? Maybe. It happens. It's like sitting in a public place, trying to read a book. Some guys take that as a hint that you really need something better to do with your time. Headphones help, but in my rush to get out tonight, I left mine at home.

"Fire?" I say.

"You're running like there's someone on your tail. Or are you just trying to get done before dark?"

He jerks his chin up, and I see that the streetlights have come on. It's almost nine, and dusk is falling fast.

I glance at him. He's smiling at me again, and I don't like the smile. No more than I like him pointing out that it's getting dark.

I laugh. "No, I'm not afraid of the dark. Just trying to burn off a big Sunday dinner."

I cross at the light, veering off my usual course to make a sharp left. He follows.

"You shouldn't be out after dark in this neighborhood," he says. "That's just asking for trouble."

"It's never been a problem before," I say.

I kick it up a notch. He does, too.

"I keep thinking I've seen you somewhere," he says.

"I work downtown here."

"No, it's . . . Wait. I know. The news. You're the one who said you saw the boy. That murdered chick's kid."

The way he says "murdered chick" makes my hackles rise. It also nudges a memory, but it flits by before I can catch it.

I take the next right, heading back. That seems to be the only way I'll lose this guy.

Except I don't want to lead him to my front door.

Damn.

Where can I go . . . ?

Coffee. That's the first idea that springs to mind, not surprisingly, given that I spent most of yesterday in coffee shops. There's a twenty-four-hour diner a block from my place. I've been there often enough that I know most of the servers. If this guy follows me in, they'll see my "problem" and help me shake him.

"So you think she had a kid?" he says.

I start to say yes. Then I remember what I was just thinking. Squelch my pride. Protect the boy.

"No, I made a mistake," I say. "The woman who died didn't have any kids."

"How do you know that? The cops haven't ID'd her."

My gut freezes. Then I shrug. "That's what they told me."

"So the police *have* ID'd her?"

"They never said that. They just told me there wasn't a boy. I was mistaken."

I cross the road. He keeps pace.

"You're sure?" he continues.

"Yes, I'm . . ." I trail off as I look at the guy. As I *really* look at him.

He's not a jogger. He's wearing sweatpants

and sneakers, but they're leisure pants and designer high-tops, both meant for style, not running. There's a bulge in his waistband. The bulge of a handgun.

That's when I remember thinking his voice sounded familiar. It *is* familiar. I heard it just last night, through a closet door. He's the guy from Zodiac Five. Denis Zima's friend.

Stay calm. Just stay calm.

I look over at him. "Are you a reporter?"

His surprise is almost comical. "Hell, no. I just remember seeing that on the news, and thinking it was a helluva thing. That chick getting bumped off for her kid. That's what it seemed like — some sicko killed her for her little boy. Some pervert. But when I looked it up later, seeing if they found the kid, I find out the police didn't believe you. That pissed me off. They do that sometimes, with women. They don't believe them."

"Well, in this case, they were correct. I was mistaken."

"Are you sure?"

I glance at him. "What difference does it make?"

"I'm curious, okay," he says, and there's a faint growl to his voice, one that warns he's just about done playing nice.

"I saw a woman with a boy," I say. "It

246

wasn't the same woman. She just had a similar look — young, blond, slender."

"And she had a son?"

"Maybe? She was with a kid. About eight or nine."

"Eight or nine?"

I shrug. "Maybe older? I don't have kids, so I can never tell."

"What were they doing?"

"Hmm?"

"The chick and her kid. What were they doing when you saw them?"

I'm about to say they were on the swings — just make something up. But when I see his expression, I realize I don't want to give anything away.

"Look," I say. "I get it. You don't want me to know you're a reporter. But it's obvious you are. No one else asks me these kind of questions."

"Except the police."

"Yes."

"So the police asked you?"

I turn another corner. The diner is a block ahead. I only have to get that far.

"The police didn't ask me much of anything," I say. "Because they didn't believe there was a child, and it turns out they were right. I made a mistake. An embarrassing mistake. Now, if you'll just leave me alone please —"

He elbows me. It's so fast and sharp that I never see it coming. His elbow strikes my bad shoulder and I stagger with a gasp. Then he grabs that same shoulder and shoves me hard into a narrow passage between two buildings.

"What the hell?" I say as I recover. "This is not the way to get a story."

His hand goes to my throat. Again, I don't see it coming. I don't expect it. He may have knocked me into this alley, but that was just a fit of temper, and he'll see he's made a mistake and cover it up.

Did I bump your shoulder? I'm so sorry.

That's what I expect. Just stand firm, and he'll back down and regroup. Instead, there's a hand at my throat, and then he's slamming me into the wall, my feet barely touching the ground.

"Let's try this again," he says. "I want to know everything about that kid. Understand?"

I glower at him, and he lifts me by the neck until I'm on tiptoes . . . and his T-shirt rises up over his waistband.

I wheeze for breath and nod frantically.

"Good," he says.

As he lowers me down again, I grab the gun. Grab it and jab the barrel into his stomach. He grunts in shock and jerks back, like I've sucker punched him. Then he sees the gun.

"What the — ?" he begins.

"Did I mention that I'm not worried about running at night? I can take care of myself. Now step away."

He grabs for the gun. I *do* hit him in the stomach then. A hard jab to the solar plexus that has him bent over, gasping.

"You said you thought that boy was grabbed by a pedophile," I say. "Well, maybe that's because you know all about them."

"Wh-what?" he manages between gasps.

"You're taking way too much interest in a missing kid." I start backing out of the alley, gun still aimed at him. "I think maybe I should call the police. Have them find out why you're so interested in little boys."

He makes a run at me, but the gun — or the look in my eyes — stops him.

"There is no little boy," I say. "I made a mistake. I don't know what your problem is, but you need to stay away from me, or I *will* make that call."

I keep backing from the alley. When I reach the sidewalk, he makes another run for me. A car comes around the corner just then. My back's to it — the driver can't see the gun — but he does see Zima's thug. He hits the brakes. The thug stops short. I continue backing toward the car. When I hear it coming my way, I lower the gun and hide it.

The whir of a window rolling down.

"You okay, ma'am?"

It's a teenager wearing a fast-food-restaurant uniform.

"Someone's following me," I say. "Would you mind giving me a lift for a block or two?"

"Uh, sure. Hop in."

He shoves a backpack off the passenger seat. I climb in, never turning my back on Zima's man, who stands there, watching and seething.

I shut the door. "Drive past him, please."

The kid nods and does that. Zima's man stays on the sidewalk and watches us go.

"You okay?" the kid asks.

"I was out jogging, and that guy decided he wanted to run alongside me. I wasn't looking for company. He really wasn't taking the hint."

"Jerk."

"If you could just turn right at the next intersection, I'll get out there."

He does and then insists on driving another block before pulling over. I thank him and try to give him twenty bucks. When he refuses, I start getting out and tuck the money under the seat. Then I thank him again and take off.

TWENTY-FIVE

I head to my apartment building. I keep an eye out, but there's no sign of Zima's thug. I hover inside the door to be sure no one has followed. Then I zip up the stairs and to my apartment and . . .

Someone has tried forcing open my door, but I installed a double-cylinder jimmy-proof dead bolt. I used to rob homes; I know how to secure one. The intruder couldn't break that. Still, I open it with care, and when I move inside, I have the thug's gun in my hand.

My apartment is empty.

I secure it behind me. As soon as I step in, though, I don't feel like I usually do, the dead bolt turned, the world shut out, me safe behind the door. I feel vulnerable, as if I've trapped myself by locking that door, and any minute now, whoever tried to break in will return with someone more capable.

There's a moment where I wonder how

they found my apartment. I'm still in shock from what happened in the alley. Having one of Zima's thugs pump me for information while pretending to be a fellow jogger is reasonable. Having that same guy toss me into an alley and slam me against a wall is not. So I'm still reeling from that, which explains why I don't see the obvious right away.

How did they find my apartment? Well, I'm pretty sure that thug didn't just happen to be wandering around my neighborhood when he spotted me. I gave my name on TV, and they've tracked me to my apartment. That thug wasn't just pumping me for information — he was distracting me while others broke in.

I pack an overnight bag. Then I clear my apartment of every sign that I have a daughter. I told the thug that I don't have kids, and he didn't argue, which suggests they haven't dug that deep. So I hide evidence of Charlotte, and I take everything that suggests I was investigating Brandon's disappearance. Then I climb into the car, and I drive.

I intended to go to a hotel.

This is not a hotel.

I'm sitting in a driveway, staring at a house

that used to be mine. I see a car in the drive that used to be mine. And inside that home is a family that used to be mine.

I sit in that drive, and I cry. I can't help it. I slump over the steering wheel, forehead against it, and I cry.

I think of all the times I pulled into this drive and took it for granted. Pulled in and just wanted to get Charlotte out of the car, because she was fussing, and it'd been a long day of errands. Wanted to get her out and put her down for a nap and rest, just rest.

I loved my life, but I'd be lying if I said there weren't times I wanted to escape it, too. Times when I longed for Charlotte to sleep so I'd have a few moments to myself. Times when I'd be making dinner and wish someone would cook it for me, wish I'd be the one coming home from work. Times when I even thought, *Dear God, what have I done?*

But that despair and regret never lasted long. The pressures and, yes, the loneliness of being a stay-at-home mom piled up, and I caved under it for an hour or two. Felt sorry for myself. Envied other lives. Far more often, though, I'd be in the yard with Charlotte, and I'd see other mothers hurrying to work, herding kids into the car, and

I'd be so glad that wasn't me. I'd be in the park with her, see the snarl of the morning commute, and I'd count my blessings. Staying home wasn't for every parent, but it'd been what I wanted. Just give me a few years with my daughter — with all my kids, including those yet to come — and then I'd happily return to the workforce and find satisfaction there.

I had that. And I didn't lose it. I gave it up. Now I sit in the car and look at that house, and I cry.

I came here to warn Paul. Tell him what's going on and make sure he realizes the danger.

That's it.

No, that's not it. I came here for sanctuary. To tell Paul of the danger, yes, but then hope he'll ask me to stay. Hope he'll *let* me stay, just for the night.

I am afraid, and this is my home, and I desperately want to be here, where it's safe. With Paul, where it's safe. With Charlotte, where I know she's safe, where I can watch out for her.

Too bad.

I can't put this on Paul. I do need to warn him, but that can be accomplished with a phone call.

As I put the car into reverse, the front

door opens. Paul steps out. His shirt is half-buttoned, his feet are bare, and his state of undress reminds me what he'd been doing earlier. Taking Gayle's daughter to the train station. Presumably with Gayle, who might be in the house right now.

I start to back out. He raises his hand for me to stop. I put down the passenger window as he walks over.

"I'm sorry," I say. "I wanted to talk to you, but I should have just called."

He leans down to the open window. "Come inside."

I shake my head. "I don't want to interrupt your evening."

"I'm working, Bree. Interruptions are welcome."

"Gayle isn't here?"

His brows knit.

"You looked . . . I thought Gayle might be here."

He glances down at himself, and it takes a moment for him to realize what I mean. "No, Aubrey, you didn't 'interrupt' anything. Charlie's in the house. I got comfortable because the office is stuffy. The air conditioner isn't working right again."

"You need to clear the weeds from the unit. They choke the fan. Here, let me do that, and then I'll go."

256

I turn off the car. When I get out and head for the backyard, Paul steps into my path.

"You aren't here to fix the air conditioner, Bree. Come inside and talk."

"I'll explain while I fix it."

He sighs but follows me into the yard. I'm glad for the darkness. It hides the play set and the sandbox and everything that will remind me of Charlotte and our life here. As I'm making my way to the air-conditioning unit, I smack into something in my path. It's a hammock. My hammock, still stretched between two trees.

Paul bought it for me to read on while Charlotte played. I remember laughing at the thought that I could laze out here, reading, instead of chasing her. I did use it, though, when she was napping. I'd read and relax with the baby monitor beside me.

I remember Paul reading outside in a chair, and I'd tried to convince him to use the hammock.

"That takes far more motor skill than I possess," he'd said.

Yet it's still here. As if I never left it. As if I could grab a book and settle in —

I push past the hammock as Paul flips on the deck lights. Sure enough, vines choke the AC unit. As I pull them off, Paul says, "I can do that."

"Got it."

I keep tugging.

"Bree?" he says.

I don't look up.

"I know you came here to explain," he says, "and you know I don't want to hear it."

I'm about to say no, that's not it, but he continues.

"I really don't," he says. "I need some time. But if you're worried that I'll keep Charlie from you, don't be. Please. I already said I wouldn't and . . ."

He exhales and leans against the deck railing, as I untangle vines below.

"I know who you are," he says. "Who you were."

I try not to tense.

"I don't just mean what you did," he continues. "When we talked this morning, you said you gave away the money."

"Not all —"

He continues as if he didn't hear me. "That made me dig where I told myself I wasn't going to dig. Into your life. Who you were. You didn't get that shoulder scar from an accident that killed your parents. But they are gone. Both of them."

I go still.

"You didn't lie," he says. "Not entirely.

258

Your mother died in a car accident when you were two. You were found in the car a day later. I think of Charlotte and try to imagine —" He inhales. "I *can't* imagine. I only know that something that . . . horrific . . . would have an impact. A huge one."

"It's not an excuse —"

"You grew up on army bases. No siblings. Your dad never remarried, and he was often deployed. I remember all the times you'd fly into a panic, worrying that you weren't a good parent, that you didn't know how to be, and I never understood why you'd get so worked up. Now I do."

"It wasn't that bad," I say. "I'd stay with good people when he deployed. I wasn't neglected or abused. My dad loved me. We were close."

"Until he took his life."

I stiffen.

"I'm sorry," Paul says quickly. "That sounded harsh."

"It was harsh. There's no nice way to put it. I was away at college, and he came home from deployment, and he was worse than usual. I kept telling myself talking to him on the phone was enough, that I'd get him help when I got home on break and then —"

I snap a vine so hard it slices into my

finger. Blood wells. I wipe it off before Paul notices.

"That's when it happened, isn't it?" Paul says. "You dropped out of college, and Ruben took advantage —"

"No." I meet his gaze. "There aren't excuses, Paul. I wasn't tricked into what I did. I chose it. I was angry, and I was stupid, and I chose it."

"Who'd you give the money to?"

I flail, hands flapping, before I quickly return to the vines. "It doesn't —"

"Bree?"

"I kept a third."

"And the rest?"

I hesitate. Then I say, "One-third to a PTSD group. The rest was anonymous gifts to people who needed it, mostly around the base."

"Rob from the rich, give to the veterans?"

He smiles, but I shake my head vehemently, my eyes filling with tears.

"Don't," I say. "I was young. I was angry. I was stupid. I didn't do it for others. That's just how I used the money, because it wasn't about the money. Young. Angry. Stupid. That's all."

He nods. "Okay."

I resume pulling vines. "I knew the statute of limitations had run out before I married

260

you, Paul. No one suspected me. I wasn't fleeing anything but my own mistakes." I look up at him. "I wasn't looking for safe haven."

He shifts, as uncomfortable as I was discussing the money. He opens his mouth, and I know he's going to tell me not to pursue this, so I quickly say, "I left because I thought you were unhappy. We were drifting apart, and that's a lousy reason for ending a marriage, but I didn't want it to get worse. I thought if I mentioned the problem, and you agreed that it wasn't fixable, then I'd leave. I took the risk that you'd agree. I felt like I had to. For you and for Charlie. Now I know *why* you weren't happy, and I wish to God I could go back to the day we met and tell you the truth, but I can't."

I rip off another vine, my attention back on that.

"You couldn't," he says after a moment. "Not when you'd first met me. It was too soon. But I wish you had, at some point. At any point."

"I know. I just . . . The further it went, the more afraid I got. The easier it seemed to just *become* someone else."

"Were you?" he asks softly. "Were you actually someone else, Bree? Or were you just pretending to be?"

"Was I pretending to be your wife? Charlie's mommy? No." I look at him. "Pretending to be happy? No. But the person you fell in love with, the one you married, you had a child with, that wasn't the whole me, and I'm sorry."

He says nothing. I bend and snake out a last bit of vine.

"So, MIT, huh?" he says, and when I look over, he's smiling. It's not his usual smile — it's a little sad, a little confused — so I just nod.

"When you're done with the AC, my desktop has been acting up," he says. "Think you can fix that, too?"

I find a half smile for him. "Probably." I straighten. "Let's see if this works."

"It should." A long pause. "Will you stay for coffee?"

"I will, but only because all this isn't what I came to talk to you about. Let's go inside."

TWENTY-SIX

We sit at the kitchen table, and I tell him everything, as succinctly as I can. I explain how I identified Kim Mikhailov, linked her to Denis Zima, went to Zima's club and overheard that conversation . . . and then had Zima's thug menace me on my jog tonight.

"So, my concern is . . ." I begin, and then I trail off as I catch his expression and realize he's no longer hearing me. He's just staring.

"I'm okay," I say carefully.

"I can see that." He pulls back and rubs his hands over his face.

"Paul?" I say. "Are *you* okay?"

"My wife just told me how she identified a dead woman, staked out a Russian mobster's nightclub, taped a covert conversation from the closet, and then overpowered one of his thugs."

"I didn't exactly overpower —"

"You took a *gun* from a man who wouldn't hesitate to use it on you."

"It was in his waistband. He hadn't pulled it. I knew what I was doing."

"Yes, Aubrey, that would be my point. You knew what you were doing. With all of it."

"Oh."

Earlier I said the woman he married wasn't the whole me, and now I see the truth of that in his expression. He's known I'm a thief, a tech whiz, but it hasn't penetrated until this moment. He's looking at me the way he'd look at a stranger. Because he's realized that's what I am.

A stranger he married. A stranger who bore his child, who is now helping raise his child.

I take a deep breath. "Yes, I grew up knowing how to fight back. I learned some martial arts, some marksmanship. Part of that was because I planned to go into the army, but part was because my father knew that as a woman I might need those skills outside a battlefield. You're wondering now how much of that I've passed on to our daughter. You've seen our pretend sword fighting, our roughhousing. I haven't initiated any of that. Maybe whatever makes me crave exercise is what makes her love physical play, too. I'm not trying to turn her into me, Paul. I wouldn't do that."

"That's not —" He shakes his head. "Your father was right. Harnessing that physicality to defend yourself was a good idea. I hope to God that Charlie is never pulled into an alley, but if she is, I want her to be able to do what you did. To fight back. To escape. I just . . . You're not . . ."

"The woman you thought you married."

A long silence.

I put my mug down with a clack. "I'll leave in a minute, Paul. I just wanted you to know what happened. I off handedly mentioned that I didn't have kids, and Zima's thug didn't bat an eye, so I'm hoping that means they don't know about Charlie. I hid everything of hers in my apartment, so if they finish breaking in, they won't find it."

"*Finish* breaking in?"

"Someone tried while the thug distracted me. That's why I left. I'm going to a hotel, but I wanted you to know what happened, in case you think that endangers you or Charlie."

He shakes his head. "I don't. You said this thug didn't even believe you saw Kim with a child. That's what he said on the phone. He must have tracked you down to see what you'd say in person. When you brushed him off, he snapped. Men like him aren't ac-

customed to that sort of treatment. You supported his conviction that there's no child,
though. That's what he'll take back to Zima
— even *you* have retracted your story. The
boy is safe somewhere, and his aunt is probably on her way to get him."

"Yes, but be careful, please. Lock the
doors. Arm the security system. I'd offer to
look after Charlie tomorrow, but that's not
a good idea. Is there anyone else who can
take her, so she's not at daycare?"

"I'd stay home, but I have trial. Gayle's
taking a few days off. Maybe I could ask . . ."
He doesn't finish.

"That's fine with me."

He nods, but it's absent, his gaze distant.

I rise. "If anything else happens, I'll let
you know."

He gets to his feet before I can leave. "You
should stay here tonight."

"I'll be fine. I'll get a hotel —"

"No, stay. That's safer, and Charlie will
like to see you."

I hesitate. "I don't want to confuse her.
Having me here . . ."

"We'll tell her that you stopped by for
breakfast because you didn't get to see her
on the weekend."

I nod slowly. "Okay, I'll take the futon in
your study."

266

"I'll take the futon. You have the bed."

I think of that. Of sleeping in my old bed. Of waking in the night, thinking I'm home. Waking in the morning, thinking I never left, and these six months have been a bad dream. And then realizing the truth.

"No," I say. "Please. I don't . . . I'd rather take the futon."

He nods and goes to find bedding for it.

I still wake in the night. Wake smelling my home. Then I remember what woke me. I'd dreamed of Charlotte finding me on the futon, and seeing my purse, and going to check whether I brought her anything and pulling out the thug's gun —

I inhale so sharply it hurts. Then I scramble for my purse, only to remember that I left the gun in the car. I put it under the seat.

Did I lock the car doors? I'm sure I did but . . .

I slip outside. The car *is* locked, but I open it and move the gun into the glove box. Then I lock that. Lock the car next. Go back inside, lock *those* doors and rearm the security system. I hear a noise overhead, the creak of a footstep. Paul appears at the top of the stairs.

"Aubrey?" he says, and there's a note in

his voice, as if I'm not the only one who is confused, finding me here. Then he shakes off sleep and comes down the steps. "Is everything okay?"

"I had a nightmare about the gun," I say. "I was just making sure it was secured."

He nods, and that sleepy confusion lingers in his eyes. He gives my arm a squeeze and leans over to kiss the top of my head. Then he stops, as if realizing what he's doing, simple reflex.

I squeeze his arm in return and murmur something as I slip back to his office to sleep.

I wake on that futon and . . . God, this is hard. Harder than I would have ever imagined. I haven't been back to this house since I left, and I didn't think that was intentional, but I realize now that it was. I stayed away even when I had reasons to come there, when I'd need something for Charlotte on the weekend and Paul wouldn't be home, and he'd say, "Just go grab it. The key's in the usual place." I went without rather than set foot in this house.

I remember once, as a child, we got a home off base. Dad didn't care much for the base housing options, and there were good places to rent elsewhere. I had a house with a yard and a pool and a purple bed-room with sunflower curtains. I made friends with a girl next door and a boy down the street, my first non-military friendships. We spent the summer exploring the ravine and forest behind our house. When Dad got transferred, I ran away. After we left, I cried every night. He painted my new room purple. He bought me sunflower curtains. And I hated them, because I'd wake up and think I was back there.

That's what this felt like, only ten times worse. I'd been happy in that other house, but I'd never been an *un*happy child. I'd just found something special there. In this home, with Paul and Charlotte, I'd been unbelievably happy. Now I wake on the futon, and I want to grab my overnight bag and run, still wearing my nighttime sweats.

I don't, of course. That's as childish as running away from my father, and I'm no longer a child. I suck it up, and I slip into the kitchen, and I make coffee. I notice Paul has bought one of those K-Cup brewers, and I have to smile at that. He never could make proper coffee, and he'd happily given up his K-Cup bachelor machine when we moved in together. Now the old brew pot is shoved back on the counter, dusty and unused. I find coffee in the freezer, right where I kept it. The *same* coffee I left there. I push back pangs of grief, and I brew a pot. I open the cupboard, and I reach for his cup and . . .

It's gone.

We had a set of *Lady and the Tramp* coffee mugs, ones we bought at Disney World. When you pushed them together, the handle cutouts formed a heart. Couple mugs. Tossed out, I presume, until I spot them at the back of the cupboard. I take out two generic ones. Fill them. Feel another pang as I add his cream, never pausing for a second to remember how much he takes. I fix his coffee by motor memory.

When I lived here, I'd get up early to make coffee and wake him with his mug. Once I have this one ready, I'm halfway up the stairs before I remember this is no longer my place. Our bedroom is *definitely* not my place. It's the one spot in this house I shouldn't enter. I'm heading back down when I hear his footsteps in the hall. Then, "Bree?"

I hold up the mug. He comes down. He's pulled on sweatpants, but that's it, and I notice he's lost weight. That thickening through his middle is gone, the early stages of a spare tire reversed, and I feel a stab of pain even at that. It's a sign he'd made a conscious effort to lose that extra weight in preparation for dating.

Can't blame him for that, can I?

He takes the coffee, and I'm about to head down to the kitchen when he says, "Do you want to wake Charlie?"

I frown, thinking it's too early. Normally I'd get him up and off to work and then relax with a second coffee until Charlotte wakes around eight, maybe even nine if I'm lucky.

That's how we did things when Mommy stayed home. Mommy no longer stays home, and Daddy needs to drop Charlotte off on his way to work.

I nod and slip past him. I climb the steps to my daughter's room, for the first time in six months. I open the door, and I see her sleeping and . . . The crib is gone. She's in a bed. Her own bed. My baby sleeping in a regular bed. My baby growing up . . . without me.

I've been so careful, stifling the pangs of grief, feeling my eyes well, allowing no more than a single tear to slide down my cheek. Now that self-restraint snaps. It starts with a burst of tears, and then I'm sobbing.

"Bree?"

It's Paul. He's right behind me. He must have been there the whole time, and when I

271

turn, he quickly puts his coffee mug on the bannister.

I close Charlotte's door. "I-I can't," I manage between heaving breaths. "I-I'm sorry. I need . . . I need to go."

I bolt for the stairs, tears blinding me. I hit his coffee mug, and I hear it crash. I let out a gasp and a frantic apology. Paul's arms go around me. I think he's just keeping me from tumbling half-blind down the stairs. Then he pulls me against him.

At first I resist. I smell the faint scent of night sweat, and I feel his skin against my cheek, and I hear his heartbeat, and my brain screams that this isn't mine, not anymore. It's like seeing Charlotte in her new bed. I want to flee while I still can. But Paul pulls me into a tight embrace, and he whispers in my ear that it's okay. I collapse against him. He pats my back with one hand and holds me with the other, and he tells me it's okay, and I hear permission to break down, to fall apart. So I do.

I sob against his chest until the pressure finally eases, until I can lift my head to say I'm all right. I look up and . . . he kisses me. His mouth goes to mine, and there isn't a moment of surprise in that, not a moment of hesitation either. He's kissing me, and my arms go around his neck, and I'm kissing him back and oh God, I've missed this. I've missed him so much. Time blurs as I pour that longing and need into my kiss. I forget where I am. I forget whatever I should be doing. I certainly forget that I should not be doing this. Or maybe I do remember that last part . . . and I just don't care.

It's a deep, desperate kiss, and the next thing I know, I'm in our bedroom. He lowers me onto the bed. Or maybe I pull him down onto it. I have no idea who does what — I only know that neither one needs to prod the other. I'm on the bed, and he's over me, and we're still kissing. He has my shirt up, and I'm tugging down his sweatpants, and it comes as naturally as fixing his coffee. Motor memory, the hungry kiss, and then both of us falling into bed and —

His phone buzzes. I glance over to see it standing on the charger. Paul puts his hands to my face, getting my attention and ignoring his phone, but when I see the name that flashes, I pull away. He glances at the phone. He sees the name — he must — but it doesn't seem to register. He only lowers his mouth to mine again. I pull back and scramble from under him.

"Gayle," I say.

There's still no reaction. Or if there is, it's

confusion, like I'm speaking an unfamiliar name.

I wave at the ringing phone as I clamber off the bed. "We can't. I'm sorry. I shouldn't have — That's not right. You have . . . Gayle."

He gives a soft — and uncharacteristic — curse and hits the Ignore button. By then, I'm at the door. He doesn't come after me. He just sits on the edge of the bed, face in his hands.

"I'm sorry," I say again. "I shouldn't have —"

"It wasn't you."

"It's . . ." I inhale. "Habit, right? Being here. It's just habit. I'm sorry. I'd never — I know you have . . . someone . . . and I wouldn't try to do that. It's disrespectful."

"Disrespectful." He gives a short laugh and shakes his head.

"I'll go," I say. "I shouldn't have been here. I'm sorry."

As I turn, he says, "No," and rises to his feet. His hand lands on my shoulder. "Charlie would love to see you. If you'd rather I wake her, I'll do that."

"No, I can. It was just . . ." I twist to look back at him. "I see you got her a real bed." I smile when I'm saying it, but that starts the tears again, my eyes filling. I wipe them away. "Sorry, it's just . . ."

I'm missing her life. I'm missing so much of it.

Missing you, too. Missing both of you.

He gives me a one-armed hug, more careful now. "I know. You go get her up, then, and I'll shower and dress. There's cereal and bagels. She goes back and forth between them."

"Do you have eggs?" I ask.

He hesitates, and when he forces a smile, it's a little awkward, a little sad. "That would require me knowing how to cook them."

I nod. Then I murmur that I'll figure out something and slip from the room. As I go, I hear him pick up his phone to call Gayle back.

Twenty-Seven

I hold it together for Charlotte. That's easier than I feared. She's thrilled to see me, even though I'm quick to explain that I just stopped by. It doesn't matter. She wakes with a bounce, as always, and there's no time to grieve for what I've lost. I get a taste of it this morning, and I'll take that as a gift and make the most of it.

I find bacon in the freezer — bacon I'd put there. I thaw it and whip up pancakes, also from my legacy baking ingredients. Paul comes down, and we eat, and the awkwardness disappears with Charlotte there, talking a mile a minute.

"So you're taking her to Gayle's today?" I ask.

He stops with the fork halfway to his mouth. Then he shakes his head. "I changed my mind. Gayle will have brought work home, and Charlie is a full-time job."

"I has job?" Charlotte says, following our

conversation.

"Yes," Paul says. "A very special job, but it might be too hard. I need you" — he leans toward her — "to be good for Mrs. Mueller. You're going to stay with her today."

"And Becky and Pete?"

"Yes, you're staying with Mrs. Mueller, and her son Pete and her cat Becky."

Charlotte squeals. "Noooo. Becky is girl. Pete is dog."

Paul frowns. "Are you sure? Becky kind of looks like a little girl, but I'm pretty sure Pete is a rat. A huge rat, like Matt."

"Pete is dog!"

"Chihuahua," Paul murmurs to me.

"Ah," I say. "Well, I can see where you'd get confused." I turn to Charlotte. "I bet Pete loves Matt."

Charlotte shakes her head, curls bouncing. "No. Pete scared of Matt. Becky like Matt."

"The Muellers moved in down the road," Paul says. "Becky's four. Her mom has offered to take Charlie anytime daycare doesn't work out, so I called this morning. I also let the daycare know she'd be away."

"Thank you."

He's about to speak again when his phone rings. He checks the screen. Hits Ignore.

"I'd like to talk to you later," he says.

"More about what's going on. And I would rather you didn't go back to your apartment without me. Well, without *someone,* but I'd prefer it to be someone who knows what's going on, and I'm guessing that's just me?"

"It is."

"We'll discuss —" His phone buzzes with a text. He flicks it to vibrate without checking the message. "We'll discuss . . . nighttime arrangements then. If you'd be okay coming back here for dinner . . ."

"Yes!" Charlotte says. "Mommy come dinner."

"I will," I say, then add quickly for Charlotte, "this one time."

"Good, Charlie can watch a movie while we talk. What time are you done — ?" Paul says.

His phone vibrates.

"I think someone's trying to get hold of you," I say.

"Just work. I'll call back in the car."

"Over Bluetooth, I hope."

His eyes crease in a smile. "Yes, over Bluetooth. Now, if you wouldn't mind getting Charlie ready, I'll tidy up here."

Charlotte's dressed and only needs to brush her teeth, so when I come back, he's still clearing the breakfast dishes.

"I'll tackle those," I say. "You go on to work."

I'm brushing past him to clear the table when his phone vibrates again. I see that it's Gayle. He stuffs it into his pocket. I hesitate, debating. Then I say, "I would like you to let Gayle know that I was here last night."

His brows rise.

I put the mugs into the dishwasher. "I'd rather you told her and explained than have her find out later. I don't want to cause trouble for you."

"You're not —"

"Please? Humor me? I just . . . I want you to be happy."

He nods abruptly and mumbles something. Then he calls for Charlotte to grab Matt and tells me he'll see me tonight, and they're gone.

I'm at work, and I'm happy. Happier than I've been in a long time. More at peace than I've been in a very long time. Paul knows my secrets. All of them. And we have moved past it. Not to marital reconciliation. I'd be lying if I said I don't still hold out hope for that. This morning, when we'd been in bed together and I realized who was calling, yes, I hoped he might say it didn't matter . . .

and let us finish what we started. I'd entertained the fantasy of him admitting it was over with Gayle, and he wanted to try again with me. That only lasted a moment. If it did happen, I'd have worried it was temporary, lust clouding his judgment. If there's any hope of reconciliation, it won't come today or even tomorrow. I can't push either. He is the wronged party, and that choice must be his.

I am happy because we've achieved something less life-changing but even more important. Personal reconciliation. He knows my secrets, and yes, they have hurt him. Yet that hasn't marked the beginning of an icy-cold post-separation wasteland, where I can no longer reach him, no longer talk to him, no longer co-parent with him. We're returning to equilibrium, and if that's the best I can hope for, then I'll take it.

I think Paul was right. Zima's goon was testing me last night. Menacing me in hopes of proving — or disproving — my story about a missing child. No one wants there to be a missing child. It's inconvenient. If I'm the only person who says there was one, and I've retracted my claim, then the thug can go back to Denis Zima and say, "That chick was wrong."

You don't have a son, Denis. There's noth-

ing to see here. Let's move along.

We're short-staffed at the library today, so I'm doing mom-and-tot story time, which I love. I'm good at it, too — I do all the voices, and I'm definitely not afraid to be silly. I'm hoping that if I impress Ingrid, I'll get to do more programming, especially with little ones. Now that Paul knows about my past, there's nothing to stop me from going back to school part-time. Get a degree in library science. I'd also like to throw my tech skills into the mix. Play to my strengths and my interests, after so many years of hiding them.

God, that feels good. I don't know if I ever truly realized the weight of those secrets. Once it's lifted, the possibilities roll out before me like a red carpet. I can get my degree and a proper librarian job. I can use my inheritance money to buy a condo. I can openly negotiate child custody with Paul, now that I don't have to worry about him digging into my past.

I can breathe again. That's what it feels like. I can finally breathe.

I'm helping the little ones check out their post-story-time books when my phone buzzes. It's under the counter, and I glance at it while the screen is lit up. It's an incoming text from a number I don't recognize.

I'll admit to a jolt of fear when I see that, as a million horrible scenarios run through my mind. Life is going too well this morning, and the universe will surely stomp out my joy with a text from Zima or his goon.

I whip through the checkouts. Then I surreptitiously unlock my phone. The text is a video with a still of Charlotte climbing a slide. I smile. Paul must have given Mrs. Mueller my number.

I'm about to text back a "Thanks!" when Ingrid appears from the stacks. I slide my phone under the counter, and I head out to shelve books. As I'm leaving the desk, a mother stops to gush about my story-time skills . . . just as Ingrid is passing to overhear. When I come back from shelving, she tells me several of the parents commented, and Nancy has been talking about giving up story time, and maybe I could take it over. It is the icing on my cupcake-perfect morning. Ingrid and I talk, too, really talk. At break time I grab my phone to continue the delicious sweetness of my day by watching my daughter play.

I sit in the staff room with a fresh cup of coffee and a doughnut dropped off by a patron. I hit Play on the video. I watch Charlotte and a preschooler tear through the tiny playground in their neighborhood.

I smile as I enjoy the video and my dough-nut. Then I see a woman holding a Chihua-hua on a leash. She's close to the girls, keep-ing an eye on them. This must be the neighbor — Mrs. Mueller.

I think that . . . and then I pause. If that's Mrs. Mueller, who's taking the video?

Maybe her spouse works from home. Or has the day off. That makes sense. Except, when I start thinking about that, I notice another oddity. No one turns to the camera. No one waves at it. No one smiles over at it.

If this videographer is with Mrs. Mueller, then the kids know they're being filmed. There isn't a chance in hell that two pre-schoolers wouldn't look over at least once.

A chill slides between my shoulder blades.

I flip to the text message and send back: Who is this?

A response comes within seconds: Are you sure you don't know anything about that little boy, Aubrey? Maybe my video jogged your memory?

My fingers tremble as I hit Call to dial the number. No one answers. I send back a text: I told you there isn't a little boy. I made a mistake.

The response: I don't think you did.

Then: You have such a pretty little girl.

My heart slams against my ribs. I start to compose a response, but I can't untangle my fingers to write anything coherent. I dial Paul's number instead. It goes straight to voice mail. I pull up his office number from my contacts, and I call. He has a new admin assistant, but when I tell her who I am, she says Paul's in court, and she'll take a message. She'll make sure he gets it on his next break. I leave a message. *Call me back. It's urgent.* She promises to get it to him as soon as she can.

Next my fingers hover over Laila Jackson's number, but it'll take too long to explain. I go to directory assistance and begin searching for the Muellers' number. I have the name and the street. They only moved in recently, though, so I don't know if there's much chance . . .

Yes! They have a home number, and it's listed.

I call. No one answers. I leave a message saying who I am and that I'm worried about Charlotte and could they call me back right away.

"Aubrey?" Ingrid appears. "I'm going to need you to end your break early. The desk is swamped."

"Actually, I have to go," I say.

"What?"

284

I'm about to lie. Say I'm sick. But I stop myself — no more lies, not when the truth is a perfectly valid excuse.

"My daughter is in trouble, and her dad's in court today. I need to leave."

"All right, come help me with this, and we'll call someone in to cover for you."

"No, it's urgent." I hold out my phone. "Someone just texted me a video of her as a threat."

"What?" Her face screws up, not in horror but confusion.

"It's connected to that missing boy. I-I'll explain later." I grab my purse. "I can't reach the sitter, so I need to go check on her."

"If your daughter really is in danger, call the police."

I don't miss the way she says "if."

"I will," I say. "On my way there. I just need to be sure Charlotte's okay. I'll be back in thirty minutes."

"No." Ingrid steps into my path. "I need you up front, Aubrey, and I've had enough of this nonsense. If you are legitimately concerned, call the police. Then do your job until I get someone to cover your shift."

I fight the panic coiled in my gut. That video came in nearly twenty minutes ago. Whoever sent it is toying with me, and the longer I argue with Ingrid, the later it'll be before I can leave.

"I'll help you with the desk," I say. "Five minutes. I'll check people through and then —"

"I said no, Aubrey. You will stay until —"

I swing past her and break into a jog.

"If you leave this building, do not come back," she calls after me. "I have had enough of your . . ."

I don't hear the rest. I'm already flying out the door.

TWENTY-EIGHT

On the drive, I call Laila Jackson . . . and get her voice mail. I don't leave a message. Not yet. First I want to be sure Charlotte is okay. When a call comes in moments later, I glance at the screen, hoping it's Paul. It's Ellie Milano. I let it go to voice mail — whatever she has to say, I don't need the distraction right now. She doesn't leave a message.

I drive straight to the park. It's nearly empty, and I can tell in a sweep that Charlotte isn't there. I spot one of the moms I knew from before. I pull over, jog to her, and ask if she's seen Charlotte.

She gives me this look, her eyes narrowing, and then she says carefully, "No, I haven't."

I wonder why I'm getting that look. Then it hits. She knows I'm not the custodial parent.

"There's a problem," I say. "Paul's in

court. I'm just wondering if you've seen her."

She says no, but I can't tell if she's still suspicious. I hop back in my car. I have the Muellers' address from the phone listing. It's a half dozen doors down from Paul's place. I pull into the drive and race to the front door.

I ring the bell. Then I knock. There's no response to either. I call, and I hear the phone ringing inside.

The car is in the drive, and they aren't at the park. Where — ?

A child's laugh echoes from the backyard. I heave a sigh of relief and race to the gate. It's a chain-link fence, and I can see Mrs. Mueller through it. The dog — Pete — races at the heels of a little girl who is not my daughter. There's no sign of Charlotte.

He's taken her. Whoever sent those photos took her.

How could I have let a stranger care for Charlotte today? Anyone could walk up and say Paul sent them to fetch Charlotte.

Mrs. Mueller sees me running to her fence, and she looks over in alarm with a called "Hello?"

I resist the urge to leap into her yard. "I'm Aubrey Finch," I call back. "I'm Charlotte's mom. Where is she?"

288

There's a long pause, as my heart hammers. I know what's coming. She sees my face. She realizes there's a problem, realizes she shouldn't have trusted that person who said he'd come for Charlotte.

Then she walks to the fence, and I see the same look I got from the neighbor at the park. Suspicion.

"I'm afraid I don't know your custody arrangement —" she begins.

"I just need to know where she is. Someone sent me a threatening video. I called. I left a message. Please, just tell me what happened."

"Charlie's napping."

I exhale and take a few deep breaths. "Okay. Thank you. Paul's in court, and I can't get hold of him. I raced over from work."

She nods. A slow nod, still wary.

"Can you wake Charlie up, please?" I say. "I'm sorry. She just . . . . She shouldn't be alone. I don't know how much Paul told you about the situation . . ."

"Only that she couldn't go to care today, and to let no one except him pick her up. He said there was a situation. I thought it was custody-related."

"What? No." Another deep breath. "Not at all, but I didn't come to take her. I totally respect your concern, and I thank you for being careful. The problem is that I've found myself caught up in a police investigation, and there had been threats. Not against Charlotte, but Paul and I were still cautious. I just received a video that clearly targets her." I hold out my phone. "It's one of you with her in the park."

She takes the phone, brows knitted. She presses Play and her eyes widen.

"Mommy?" The little girl runs over, dog tumbling along behind. Mrs. Mueller motions for her to come closer and says, "We're going to get Charlie up. I think she's napped long enough." She opens the gate. "Come and sit on the deck. We'll be back in a moment."

"Thank you."

Charlotte is awake, and Paul is on his way. His admin assistant got the message to him as soon as court ended. He called, and I said everything was fine, but he wanted to come get us.

I sit outside with Mrs. Mueller for a very awkward hour before Paul arrives. The first thing he does is apologize to her. He shouldn't have put her in this position, and he wouldn't have if he'd had any idea this might happen. He's also quick to say I warned him. I appreciate that, so it doesn't sound as if I'm the one who underplayed the danger.

We drive to his house. I check the locks before we go in, but there's no sign anyone tampered with them. He tells Charlotte to go brush her teeth, and we'll all go for ice cream.

"You're telling her to brush her teeth *before* ice cream?" I say as she races off.

He screws up his face. "Okay, that makes no sense. I'm not thinking straight."

He looks exhausted, as if he ran all the way from Chicago. I resist the urge to give him a hug, and I offer a smile instead, saying, "I'm teasing. You know that."

He nods. "I do. I'm just . . ." He looks at me. "I'm sorry, Bree. You were worried about that guy, and I blew you off."

"You didn't blow —"

"Some thug came at you with a gun last night. Obviously, he was serious. I just thought . . ." He throws up his hands. "I don't know what I thought. Men like that often have guns, and he didn't pull it, so I presumed he was just trying to intimidate you."

"If I thought Charlie was in actual danger, I'd have said so. Sending her to a sitter made sense."

291

Charlotte races in, saying, "Ice cream! Ice cream!"

Paul looks at me. "I thought we'd go to Elsa's Castle. She can play while we talk. Is that all right or do you need to get back to work?"

I had called Ingrid as soon as I got off the phone with Paul. I said Charlotte was fine, and I was just staying with her until he arrived. She coldly informed me that there was no need to come in today. Nor any need to come in tomorrow.

"I have the day off," I say.

We sit outside at the ice cream parlor and watch Charlotte on the play equipment while we talk. She ate half her ice cream and then wanted Mommy to come play, but as soon as Paul said he needed to speak to me, she zoomed off.

"That was easy," I say. "The last time I tried to get her to play alone, you'd have thought I was sentencing her to a year of solitary confinement."

"She's just happy to see us . . ." He shrugs.

"Together." I glance over at her, and she's climbing while smiling at us like a grown-up watching her kid on a date. "Do you think we're giving her . . . I don't want to . . ."

"She's fine, Bree. Now tell me what happened."

I do, leaving out the part about Ingrid.

"I thought it was the sitter sending the video," I say, "or I'd have looked at it sooner."

"Honestly, that's what I thought, too, when I first saw it."

When I blink, he makes a face. "Sorry, did I mention I'm not running on all cylinders?" He takes out his phone. "I got the same video."

"What?"

He shows me. It was sent a few minutes after mine, while he'd been in court. He didn't see it until after he got my message. The text accompanying his reads: Your ex is sticking her nose where it doesn't belong. Tell her to stay out of our business, and we'll stay out of yours.

My gut twists. "I'm sorry, Paul. I'm so—"

"Stop. You did nothing wrong, Aubrey. You were trying to help a little boy, and I don't know what Zima's problem with you is."

"He thinks I know more. Somehow he's found out I'm investigating, and he isn't buying my story that I made a mistake about Brandon."

"Did you report the video?"

"I wanted to. I called my police contact

293

but got her voice mail. Now I'm wondering if my contact is the one who's telling Zima that I know more. She's the only person who *realizes* I know more." I exhale. "And I'm being paranoid thinking that, aren't I? Suspecting a cop of being in a mobster's pocket."

"It wouldn't be the first time, unfortunately. It's rare, but yes, if you give me a name, I'll run a few discreet checks."

I give him Laila's name and everything I know about her. Then we discuss the video itself. I'd asked the sitter if she'd seen anyone videotaping in the park. She hadn't.

"From what I can tell," I say, "it was taken from the east end of the park. There's new construction there, so I'm wondering if whoever filmed it was tucked in there, out of sight —"

My phone rings. It's Ellie Milano again. I motion to Paul that I'm going to take it, and he nods and then heads over to watch Charlotte.

"It's Ellie Milano," she says when I answer. "You called me yesterday about Brandon."

She said his name. She actually said his name. Please tell me that means she knows he exists — and she's not parroting back the name I used.

"Who are you?" she asks.

Now I hesitate. Two days ago, I'd have given my name, address and whatever else would convince her that I wasn't some crank. That's changed. I glance at my daughter, running to jump into Paul's arms. That *has* to change.

"I'd rather not say," I say. "I'm sorry, but getting involved in this has caused trouble for my own family. I'm going to ask you to call the Oxford Police Department. I reported seeing Brandon to them. They have no evidence to corroborate my story, so they aren't looking for him, and the fact that you told them he doesn't exist really didn't help."

"Wait!" she says, as if expecting me to hang up. "I'm sorry. I'm just protecting my nephew. That's what Kimmy wanted. It was" — her voice catches — "the only thing she wanted, the only thing she cared about."

That catch reminds me this is a woman in mourning, and my tone softens as I say, "I'm sorry."

She takes a deep breath. "You were trying to help. I didn't dare admit you were right, but I should have been polite about it."

"You were thinking about Brandon. His situation. Kim was afraid for him."

"*Terrified* for him."

"Terrified of his father. Denis Zima."

"Is that his name?"

"She never gave it?"

"She refused," Ellie says. "She said it was a guy she'd been with in LA, and his family was into crime." A harsh laugh. "God, that sounds like being into fashion or the music industry. They were criminals. That's all I know. She left him when she got pregnant, and her plan was to hide Brandon until he was school age. By then, she figured it'd be safe. He was going to school this fall, and she was so excited." Her voice hitches in a soft sob.

"But he will go to school now," I say. "He's safe with whoever she gave him to —"

"No, he's not."

"What?"

She takes a deep breath, as if calming herself to speak. "Kimmy always told me as little as possible, for my own safety. I knew about Brandon. I've visited them, but my kids don't even know they have a cousin. She was *so* careful. She said, if anything ever happened to her, she had arranged for someone to take Brandon. I said no, I wanted him. He should be with family. I convinced her I was right, and I think she was relieved. That's what she wanted.

Brandon to be with me. She just didn't want to assume I'd be okay with it."

"So you were supposed to take him from whoever had him."

"Right. She gave me an address in Chicago. If anything happened to her, I'd get a call, and then I should go to this address. It wouldn't be safe to give me the address over the phone, so I needed it in advance. The day before she . . . before she was murdered, she called to see if I still had the address. I asked if anything was wrong. She laughed. Said she'd had a nightmare that I'd lost the address, so she was checking. She did things like that, so I never questioned it. I should . . . Oh God, I should have questioned."

"She didn't want to put you in danger."

"I know." Another deep breath. "Then the police phoned about Kimmy, and I flew into a panic because no one had called about Brandon. You did, and I thought for a second *that* was the call . . ."

"But it wasn't."

"No, and I was already on my way to Chicago. I thought maybe his caregivers couldn't get through or they'd lost my phone number. I told myself everything was fine, Brandon was fine. But then I got to the address where he was supposed to be . . ."

"And he wasn't there."

"*No* one was there. It's an empty house. I freaked out. I searched it for any sign that he'd been there, and there was nothing. Now I'm in Chicago, and my husband thinks I'm making arrangements to bring Kimmy's — to bring her home — but I haven't even spoken to the police yet. I just keep waiting for that call, and circling back to the address, in case I missed them and . . . And I don't even know what to do."

I open my mouth to say I'll be right there. It's the first thing that comes. Then I see Paul, lifting Charlotte onto the play structure.

I can't do this. For the sake of my family, I cannot do this.

Yet I can't say that either. There's a woman in crisis on the other end of this line. A woman whose sister has been murdered. Whose nephew is missing. I will not say "I can't help you" and hang up.

"My husband is a lawyer," I say. "A criminal attorney. He's right here. He knows what's been going on. May I get his advice and call you back?"

There's a pause, and I'm not sure if she's hesitating about me explaining to Paul or

298

she just doesn't want to let me go. When she gives a reluctant yes, I promise to call ASAP and disconnect.

Paul catches my eye, and I only nod, letting him know I'm off the phone. He's playing with Charlotte, and I don't want to interrupt him. After a moment, he comes over and says, "Is everything okay?"

I tell him what's happened. When I finish, he pushes his glasses up his nose and pinches the bridge, his eyes shut. It's a gesture I know well, the one he'd make if I came to him with a problem after a long day of work. It means he's too exhausted to deal with this, but he won't say that. He never says that.

"I'm sorry," I say. "You don't need this —"

"Aubrey?" He meets my gaze. "Don't."

"I just —"

"You're trying to help this woman. I want to help you. I'm just thinking that it's a mess. An unfortunate and tragic mess, and I'm not even sure what to tell you. I know what you need to tell *her,* though. Call the police."

"Go to them, not me. I should stay out of it."

"I'm not saying that either. Charlotte is fine. I'm taking her to my mother's for a few days. If you want to help this woman, then I will do what you needed me to do from the start — support your decision. But at this moment, she needs to tell the police everything. Not this Officer Jackson. Let me check her out first. Have Ellie contact the detective in charge of Kim Mikhailov's murder and tell them about her son. Tell them what's happened."

I nod. Then I make the call.

TWENTY-NINE

Ellie won't contact the police. Kim didn't trust them, so she doesn't either. I can't do it myself, not when she's adamantly opposed. So I'm stuck. I tell myself that's a good thing. I cannot get involved. I have already endangered my child getting involved. Ellie needs to handle this, and with any luck, she'll realize that the best way to do that is to involve the police.

I will not feel guilty about telling her I can't help.

I won't.

I do, of course. But I've made the right choice, and I need to let it go.

We're driving to the house. Paul is taking Charlotte to his mother's tonight, and he'd like me to come with them for the drive.

I shake my head. "I've never been your mom's favorite person. Apparently, she had good instincts."

Paul's hands tighten on the steering wheel. "I'd like to put that aside for now. Please."

I glance back at Charlotte, asleep in her seat. "I'm not trying to start a fight."

"I know. But I need to set it aside. I'm here to help you. I'd like . . . I'd like us to get past this, which means at some point, yes, we need to hash it out. Under the circumstances, though, it's counterproductive. I'm not over it, but I'm not as angry as I was. I'd like to put the rest on pause."

"Okay."

"As for my mother, I don't think I ever dated anyone who lived up to her expectations. You were too young for me. Too different from me. She thought you were after a husband with a good job, and then you'd leave and take half my money."

"A gold digger."

"A gold digger with very modest aspirations."

I laugh at that.

"Obviously, she was wrong," he says, "though it did make me more sensitive to the issue of why you married me when I found out —" He stops short. "And that's not dropping the subject, is it?"

"No, but I understand."

He sighs and leans back against the headrest. "I say I want to put it aside, but that's cowardice. I want to forget it. I want to pretend . . ."

"It never happened. Because when you remember it did, you question whether I should be here, whether you should be helping me."

He makes a face. "Not like that. I accept that you didn't marry me as a shield to hide behind. But you *did* lie, and you did deceive me, and I do feel betrayed. I do feel like I married a stranger. I'm just . . ." His fingers tighten on the wheel again. "I'm hurt."

"If I could start over, I'd do it differently. But I understand that there's no undoing that now. There's no making up for it. Which means I appreciate this all the more, Paul. I really do."

He nods. There's silence, then. So much silence, before he says, "If you won't come to my mother's, will you at least stay at the house?"

I hesitate.

"I'd like you to stay there, Aubrey," he says. "With the security system and . . ." He glances to make sure Charlotte's asleep, but still lowers his voice. "That gun. Just stay there, safe, until I return. Please."

"All right."

I've been at Paul's place for about two hours when he calls. That's what I must think of it as. Paul's place. Not ours. Not even "my old house." That's a dangerous path. He bought it. I left it. Now it is his.

Paul calls about Laila Jackson. His contacts have gotten back to him, and the word is that while she can be "difficult" and "ambitious," there's never been any hint of corruption.

"As my one contact said," Paul says, "she's more likely to be the person reporting corruption. In hopes it'll free up a job, he says. Which isn't fair. She's a woman of color, and she's ambitious, and that doesn't always play well with the good old boys. But someone like that isn't going to risk her career for a quick payday from the mob. Even those who don't care for Laila Jackson say she's good at her job."

"Should I report the video directly to her, then?"

"I would. You know her, and that's more useful than placing a call to the switchboard. I could give you a contact of mine if you'd prefer . . ."

"No, I'm okay with Laila. She's not my

biggest fan, but sometimes that's helpful. She'll be straight with me. I'll tell her about my encounter Sunday night and the video today. I won't mention Ellie Milano."

"Unless it means lying," Paul says. "If she asks you anything where you'd need to lie to protect Ellie's privacy, I would strongly suggest you don't. Just avoid volunteering information."

"Got it. Oh, if Laila wants to speak to me in person, should I go to the station?"

He pauses. "I'd rather she came to the house. I'd like her take on this — how much danger you might be in personally — before you go out alone. She'll bring her partner to take the report, and I'll be home in about ninety minutes."

"Great. Thank you."

I call Laila. She's out on patrol, but when I ask if I should report this to another officer, she's quick to say no. Less than an hour later, she's on the doorstep. And she's alone.

"Where's Officer Cooper?" I ask.

"Buried in paperwork. He said I can handle this."

I hesitate in the doorway, not moving aside to let her in. "I thought police were supposed to work in pairs."

"Technically, yes, but I know you, and this

is part of an on-going case. A case he'd rather not bother with."

When I still don't move, she arches her brows. Then she laughs. "Ah, you think this is suspect, me showing up alone."

She holds out her phone. On it is a text string between her and Cooper, where she tells him "that Finch woman" wants to report an incident, and he grumbles. She says she'll take it.

"Yes," she says as she puts her phone away. "I was dismissive, because I *wanted* to talk to you alone. Coop is . . ." She seems to check herself and says, carefully, "Let's just say that I'm sure you thought he was the one taking you seriously about the boy, and I was the one blowing you off, but that's not the way it worked. While I was suspicious, I still investigated. Mostly alone. Whatever you say to me tonight will go into an official report, and you can call the station later to verify that."

I back up. "Sorry. I'm just a little suspicious myself right now."

"I see that."

As she walks in, her gaze moves through the hall, taking the measure of this house.

"It was my choice," I say.

"Hmm?"

"Before you draw any conclusions about

306

why I'm in that crappy apartment while my husband lives here, it was my choice."

"Ah."

She's still looking as she walks through. Then she stops at a photo. It's the three of us — Paul, Charlotte, and me — at the beach.

"Wandered a bit, did you?" she says.

"What?"

She shrugs. "I don't blame you. I think I'd go nuts in a place like this. Especially with a toddler. You got bored and wandered."

"If you're asking whether I cheated on my husband, the answer is no. I'm not living in a lousy apartment out of guilt. Our marriage didn't work out, and Paul was the one who bought this house, so I left him with it. That seemed fair. As long as he was staying, our daughter should, too, at least until we straighten out the divorce. Also fair."

She studies me. Then she nods. "Okay, I can understand that."

"So, if you're done questioning my life choices . . ."

"Hey, you're suspicious. I am, too. We both want to know who we're dealing with. Why don't we sit, and you can give me your statement."

THIRTY

I tell Laila what happened with Zima's thug. By the time I finish, we don't need a functioning air conditioner to chill the room — her look does it just fine.

"This happened last night?" she says. "And you didn't contact me?"

"I handled it."

Her face hardens, eyes flashing. "You are not *supposed* to *handle* armed stalkers, Aubrey. You are supposed to call us."

"Somehow I didn't think he'd wait while I dialed 911."

"You know what I mean. As soon as you got away, you should have called me. This is connected to the case. It's not a matter of whether or not you can handle it yourself. I needed to know."

"And I needed to know you could be trusted with that information."

"Are you questioning my competency as an officer."

"No, I'm saying that you and I got off on the wrong footing, and I wasn't ready to trust you. Now I am. Which is why you're here."

"This is a police investigation. You don't get to decide —"

"I handled it the best I could. I was very, very clear to this thug that I thought I'd misunderstood the situation and didn't actually see a boy. There was no way I'd let Denis Zima think he has a son out there. I said I made a mistake. That I *definitely* made a mistake. He didn't like that answer."

Laila chews this over, and I can tell she's debating whether or not to pursue our disagreement. After a moment, she says, "Did he seem to think you were lying?"

"I'm not sure. It's the same guy I taped on the phone. I'm sure of that. That night, he told whoever was on the line that he thought I was wrong. That there was no kid. So he might have just been pushing me around, making sure I stuck to my story. That's what Paul thinks, and I'd tend to agree."

"Can you describe the man?"

"I can do better than that. I have a name. Hugh Orbec."

She looks up at me.

I shrug. "I had some time to kill. The man

I heard on the phone knew Kim, so he dated back that far in Denis Zima's life. Social media is a wonderful thing for tracking friends. That's what Orbec is. He's three years older than Zima. Worked for Zima Senior, who lent him to Denis for the LA clubs. They apparently became close, and when Denis quit the underage-strip-joint racket, Orbec followed him. He's head of operations for the Zodiac chain."

Laila's quiet, and I feel the temperature drop again.

I sigh. "Now what have I done?"

Her gaze meets mine, hard as steel. "Potentially ruined our case against the man, that's all. If a defense attorney found out that you'd positively identified your attacker as Hugh Orbec *before* you gave your statement, he can claim your recollection is based on Orbec, not the man in the alley."

"It doesn't matter. I'm not filing a complaint about what happened in the alley. There's no point. I'm not injured. He didn't pull his gun. He probably even has a permit for carrying it. If I complain, I'll only make a dangerous enemy. My complaint is about what happened next."

I tell her about the video. Then I show it to her, along with the text.

"I'm not claiming *this* is Orbec," I say.

"When I spoke to him, I off handedly said I didn't have kids, and he never questioned that. If he sent the video, I'd think he'd reference that. Say something like 'I see you *do* have a kid.' "

"Maybe. But that's hardly proof that it wasn't him." She takes my phone and rereads the texts.

"It also doesn't quite fit with Orbec," I say. "Why keep pushing if you *want* me to stick to my story? To say there was no kid? What reason would I have to lie about being wrong . . . after he threw me into a wall?"

"But you did."

"To protect my family and Brandon. As far as Orbec knows, though, I'm just some lady from the suburbs claiming that a dead woman had a kid. To him, I don't know who Kim is. I don't know Denis Zima's connection. I've done nothing more than witness something . . . and then retract my statement. Why keep harassing me?"

"Because someone realizes you're more than you seem, Aubrey. Someone knows you're involved. Someone knows you've been digging."

Which is the answer I don't want. Of course I realize that's the most obvious explanation. I just want her to give me one that means these people will leave my family alone.

I'm about to ask her advice when Paul gets home. He greets Laila — handshake, introduction, civil but not overly warm. He feels the chill in the air. I know he does — he keeps sneaking glances at me, gauging the situation.

When she asks to see his video and texts, he gives them to her. She forwards them to herself at the station, as she did mine.

"We'll be investigating." She turns to me. "By *we,* I mean the Oxford Police Department. Not you, Aubrey. You are to stay out of this. Understand?"

I can barely unhinge my jaw to answer. "I understand."

So, once again, I'm on my own. If I had any hope of an alliance with Laila, it evaporated in that conversation. She's a cop, and I'm not, and that is a line she's not letting me cross, no matter how helpful I've been.

I don't know if I'll dig deeper. No, that's a lie. I will dig. I must. I just won't be out there, sneaking into clubs and playing spy anymore. Or jogging at nightfall in my neighborhood.

Paul and I talk after that. He orders dinner in, and we spend the evening talking and polishing off a bottle of wine. He knows I'll investigate the phone number and video. He doesn't even ask about that — just proceeds as if it's a given. Which proves that while he may not have known the particulars of my life, he does know me.

I consider making sure he tells Gayle that I'll be staying over again. I might say I'm protecting their relationship, but I'm really protecting ours. I don't want to be the cause of their breakup, something he can later resent me for. Nor do I want to give her any reason to peg me as the evil ex wriggling back into his life.

I don't say anything, though. I did this morning and to keep harping on it is interfering. He knows Gayle. He'll know whether he needs to keep her apprised of the ongoing situation.

So we drink, and we talk. Mostly about the case. A little about Charlotte. Nothing about us. When it's time to retire, I take the futon and he heads upstairs to bed.

I am in the car where my mother died. I see her reach for me. Feel her hand wrapping around mine. Hear her tell me it'll be all right, that someone will come.

I know no one will come. I see her smiling at me, and I know she will die if I don't help. I know I could wriggle out of my seat. I've done it before. I'm not supposed to, but I could. Yet I don't.

I don't escape and go for help. I don't scream for someone to come. I don't scream for someone to save my mother. I just sit there . . . and I watch her die.

The nightmare stutters to a stop. Rewinds. Starts over.

This time she begs for help. This time she undoes my seat so I can get free. This time the car door lolls open, giving me no excuse, and she's begging, *begging,* me to go for help.

I ignore her. I pick up a toy, and I play with it, and I ignore her.

Inside my head, I'm screaming at myself to do something. Screaming so loud. But all I do is play with that damned toy, and I want to knock it from my hands and —

"Aubrey? *Aubrey.*"

A hand grips my shoulder, and I think someone's there. Someone's come to save my mother.

Someone has finally come.

The hand squeezes, and my eyes fly open, and it's Paul. He's crouched beside the futon, his hand on my shoulder.

I scramble up, looking around, blood

314

rushing in my ears and drowning out his words.

Nightmare. He's telling me I was having a nightmare.

I know that. But it doesn't matter. I'm still shaking and gasping for breath.

"I'm okay," I say. I'm not, but I say it anyway.

"You were calling for your mother," he says. "For someone to help your mother." He wipes a finger over my cheek, and I realize it's hot and wet with tears. "It was about the accident, wasn't it?"

"I didn't get help. She unbuckled me and told me to go get help and . . ." I squeeze my eyes shut. "No, that's not how it happened. Or, I don't think that's . . ."

"It isn't," he says. "I read the police report. You were buckled in your seat, which was jammed shut by the accident."

"I could have wiggled out. I could have —"

"Bree?" He puts a hand on each shoulder, turning me to look at him. "You couldn't have. Your mother would have never expected you to. You were barely two."

"No one came," I say. "She was there all night. She was alive all night. They could see the car in the field. And no one stopped."

His arms go around me, and I collapse into them, sobbing.

THIRTY-ONE

Over breakfast, Paul asks whether I've heard from Ellie.

I shake my head. "She never called back. I hope that means she contacted the police and doesn't need my help. She only reached out once, in hopes . . ." I shake my head, gaze on my plate, and I don't finish.

"She reached out in hope," he says.

I nod, and I sip my coffee.

"You want to help her," he says. "You feel bad about refusing."

I shrug and keep drinking.

"That's what the nightmare was about," he says. "No one stopped for your mother. No one helped. And now you feel like you're doing that with Brandon."

I take a deep breath. "Rationally, I know better. He's not lost in a field, with no one looking for him. Ellie knows he's gone. She's his aunt. It's her responsibility to call the police."

He eats quietly for a moment. Then he says, "If you want to contact her, that wouldn't be a bad idea. Try to convince her she can trust Officer Jackson. If she still won't . . ." He takes a deep breath. "I need to work at the office this morning, but I'm taking the afternoon off. Whatever you do about Ellie, please don't physically investigate until I'm here. I know you can look after yourself, but I can watch your back. I'd like to watch your back."

I agree.

Before Paul leaves, he tells me I should take a nap.

"I know you won't," he says. "But you had a rough night, so I'm going to suggest it anyway. If you're calling Ellie, maybe wait a bit. Give her time to wake up and realize she needs to contact the police."

"I'll do that."

"You gave Officer Jackson Orbec's gun, right?" he asks.

I nod.

"Then since you have the day off, I'll ask you to stay in with the security system set. Obviously, you can tell me where to stick my advice . . ."

I smile. "I'd never do that. But yes, I know it's just a suggestion. A wise one. I'm going to spend the morning online. I won't hack anything from the home Wi-Fi, though."

"Hack?"

"Er, sorry. I meant —"

He presses a finger to my lips. "You meant hack. I get it. Maybe someday you'll explain *that* part, but for now, as long as you don't 'hack' government security, I'm not too worried about it. We have an open Wi-Fi channel. If anyone reports hacking, I'll blame it on Mrs. McDonnell next door."

"Eighty-year-old invalid Mrs. McDonnell?"

"She needs a way to spend her time."

I laugh. "Okay. I'll be careful, though. I'll mask the IP."

He shakes his head. "I'm not even going to ask what that means. I'll be home by one, and I'll bring lunch. Be safe."

He leans forward to give me a goodbye kiss, as he did every morning of our marriage. Then he stops and pulls back, mumbling something.

I kiss his cheek, a quick peck. "Old habit, I know. If this gets too cozy for you, just say the word. I can stay in a hotel."

He gives me an awkward, one-arm hug. "It's fine. I'll rest better with you here."

"You know I appreciate it."

"I do. Now arm the system as soon as I leave."

"Yes, sir."

I don't nap, of course. I couldn't sleep even if I wanted to. I have a job to do, which will keep me from fretting about many things . . . including the fact that I may not have an *actual* job. I told Paul that I have the day off. That's true. It's just not a scheduled one.

I called Ingrid last night to tell her that I'd reported the video incident, and I gave her Laila's number to follow up on that. She said that was fine . . . but that my job was under review for "other reasons," and I should stay home until they decided the future of my employment with the Oxford Central Library.

I pull up the video from yesterday's threat. I keep feeling like I should be able to get something from it. That's not my area of expertise, though. I analyze the metadata, but there's nothing useful there. I already knew the date and the location and there was little more I could gather from the data. On to the video itself then. It's less than three minutes long, which makes it easy to parse and view frame by frame.

I hope for some secret in those frames. I

don't know what. A reflection of the videographer in a window? A glimpse of his shadow, with some distinctive hair or headgear? Ridiculous, I know, but I still look. The problem is that it's a distance shot, with nothing in the videographer's immediate surroundings.

I see Charlotte and Mrs. Mueller and Becky and the dog. At one point, another woman and her child join, and I think I recognize her. I can ask Paul if he does and find out whether she saw anything untoward. Otherwise, it's just a video of the park, with a house in the background and two cars parked on the street.

One of the cars catches my eye. I zoom in. The playground doesn't have a parking lot — people walk to it or they park on the street. There are two cars clearly in the video. The one that grabbed my attention is farther down, and the video only includes the back end.

I've seen that car before. I can't make out the make or model, but the rear bumper tweaks a memory. It's a luxury sedan in a neighborhood full of luxury sedans. I must recognize it because I've seen it around before.

Still, I screenshot the image for later, along with one of the neighbor and her son, for Paul to follow up on.

Next comes the phone number. For that, I do need to hack. It turns out to belong to a prepaid — surprise! I trace back to the call records. It was activated yesterday morning, and it has sent two videos — one to me and Paul — and four texts, all to us. That's it. No calls. No other texts.

I stare at that meager call log . . . and it reminds me about something. The calls on Kim's phone. I'd traced a few, including Ellie's, but there's the one that came in while I was with her in the park and a couple of times before that.

Time for more hacking. This one's easier than I expected, and I kick myself for not digging deeper before now. When a simple search hadn't returned an owner, I presumed it was prepaid. Yet when I dig, I come up with an actual account . . . one owned by Hugh Orbec. I look for the call I heard him make Saturday night, when I was in the closet at Zodiac Five, but it's not there. That suggests two phones: personal and business.

Why would Hugh Orbec be so careless, using his personal phone to call Kim?

Or had someone else used it? Denis Zima could probably get access to Orbec's cell phone. Was he setting up his old friend? I don't know. But I do make note of other numbers that called and texted with Orbec's phone. I'm doing that when my alarm goes off, telling me it's 11 a.m. Time to phone Ellie, having given her plenty of time to wake up and realize she needs to get the police involved.

That's how I greet her. Not with "Hello" or "Good morning," but "It's Aubrey. Have you called the police yet?"

She hasn't. She's absolutely convinced that if she involves them, Brandon will suffer. I try to talk her into contacting Laila Jackson. It doesn't work.

"If they didn't believe you, they won't believe me," she says. "You're a librarian. I'm a stay-at-home mom from South Dakota."

"You're Brandon's aunt. You know him. The police can't say you hallucinated a nephew."

"And then what? Where will they go from there? Whoever has Brandon murdered Kim. They'll kill him too if the cops rush in."

"So what are you going to do?" I ask. "Just hope they'll take good care of him?"

"Of course not. I'm hiring a private investigator. I've found someone. I just need to figure out how to cover his retainer.

It's . . . more than I expected. But I can do it."

I struggle to keep the impatience from my voice. "Any PI worth his salt would tell you to contact the police. Private investigators are a last resort, when the police won't get involved. If he's not telling you that, he just wants your money. How much is the retainer?"

"Five thousand."

"What? No. That's crazy."

"How much would you charge?"

"Me?" I sputter. "I'm not a private investigator. I'm a librarian, like you said —"

"Which means you're smart. Detective work might not be your job, but you're really good at it. You identified Kim. You found out who Brandon's dad is, and even I didn't know that. You are —"

"— not a private eye."

"But I'd pay you."

"I don't need money."

Silence.

I should wish her luck and sign off. *Let me know how it goes! I'll cross my fingers for you!*

I can't do that. Physically cannot.

I take a deep breath. "Can I get that address? The one Kim gave you?"

She gives it.

"Let me do some digging," I say. "I'll get back to you. If you decide to contact Officer Jackson, please do that and let me know. But hold off on hiring a PI and spending five grand you don't have. Please."

Not surprisingly, there's no public listing for the owner of that house. Still, obtaining the owner of record is easy enough through property taxes. But that requires doing exactly what Paul asked me not to — hacking into government servers. I'll wait for Paul on that. In the meantime, this triggers another thought. Kim must have been in contact with whomever she asked to take Brandon.

A scan of her prepaid call record identifies the most likely number. It's one she dialed twice in the days before her death. One call was made on the Friday, and then one shortly after she spoke to Hugh Orbec — or whoever used his phone. The initial one was short, as if she was reaching out.

I may be in trouble. I may need your help.

The second is longer, as if it was the planning call. Orbec had made contact, presumably threatening Kim, given what I'd heard of the exchange. She realizes then that she must enact her plan with Brandon, and she places the second call.

I try to trace that phone number, but I have no luck.

Paul gets home shortly after that. He's brought lunch and a sympathetic ear as I vent my frustration. First, he takes what action he can, by asking his assistant to investigate the tax situation on that house. Then he just listens.

"I don't know what to do," I say.

"What do you want to do?"

I shake my head. "That doesn't matter. I already endangered Charlie doing what I wanted to do."

"No, some thug *threatened* Charlie to scare you off. Whoever these people are, Aubrey, they're not going to kidnap your daughter. It was empty posturing. But, in the event that it wasn't, we've removed our daughter from the equation. She's safe."

I nod, but I don't say anything.

"You're right about the private eye," Paul continues. "He's scamming Ellie. You're also right to keep pushing her toward Officer Jackson. Eventually, she will have to make that call. If, in the meantime, you want to keep digging, I don't see any problem with that. As long as 'digging' doesn't mean marching to that club to confront Denis Zima."

I chuckle. "I'm not that stupid."

He takes another plate of pad Thai. "On that note, I also had my clerk dig into the Zimas. It's an interesting situation, and I'm not sure what to make of it. Denis's father definitely has ties to organized crime. It's the kind of scenario where everyone knows he's breaking the law, and no one can prove it. They even tried doing an Al Capone by going after him for tax evasion. He's very, very careful. He has good connections to the Russian mob through his wife's family. So Denis grew up right in the heart of that. There are all kinds of rumors about his old strip club in LA. The most pervasive was that it wasn't just selling underage strippers, but underage girls themselves."

"Prostitution?"

"More like sex slavery."

"Do you think Kim was part of that?"

He takes a bite of his food before answering. "On the surface, that makes sense. Teenage girl starts dancing in his club and then gets together with him. It seems very . . . suspect."

"Uh-huh."

"But I'm not sure it's as cut-and-dried as it seems. Kim stayed with Zima after he closed the club. And he's the one who closed it. The rumor is that he had a falling-out with his parents and decided to go straight."

"He closed the strip club and started the Zodiacs."

"It's more than that. Apparently, he started to cut a deal with the feds, turning on his parents. He told the feds that he had information. He asked for witness protection for himself and Kim. She was using another name at the time, but it was clearly her. They were brokering a deal with him when he backed out. He said he'd made a mistake, and he didn't have anything for them."

"Was it grandstanding? He wanted something from his parents so he threatened to expose them?"

"Possibly. That's a dangerous way to get a bigger allowance, though. It's more likely that he realized the danger. Either way, it looks as if Brandon was born about ten months later."

"Which probably means he didn't go straight after all. Kim ran and hid her baby for five years. She knew Zima was dangerous."

"I'd agree. Throughout all that, Hugh Orbec was at his side. He's definitely Zima's right-hand man . . . whatever business Zima is into these days."

We talk some more. I pull up the still images from the video of Charlie. He recognizes the mother and boy, and he says he'll talk to them, see whether they noticed anyone hanging around the park or videotaping nearby. When I show him the photo of the car, he chuckles at first, and says, "Lots of those around here. Probably a lot in Denis Zima's world, too. I could try to find out what he and Orbec drive. Do you have a better shot of it? I can't see much from that angle."

"No, this is it."

I zoom in. "Do you recognize it?" I say.

He pauses, lips pressed. "Possibly? I'm not sure. Leave it with me."

I'm making coffee when Paul's law clerk gets back to him. The house is a secondary address owned by a Chicago woman named Elizabeth Kenner.

I look up Kenner. She's a retired social worker, active in several youth organizations. She's been living in Chicago for seven years. And before that? She's from Cedar Rapids, Iowa. Where Kim and Ellie grew up.

I call Ellie. When I tell her the name, she's quiet for a moment. Then she says, "Yes! Of course. Beth. She was Kimmy's outreach worker. Before Kimmy left, she had some problems. Our dad . . ."

"There were problems," I say when she trails off. "Between him and Kim."

"Him and all of us, but Kimmy got the worst of it. She was tough, and the tougher she got, the harder he . . ." She inhales sharply. "It was bad. I didn't realize *how* bad because I moved out when she was still a kid. Anyway, Kimmy got into trouble, and she was assigned a youth outreach worker. That was Beth. I met her a bunch of times in hopes I could help."

She describes the woman she remembers, and it matches the photographs of Elizabeth Kenner.

"That makes sense, doesn't it?" Ellie says. "My sister trusted Beth. When she needed help, she might have contacted her. Kimmy might even have moved to Chicago because of her."

"It does make sense," I say.

"Then we need to speak to Beth. Do you have an address?"

"I do, but I really think the police —"

"No," she says firmly. "I need to know what went wrong. Why Brandon isn't with Beth. If we call in the police, we might spook Beth. Especially if she knows what kind of person Brandon's father is. If you can't come with me, I understand. Just give

330

me her address."

I tell Ellie I'll get back to her. Then I hang up and go into the study, where Paul is working. I tell him everything.

"If you're comfortable going with her, that's probably a good idea," he says. "It would help to have a witness to whatever this woman says. I don't see any danger. This is the person Kim trusted with her child." He gets to his feet. "And I know you'd like to hear the answers firsthand."

"I would."

"I'll go with you and wait in the car."

I shake my head. "This is just an interview. I can handle it."

He hesitates. Then he nods. "All right. I do kind of wish you'd kept the gun, though. I'm not a fan of firearms, but this is one time when I can see the appeal."

"I do actually have one, in a storage locker in the city. It's even registered. But I don't have a concealed carry permit."

"Right now, I don't care. If you're already heading to Chicago, I'd like you to swing by and grab it." He pauses. "I'll drive into the city with you. I forgot a few files at the office."

THIRTY-TWO

Paul and I drive to Chicago in our own cars. I told Paul that he could follow me to the locker, if he wanted, and he does. There's no reason for him to come along. No practical reason, that is. The invitation is symbolic — this locker is what remains of my old life, the repository of my secrets. If he'd like to see that, he's welcome to. I'm not hiding anything. Not anymore.

When I open my locker, I see him looking about.

"Yes, it's kinda sleazy," I say. "This is what you get when you pay cash."

"Actually, I was thinking it's very small. This is everything you have?"

I nod and turn on the light. He walks to a rickety dresser.

"This is . . . a family piece, I'm guessing?"

I smile. "No. It's just junk. I bought the furniture to hide what's inside it, in case of a break-in."

I take out the gun and place it on the dresser. He leans in to examine the firearm without touching it, and I struggle not to laugh at that.

"You can poke around if you like," I say. "There's money. That's my inheritance, not my ill-gotten gains." I pause. "Though, considering I was living off the stolen money while saving this, I'm splitting hairs."

"It's not actual stolen cash, which is the main thing." He takes out a bundle. "If it's an inheritance, then you've already paid taxes on it. There's no reason to hide it."

"I was saving it for a condo. Then we got married, and I couldn't bring it out without raising questions, so . . ."

"So you've been living in a crappy apartment rather than use this?"

"I didn't want —" I clear my throat. "I was concerned about the custody implications."

He seems confused for a moment. Then he says, "You thought if you suddenly had money, I could unearth your past and use that to get full custody of Charlie."

I nod.

He sets the money down. "No matter how angry I got, I never considered stealing her from you, Aubrey. You are free to bring out this money and put a down payment on a house or a condo or whatever you want. If you need help making the mortgage payments, I'll pitch in. I've said before that you gave up your earning potential to care for our child. You are *owed* money for that."

"I don't want —"

"Yes, I know. You feel guilty, and you want to be fair. *This* is fair."

"I have enough for a good down payment, and once I get a new job, I'll be able to cover the mortgage."

"New job?" He pauses. "Ah, one that uses your tech skills. Good. I was going to suggest that." He catches my expression and says, "Which isn't what you meant at all, is it?"

"I'll be fine. Now, I've got my gun so —"

"What's happened with your job?" He pauses. "This better not have anything to do with you rushing off after Charlie on Monday."

I don't need to answer. Again, he sees it in my face.

"They can't terminate you for that," he says. "Legally —"

"I don't want to work someplace that doesn't want me. Legal termination or not. If they fire me, I'll wave around the threat of a lawsuit, but only to negotiate a decent reference. I appreciate the outrage, but I've got this. Now, if you're ready to go . . ."

He looks around. "Money and a gun. Is that everything you have here?"

I shrug. "There are a few mementos."

"May I see them? If you have time?"

"I do."

I've spoken to Ellie by phone, and I've seen her on Facebook, so it's hard to remember that we haven't actually met. She is what I saw online — an older, more full-figured version of her sister. I meet her in her hotel lobby, and we head out.

Chicago is the third-largest city in the U.S., and I'd be lying if I said I got to know it well in my few years there, before I moved to Oxford with Paul. I got to know my apartment neighborhood and my work neighborhood. That's normal for me, after a life spent moving around army bases. I focus on my narrow sphere. It's only in Oxford that I feel I "know" the city.

So I set my GPS for Beth Kenner's address, without knowing where it'll lead. As it turns out, it takes me to a neighborhood that was probably a former suburb. Winding streets. Massive trees. Post–World War II houses that look mass-produced from two basic molds.

We park around the corner from Beth's

place. I know there's no danger here, but I'm being careful. I can't help it. The address leads us to a cute bungalow with a steep roof and massive front picture window. There's a car in the drive, which I hope means she's home.

When I knock, I hear sounds within, but no one answers. I put my ear to the door. It's gone quiet.

I knock again. Ellie leans to look through the picture window, and I reach to pull her back.

"Careful," I whisper. "I don't like the sounds of —"

Footsteps patter across the floor inside. A lock turns. Then another. A small, white-haired woman throws open the door with, "Ellie!"

She opens the screen and ushers us in. "I was out back reading. Then I heard the bell and saw your friend through the peephole. I thought she was selling something. Come in, come in."

She keeps prodding us until we're in the living room. Then she hugs Ellie.

"It is so good to see you," she says. "Are you here visiting Kimmy?"

Ellie looks at me. I wince. The older woman looks from me to Ellie.

"Is something wrong?" she asks, her words

336

slow, her back tightening.

"When did you last hear from Kim?" I ask.

She settles onto the sofa, her hands fluttering. "Oh, I'm not even sure. We get together now and then. But it's been a few weeks. Is she all right?"

"She . . ." I look at Ellie, but she's frozen. "I'm sorry, but she's been killed. That's why Ellie's here. We thought you knew."

Beth stares at us. "Killed? An . . . accident?" Her voice rises in a way that says she hopes that's what I mean, but she knows better.

"She was murdered," I say. "It was in the news."

She looks at me blankly, and I remember we're in Chicago, not Oxford. I'm sure Kim's death made the news here, but not the way it had at home. Kim hasn't been identified officially either. There's no reason Beth *would* know.

"I'm sorry," I say. "So you haven't heard from her in weeks?"

She nods, but even if I didn't know better, I'd see the lie in her expression.

"I know that's not true," I say gently. "I have phone records. I know she spoke to you twice before her death. Once on the Friday before she died and once the Sunday before."

337

I can't prove the number was Beth's. Not yet. But I must sound convincing, because she goes still.

"It was about Brandon, wasn't it?" I say. "You were supposed to take him."

She glances at Ellie.

"I know about the house," I say. "Your country place. That's the address Kim gave Ellie for picking up Brandon if anything happened to her."

Beth exhales. "Yes," she says. A moment of silence then, again, "Yes. I was supposed to take Brandon in an emergency. Kim called me two weeks ago. She was worried, and she wanted to make sure I was around, in case she needed me to take Brandon. Then she called back a few days later and said she'd found another way. She said everything was okay, but she was taking Brandon away for a while, just until . . . his father left town."

"His father was *in* town to open a new club."

She nods and seems relieved that I know who Brandon's dad is. "She was worried with Denis being in Chicago, but she found a solution. She said she had something Denis wanted, and if she gave it to him, everything would be fine. She'd do that and then take Brandon on vacation until Denis

338

left Chicago, just to be safe. That's the last I heard from her."

Beth offers coffee after that, but neither of us is in the mood to socialize . . . and I don't think she is either. Ellie tells Beth that she'll let her know about funeral arrangements.

Beth has no idea who might have Brandon. We're all holding out hope that Kim really did make alternate arrangements. Better and safer ones that she didn't dare tell Beth, for fear even that would endanger Brandon.

That is our hope. That he is with someone, and that person has Ellie's number but has chosen not to contact her until they know what's going on with Kim's murder. Solve that first. Put Denis Zima behind bars. Then Brandon will be safe.

Yet, according to Beth Kenner, Kim thought she already had a way to keep him safe. She said that Zima wanted something from her, something that was presumably not Brandon himself. If she handed that over, Zima would stop pursuing.

I've presumed that Kim was on the run all these years to hide Brandon from his father. What if, instead, she was in danger because she took something else when she left.

When I broke ties with Ruben, I'd considered preventative measures against future blackmailing. Hack his own computer. Tape an incriminating conversation. Gather some intelligence I could use if he ever came after me . . . as he eventually did with Paul. I'd decided against it because that is a dangerous game. I already knew things I could threaten Ruben with. Gathering extra would only make him all the more determined *not* to let me walk away.

What if Kim took out her own insurance policy? Her getting pregnant was like me getting shot — a wake-up call, probably fueled by a generous dose of panic. We needed to escape. Immediately. Yet neither of us was a wide-eyed naïf. We knew who we'd gotten mixed up with, and we knew our past could come back to destroy us. So we went into hiding. But I'd left knowing I had a small insurance policy against Ruben and deciding against a larger one. What if Kim — being younger and more desperate — grabbed the big insurance policy before she left . . . only to realize later that having it further endangered her child.

If Kim took something incriminating, she thought it'd be insurance. What she would have discovered is that Denis Zima would happily kidnap his own son and use him to

get what she stole. Then he'd keep the boy
and kill Kim.

That means whoever is holding Brandon
might want the same thing: Kim's insurance policy. And if they don't get it? We're
not talking about a father taking his child.
We're talking about a bargaining chip that
will lose its value once no payoff appears.

This must go to Laila Jackson and the
police. Once I get away from here, I'm pulling over and calling her. I'm thinking this as
I climb in the car, having not said a word to
Ellie since we left Beth Kenner's. I'm about
to tell her when I'm idling at a four-way
stop and see the driver in the vehicle across
from us.

It's the man who accosted me Sunday
night.

Hugh Orbec.

There's a moment, of course, where I
think I'm wrong. I catch a glimpse of a man
who resembles him, driving a Dodge Charger, and I think I'm mistaken. Then he looks
over — not at me, just a casual glance
toward my vehicle as I pass — and there is
no question.

That's Hugh Orbec . . . and he's heading
in the direction I just came.

Toward Beth Kenner's house.

At first, I'm sure he's followed me. But

that makes no sense considering he drove right past. Even if he knows what I drive, this isn't my car — Paul insisted we switch vehicles after the storage locker, giving me an extra layer of privacy.

If I've led Orbec to Beth Kenner, it's not physically, but in another way — he's following my virtual footsteps or tapping my phones or he's arrived at the same conclusion independent of me. He's been doing amateur detective work of his own, and he thinks Brandon is with Beth.

How Orbec got here doesn't matter. The important thing is where he's going — to the home of a retired woman who lives alone, who tried to help a young woman in need, and is now going to suffer for it. If Orbec thinks Beth has Brandon, he's not going to take "Sorry, you're mistaken" for an answer.

I watch as Orbec turns the corner behind me. Then I stop at the curb and throw open my door, startling Ellie from her own thoughts.

"Take the car," I say. "Drive to . . . to a coffee shop. The first one you see. Text me the address."

"What — ?"

"I just saw one of Denis's men heading for Beth's. They think she has Brandon."

Ellie's mouth opens in an O, her eyes widening. "Shouldn't I come with you?"

I shake my head. "I've got this. You get someplace safe." I want to tell her to call Laila. Call Paul. Call someone and tell them where I am. But I don't have time to explain. I have my phone. I can text her as soon as I get a second. And if I don't get one? Ellie knows where I went and why. Good enough.

THIRTY-THREE

I call Beth. She gave us her number but warned she no longer carries her cell phone around, now that she's retired. It rings three times. Then her cheerful voice invites me to leave a message. As I ask her to call back, I remember she'd been reading on the back deck when we arrived, and I curse under my breath.

I remind myself that she hadn't been quick to open the door for us. She only did so when she saw Ellie. This *isn't* a naive senior citizen — she was a social worker, and she knows to be cautious. That won't help, though, if Orbec forces his way in. Or if he surprises her in the rear yard.

I zip to the street behind hers. I can't see her yard from there, not with privacy fences and hedges everywhere.

I sprint down three houses. The driveway behind Beth's is empty, the house dark. I race into the yard. There's a six-foot fence between that yard and Beth's. I hop onto the lower rail and peek over.

She's not on her deck.

I'm about to hop the fence when my phone rings. It's Beth. I jump into her yard and then spot her at the kitchen window, phone to her ear. I answer as I cross the yard.

"One of Denis Zima's men is here," I say.

"Here?"

"I think so. Is your front door locked?"

"Of course."

She spots me as I hop onto her deck. She opens the door for me and starts stepping out, but I wave her back inside and follow. I go straight to the front door and double-check it. Both the dead bolt and key lock are engaged.

"We can leave out the back," I say. "I'll call Ellie and have her pick us up."

"If you're suggesting I hop that fence, I'm not your age," she says. "I don't even think I could climb it." She looks around. "Do we need to leave? I'd feel better staying here and dealing with it."

"This isn't the sort of person you can deal with."

She smiles at me, the kind of smile you give a very sweet but misguided child. "I was a social worker for forty years. I've

345

talked drug dealers into putting down their guns. I've talked homicidal fathers into handing me their children. I can get rid of him, dear. He'll walk away and rethink his strategy, and while he does that, we'll contact the police."

"Okay. But we can't let him see me. Can you pull the front blinds?"

"That'll seem suspicious, won't it?" She looks around. "Why don't you wait in the bedroom . . . no, those blinds are open. Maybe the back —" Footsteps sound on the front steps.

As she looks around again, Orbec rings the bell. Beth spins me toward a door off the kitchen. "The basement. Go down there and wait for me."

"I'd rather —"

"I can handle this."

I let her prod me onto the steps.

"There's a TV room at the bottom," she says. "Wait there."

The door closes behind me as the bell rings again. As soon as her footsteps retreat, I creep back to the top step and crack open the door.

Orbec is knocking now. The dead bolt clanks. Then the front door squeaks open.

I have my gun in hand.

"Miz Kenner?" Orbec says. "Elizabeth

346

Kenner?"

"Yes, that's me, and whatever you're selling —"

"I'm a friend of Kim's." Orbec goes on to weave a story about how he knows Kim and Brandon, and he was told that if anything ever happened to Kim, he's to come to this house and ask for Elizabeth Kenner.

As he drones on, I relax. Beth was right. He's not going to force his way in at gunpoint. It's broad daylight in a residential neighborhood. He's playing it cool with a plausible story. When that fails, he'll retreat to formulate a new strategy.

That's exactly what he does. Beth insists she has no idea what or who he's talking about, and when she asks him to leave, he does.

The door closes. The house goes quiet, as if she's watching him leave. Then I hear her voice, low, murmured. Something about . . .

A basement?

Did she just say something about a basement?

Is she on the phone to the police?

Why would she tell the police I'm in the basement?

She wouldn't, and she hasn't been on that phone long enough to explain the situation. She's barely had time to place a call . . .

347

She *hasn't* placed a call. Because she left her phone on the kitchen counter. She put it down before answering the door and never returned to the kitchen.

Which means . . .

I figure out what it means one second before I hear the murmur of another voice.

Hugh Orbec.

Beth just told *him* I'm in the basement. There's no other explanation.

There's no way I can get to the back door without them seeing me. I quickly shut the basement door and hightail it down the stairs. I race into the TV room. Turn on the light. Shut the door. Sprint down the hall. Open another door to find a laundry room with a window.

I shut that door and leave the light off. The window is right over the washing machine. I climb up onto it. It gives a creak, and I freeze, but the sound is covered by the thump of feet on the stairs.

The window is fixed, no way to open it. I grab a towel from the top of the dryer; then, with one eye on the door, I wrap the towel around my gun and force myself to wait.

The TV room door opens. As Beth calls "Aubrey?" I smash the window with the towel-wrapped gun. I wince at the noise but I clear the sill as fast as I can. Beth calls my

348

name again, casual, not having heard the window break. I toss the gun out and hoist myself up and . . . Damn it, this is one time I wish I hadn't kept those extra pounds.

My hips stick in the window. Beth calls again, but Orbec has already figured it out. He lets out a curse. I'm wiggling as hard as I can, pushing hard, trying —

My hips pop through just as the laundry door slaps open.

"You —" Orbec begins.

I don't hear the rest. I'm sure he's not complimenting me on my ingenuity.

As Orbec snarls curses, I spring to my feet and run. He comes after me, but for him, that means going through the basement, up the stairs, past Beth — who I'm sure will demand an explanation — and out the back door. By that time, I've vaulted over the fence and reached the street. From his footsteps, he presumes I've gone the way he saw me run — for the back fence. Instead, I've climbed the front one, and I'm already jogging down Beth's road.

My gun's put away, and I have my cell phone in hand instead, my fingers poised over the emergency button. If I hear anyone running behind me, I'll push it. I take every turn I come to until I reach a small market.

The shop reminds me of the one in my

old neighborhood, the kind that sells over-priced organic staples for those who can't bother driving into the city. Which means it's *not* like the corner stores in my new neighborhood, where Orbec could barrel in, grab me by the hair, and haul me out, and the clerks would busy themselves checking the cigarette stock.

Before I walk inside, I fix my ponytail, straighten my shirt, and then check for blood and dirt. There is some of both. I hadn't done a perfect job clearing that windowsill, and I cut my bare arm. My hands and knees are filthy from crawling out into Beth's garden. Fortunately, this is also the sort of shop that has a dog tap outside for thirsty pooches. I quickly clean my hands and knock dirt from my jeans. Then I go inside and call for a taxi.

Maybe I should be phoning the police, but honestly, I expect the taxi will come faster. I feel safe enough now, and the Chicago police would require a full explanation. If I gave it, they'd probably figure I was high on meth or oxy. So a taxi it is. As I wait I pick out a snack I won't eat — gourmet soda and veggie chips — and then chat with the cashier until my cab pulls up.

I call Ellie next. According to the text she'd sent, she's only a few blocks away, but

I can't risk leading Orbec to her. I tell her to take my car back to her hotel and stay there until I can get in touch again.

"Is Beth all right?" she asks.

It takes me a moment to remember that I'd gone back to "save" Beth. I stifle a snort at that. I haven't even processed what Beth has done. I haven't had time.

"Beth is fine," I say. "But she's working with Denis."

"What?"

"That's why Denis's thug was there. Remember how long it took Beth to get to the door when we arrived? I think she was calling him. That's why she didn't want us leaving so soon."

"Oh my God." A pause. "Are you sure?"

"Am I sure she called him? No. Am I sure she's in on it all? No. But she told me to go in the basement while she got rid of him. She pretended to do that. He pretended to leave. Then she told him I was in the basement. I escaped out a basement window."

"Oh my God." She inhales. "I keep saying that. I'm sorry. It's just . . . Kimmy was so afraid, and I kept telling her she was overreacting. We'd fight about it. I told her she was ruining her life and damaging Brandon's out of pure paranoia. Once, I even suggested she see a therapist. Kimmy didn't

351

always make the best choices, but I could not imagine she fell in love with any guy who frightened her that much. She'd never talk about him, though. She'd shut me down and say it didn't matter, that Brandon was in danger. Serious danger. And I didn't believe her."

Her voice breaks. I tell her the important thing is that she's here for Brandon now. That she believes Kim now. And, understanding the danger, she'll stay in that hotel room, right?

"I will. I absolutely will."

"Good. Put the keys under the car mat, please. I'm going to swing by and take it. I'm also getting the police involved. I know that's not what you wanted, and if you insist, I'll leave you out of it . . ."

"No, you were right. This is a matter for the police. Tell them everything."

"Okay. For now, get to your hotel. Park. Don't contact me again. I'll find the car. You stay safe."

352

THIRTY-FOUR

I have the taxi circle, so I can be sure Ellie parks and leaves before I arrive at the hotel. I find the car easily enough — at mid-afternoon the lot is almost empty. I drive straight to Paul's office. I want him with me when I contact Laila. At this point, I'm starting to feel like legal representation might be wise. No, that's an excuse. I just want to be with Paul. I'm holding it together and faking calm, but inside, I'm freaking out.

Part of me doesn't even want to speculate on what's going on here. Just shove aside any need to interpret and take the facts to Laila. But I can't help trying to figure it out. Trying to make sense of it.

Beth Kenner is working with Hugh Orbec, which means she's working with Zima. If Kim had handed over Brandon, as planned, Ellie still wouldn't have gotten that call to come get the boy. He'd have gone straight to Denis.

But now Denis is looking for Brandon, which means he doesn't have him. Kim didn't give Brandon to Beth. Did she figure out that the one person she trusted in Chicago wasn't trustworthy at all? Was Beth telling the truth about that — Kim called and pretended everything was fine, said she didn't need Beth's help after all? I think so. Something tipped her off, and she changed her plans.

But what did she change them *to*? Did she find someone else to take Brandon? Or did she turn over her insurance policy . . . and then pay for that mistake with her life?

I want to believe she found someone else, and Brandon is safe, and as soon as Denis is arrested for Kim's murder, Brandon's caretaker will decide to contact Ellie. Everyone lives happily ever after.

Thinking back to that day when Brandon was taken, I can find evidence to support my theory. Kim must have told Brandon to play for a while and then gave him a time to meet his guardian in the parking lot.

Then why did he fight it? He ran over, as if expecting to see someone he knew. Yet the man who came out of that SUV was a stranger, and Brandon fought.

Maybe in her haste to make new arrangements, Kim forgot to tell Brandon it wouldn't be Beth picking him up. Or maybe Brandon just expected a woman.

It doesn't matter who has the boy. He's safe. I'll take what I have to Laila, and the police will pick up the investigation from there.

I call Paul to let him know I'm coming. His cell goes to voice mail. I try his office instead.

"He's not here, Mrs. Finch," his admin assistant says.

"It's Aubrey, please. He stepped out?"

"No, he's gone for the day. He said if you called or stopped by, I should let you know he'd left and tell you to call his cell."

I'd expected he'd wait for me to be done. Which is silly. As far as we knew, I was on a completely safe mission to interview a friend of Kim's. No need for him to stay in Chicago, and if I'm disappointed, that's personal. I wanted him to be waiting for me. He isn't. Too bad.

"All right," I say. "He's not answering his cell, but I'll leave a message. Did he say he was heading home?"

"He . . ." She goes quiet, and then says quickly, "He was looking for Ms. Lansing."

"Gayle?"

"Yes. He came in looking for her, but

355

she'd just left. She was planning to work from home for the afternoon. He went after her."

"Ah, okay. Thanks."

I disconnect and idle at a green light until someone lays on the horn behind me.

Paul lied to me. He said he was picking up files. Instead, he was looking for Gayle. When I asked how Gayle felt about him helping me, he said she was fine with it . . . and then changed the subject.

Gayle must not be fine with it, and he went to the office to speak to her. Now he's followed her home. That's okay. It's time for me to tackle this on my own and not screw up his new life any more than I have.

I'll call Laila before I get to Oxford and meet her at the police station, where I'll tell her and Cooper the whole story. I don't need Paul to hold my hand for that.

I do call him, though. Just a quick one to say I have everything under control. The phone only rings once. Then someone answers. Only it's not Paul.

"Hello, Aubrey." The woman's voice is ice cold.

"Gayle?"

"Yes."

"Is Paul there?" I hurry on with, "This will only take a moment."

"Haven't you taken up enough of his time?"

I should wince. I should apologize. I'd just been thinking that very thing. But it's not as if I strong-armed Paul into helping me. Or sobbed on his shoulder, begging for his assistance.

"Yes," I say, injecting an equal dose of ice into my voice. "Paul comes with some baggage, and that baggage is me. But if you know him — at all — then you understand that this is how he is. I'm having a problem that affects our daughter, and he is helping me resolve it. I am very sorry if that has upset or inconvenienced you, but it is almost over. Just let me —"

"It's over *now*, Aubrey."

"Where's Paul?"

"Here. He's asked me to handle this."

I snort a laugh. "Uh, no. He hasn't. Let me guess, he's temporarily out of the room, and you grabbed his phone."

Her silence tells me I'm right. In that silence, I hear the ticking of a grandfather clock. The one at our — Paul's — house. So they've gone there, and he's stepped into the bathroom, and she's seen me call and answered.

"Paul wants me to tell you —" she begins.

"Like hell. Paul is a nice guy. A good guy.

A guy who doesn't particularly like confrontations, but he's not a coward. If he has something to say to me, he'll say it himself. Just like he would have asked me about horseback riding last Saturday. I thought that seemed odd. Turns out you lied to me, which — by the way — I haven't told him. Now hand the damned phone to Paul."

"Gayle?" Paul's voice sounds in the background, underscored by the smack of his loafers along the hall. "I thought I asked you to leave —"

Gayle hangs up.

You bitch.

You royal bitch.

I start to call back. Then I stop myself. I'm not getting into a tug-of-war between them. I don't know what's happened, but Paul's tone and his words tell me they've had an argument. If it's about me, then I'm sorry for that, but I've done nothing wrong.

I know Paul's at home. I'll be there in twenty minutes, and I'll talk to him in person. By then, Gayle will be gone.

I call Laila and leave a message saying I'm coming to the station to speak to her. I'll be there in an hour.

Whatever's happening with Beth, it's not an urgent situation. No more urgent than it has been since Kim's death. I lost Orbec back at Beth's place, and I've seen no sign of him or his car since then. I've been watching for them. Back when I walked away from Ruben's operation, I educated myself on Fugitive Life 101 — everything I needed to rest assured that no one was after me. So I know how to spot a tail. I don't have one.

As I round the corner to Paul's house, I see Gayle's car in the drive. I let out a curse, and I slow.

If they're still arguing, I don't want to walk into that. And if they're making up, I *definitely* don't want to walk into that.

I will admit that it takes some effort to decide I'm not going into that house. I know it's the right stance — the selfless choice I should make if I care about Paul. If Gayle makes him happy, he should be with Gayle. But that's me making a conscious effort to do the right thing. There's still a little part of me — okay, not *too* little — that wants to barrel in there and have it out with her and let Paul know what she did on the phone.

I love him. I would love to have him back. I'm not denying that. I just need to keep my distance until he figures out what he wants. I owe him that much.

As I pass the house, I slow. I'm looking at Gayle's car, and something's prickling the back of my mind, pushing through the warring voices of "stay out of this" and "get in there and fight for him." Those voices are loud enough that the niggling really has to push hard to break through. But it does, and I realize what I'm seeing.

The car from the playground video.

I squeeze my eyes shut and give my head a sharp shake. I'm angry at Gayle. Outraged and fighting the overwhelming urge to show her why messing with my family is a very bad idea. In that state of mind, I'm jumping to ridiculous conclusions that paint her as something far worse than a woman who wants my ex-husband.

I take out my phone and find the still image of that car. I enlarge it. I compare the two.

It's definitely Gayle's. There's a scrape on the rear bumper that matches. I saw her car at the daycare and thought it looked like the vehicle of a woman who belonged with Paul. That's why it stuck in my mind.

I remember Paul seeing this picture. I remember him hesitating. This is why he wanted to stop by the office. Not to pick up files. According to his admin assistant, Paul went there to see Gayle. True. He went to confront her about this.

The fact that Gayle's car is in the video is

not proof that she sent it. A court would see it as circumstantial evidence. But there is no other logical reason for Gayle's car to be near that park. She doesn't even live in Oxford.

Paul said she was working from home Monday. He'd considered sending Charlotte there and then changed his mind and left her with the neighbor instead. Had he told Gayle that? If so, she'd know exactly where to find Charlotte. It would be easy to follow them to the playground and shoot the video.

Shoot a video of our daughter and send it from a prepaid phone with threatening texts? Why the hell would Gayle do that?

I don't care. I'm not going to sit at this curb and ponder her motivation. This woman scared the life out of me and cost me my job. She also scared the life out of Paul — a man she supposedly cares for.

I march to the house.

I glance at her car as I pass. I even run my finger down that scrape, to be sure I'm not hallucinating it. I'm not. This is the car in the video.

The rear gate is ajar, and I swing it open and continue through onto the deck. The back sliding door is also not quite shut, as if someone strode through this way, too angry

361

to close gates and doors behind them. I'm reaching for the sliding door handle when I see something smeared across the glass.

That smear gives me pause. Paul might have a three-year-old, but he also has a housekeeper three days a week. He'd be quick to clean it himself, too.

It looks like jam or candy. A light smear of red . . .

Red.

Blood. There's a smear of blood on our back door. I grab the handle and have to forcibly stop myself.

I take out my phone to dial 911. Then I reconsider, pocket the phone, and pull my gun instead. I slide the door as carefully as I can.

Inside, it's cool and dark. Quiet, too. Completely quiet. My heart thuds faster.

What have I done?

What the *hell* have I done?

Led Orbec to Paul, that's what I've done. I traipsed off after my escape at Beth Kenner's, and I'd been so pleased with myself. No need to rush and call Paul. No need to rush and call the police. The situation is under control.

I take a deep breath. Plenty of time for self-recriminations later. Right now, I need to focus.

Ahead, I see a lamp on the floor, the shade knocked off. Signs of a struggle.

Don't run. Just keep moving. Be careful and keep moving.

I continue into the living room. And there is Gayle, sprawled on the carpet. I race to her. There's no sign of blood. No sign of injury either. She's breathing fine, sound asleep.

I grab Gayle by the shoulder. She wakes, flailing, her eyes wide.

"Where's Paul?" I say.

She looks around, as if expecting to see him standing there.

"Where is Paul?" I repeat.

She blinks. "He-he took him. The man. The one who broke . . ." She seems to lose her train of thought and rubs at her temple, wincing.

"Where is he now?"

"I have no idea," she snaps. "You're the one who brought that man into his house."

"What man? Describe him."

She describes Hugh Orbec. Then she goes on to say that Orbec broke in and knocked her out, and the last thing she remembers, he was telling Paul to come along. Orbec was taking him hostage. That's when she lost consciousness.

As she's telling me this, I search for a note.

363

If Orbec took Paul, he's left a note.

As I hunt, Gayle follows me, still talking. "I don't know what kind of hold you have over Paul, but he cannot break free of it. God knows, I've tried. It took months to even get him on a date, and then he's dragging his feet every step of the way."

"And you didn't take a hint?" I say as I check the kitchen counters.

She glares at me. "I knew what he needed. I knew what Charlotte needed. I just had to make him realize it. I finally start seeing progress, and then you slam back into his life like a tornado. All of a sudden, I can't do anything right. I fix your mess with the princess tea, and he tells me I handled it wrong, that I should have encouraged you to go despite not being dressed for it. I invite Charlotte to my daughter's party, and he accuses me of planning it at the last minute."

I'm barely listening, too focused on finding that note. If Orbec took Paul hostage, he must have left something for me. A threat. A warning. An ultimatum.

Gayle keeps talking. "Sunday evening, he calls to say you're in trouble and staying here for the night. He asks if I can take Charlotte the next day. I'm not happy about you sleeping over, but I suck it up. I figured

I'd deal with that later. The next morning, he calls and ends it. Breaks it off. No explanation. Just 'it's not working out.' "

"And that's why you sent the video?"

She looks at me.

"I know you sent it," I say. "I saw your car in it. Paul did, too. He confronted you. Didn't he?"

She chews on that for a moment, deciding which angle to play here. Then she spits, "Yes. All right? I sent it to protect Paul from his crazy ex. To show him how dangerous you are. What kind of danger you pose to his daughter."

I spin on her. "Danger I pose? The only threat against our daughter was that video. Which *you* made. You call me craz—" I bite it off and head for the back door. "If Paul dumped you, that's on you. I can tell you one thing, though. Now that he knows who sent that video, you don't have a hope in hell of getting him back."

"And you'll make sure of that?"

"I won't need to," I say as I head out the back door.

THIRTY-FIVE

I'm in Paul's car, trying to decide my next move, fighting against absolute panic, when Orbec calls.

"I believe I have something of yours," he says when I answer.

"Do you really think this is going to work?" I say. "I know who you are. All I have to do —"

"— is call the police? Do you really think *that* is going to work? Leave the cops out of this, and I won't hurt your husband, Aubrey."

"You already have. I saw the blood."

A short laugh. "That would be mine. He punched me in the nose. I have no interest in you or him. What I want is that data."

"What data?"

"Don't play coy. You're a friend of Kimmy's. You know exactly what's going on here."

"*Friend?* I met her once, for ten minutes,

in a park —"

"Do you honestly expect me to believe that? The police didn't, did they? They thought you were a whackjob. I know better. You're a friend of Kimmy's, and you know what's going on, and you're trying to help her and the boy. It's too late for her, but I'm going to tell you how you can help Brandon — and your husband."

"I'm telling you, I don't know Kim —"

"So you did all this for a stranger? A woman you met, as you say, for ten minutes? No one does that. Stop prolonging this conversation. I will call again in an hour. You will have the data. We will trade. You'll get your husband and something else you've been looking for."

"Brandon? Are you telling me you have — ?"

He hangs up.

Hugh Orbec thinks I'm a friend of Kim's. He thinks I'm involved in this, that I know her and I've been pretending to be a stranger caught up in it to help her and Brandon. Because that's the obvious answer. If I wasn't so freaked out, I'd laugh. This is what I get for playing Good Samaritan. For being the person who stops to help. It's so far outside Orbec's experience that he's rejected the possibility. I must know Kim. I must know about her situation with Denis Zima. I must know about the "data" — whatever the hell that is.

No, wait, I do know what it is. Kim's insurance policy. That must be it. Now I'm supposed to find this "data" and hand it over? Mission impossible.

I'm barely off the phone when Laila Jackson calls. I want to answer that call. I want to answer it so badly. *Ten minutes earlier, Laila, and I could have told you everything.* Now I don't dare. She leaves a message. I don't even retrieve it.

I call the number Kim had for Orbec. He doesn't answer. I consider pleading my case, my ignorance, but I know that'll do no good. Worse, he might punish Paul for it.

I try Beth Kenner next. Yes, she's part of all this, but she was a social worker. There must be a streak of goodness in her that I can appeal to, more than I could with Orbec. At least I can ask her what he's looking for exactly.

I call the number. The line is disconnected.

I could go there. Confront her . . . if she's home, which I doubt. She knows I might come back.

That leaves one option. The riskiest of all.

Stop playing with the hired help, and go straight to the top of the food chain.

Earlier, I told Paul I wouldn't do anything as crazy as confront Denis Zima. Now I'm convinced that's exactly what I need to do.

Finding Zima is easy. Men like him don't hide.

To locate him, I make a few calls. Tell a few lies. Concoct a few stories. And soon learn that Zima is at Zodiac Five, working for the day.

So he's working, maybe clearing some paperwork . . . while his thug menaces me and kidnaps my husband. Just another day at the office for Denis Zima.

When I return to the club, I see that I missed a potential escape route Saturday night. There's a fire escape with a second-floor emergency exit. I get up onto that and pick the door lock. It's easy enough — it seems Zima's security team still hasn't brought the place up to the boss's standards.

I'm stepping into the hall when Laila calls again. My phone vibrates loud enough that I quickly back onto the fire escape and shut it off.

I reenter the club. The upper hall is dark, the only light coming from under the office door. I creep to it, gun in hand. Then I put my ear to the wood. I hear the clackity-clack of someone striking a keyboard with type-writer force. It's fast spurts, patter-patter-patter, pause, patter-patter-patter, pause. At that speed, I'm wondering if it's someone else. Denis Zima doesn't strike me as the kind of guy who took keyboarding in high school.

A phone rings, and whoever's in the office lets out a curse. He answers. I've never heard Denis Zima speak, but this does seem to be him — he's telling someone in security that if the work isn't done this week, they're out of a job. He hangs up and grumbles under his breath. Then back to typing.

If there were anyone else in the room, I'd expect some conversation after that call. The silence tells me he's alone. Still, I only crack the door a half inch, enough to peer through. Zima sits at the desk, intent on whatever he's typing on a laptop. There's no sign of anyone else.

Zima pauses. Thinking through his next words. When he attacks the keyboard with fresh ferocity, I use the clatter of those keys to push open the door. He never even notices. When he pauses, though, he goes still. He doesn't look my way, but I know he senses someone there. I expect him to reach for a holstered gun. Instead his hand slides toward a closed drawer.

"Stop," I say.

His chin jerks up, as if he's surprised by my voice. Surprised by the gender of it, I presume. Then he looks over, and his eyes widen before his brow furrows. As he stares at me, I lock the door behind my back.

"You're . . . the woman from the video?" His voice inflects, as if he must be wrong.

"Surprised I actually showed up? You have my husband. I'm not going to cry in a corner, hoping you'll be nice and give him back."

His face screws up. "What?"

I move forward, gun pointed at his forehead. "If you're stalling in hope of rescue, I'd strongly advise you to reconsider. You have my husband. I can't get you what you want in exchange. So I'm a little short on options. If I hear footsteps outside that door, this turns into a hostage situation with a woman too desperate to control her trigger finger."

"I'm not stalling, Ms. . . ." He struggles, as if to remember. "Finch, right? Ms. Finch? If I'm acting confused, it's because I am. I don't have your husband. I have no idea —"

"Hugh Orbec."

He stops. "Sure, I know Hugh. He works

371

for me. He's a friend."

"He's also your hired gun. He broke into my house two hours ago and took my husband. He left a witness who described Orbec perfectly. I'd know, because I've met the man. First when he slammed me into a wall while I was out jogging Sunday night. Then today, when he tried to corner me at Elizabeth Kenner's house."

"Elizabeth Kenner?"

I tell myself he's faking his confusion. He must be, even if it doesn't seem like it.

I push on. "The woman Kim trusted to take Brandon . . . well, until she didn't trust her. For good reason it seems."

"Brandon?" Something sparks in his eyes. "My . . . you mean my son? That's his name?"

That spark hits me square in the gut. There's no way to fake that look, that glimmer, the way he perks up, as if that's all he heard, the rest only white noise.

I take a split second to regroup. Then I plow forward again, because it's all I can do. Don't hang everything on a look. Acknowledge it and keep going.

"Hugh Orbec kidnapped my husband. He called me an hour ago and said if I gave him the data, he'd return Paul."

"Data?"

"Kim's insurance policy."

When he still looks confused, I say, "Whatever she took when she left you."

He pauses. Then his eyes go wide, and he lets out a string of curses. Again, his surprise doesn't seem faked. Not unless he's an Oscar-caliber actor playing a two-bit mobster.

My gut twists. What if I'm wrong? What if I've miscalculated completely?

Keep going. That's all I can do. Just keep going.

I say, "The problem is that I don't know where to find this insurance policy. I don't even know *what* it is. I only know Kim took something from you because Beth Kenner said so."

"Beth . . . ?"

His confusion still seems real. All his reactions seem real, and I want to tell myself they aren't, but my gut says that Denis Zima hasn't the faintest clue what I'm talking about.

If he doesn't know about Paul's kidnapping, though, that means Orbec isn't acting on his boss's orders. So what the hell is going on here?

Keep going. Let this play through and hope I can figure it out.

"Beth is Elizabeth Kenner," I say. "Kim's

373

former social worker. She'd retired and moved to Chicago. I think that's why Kim moved here. Because she trusted Beth. Wrongly, as it turns out. But the point is that Kim took something of yours and Orbec wants it back, and I have no idea what he's talking about, so I'm kind of screwed."

"The thumb drive," he murmurs, as if to himself.

"Thumb . . ."

"USB drive. One of those —"

"I know what a thumb drive is. I'm just confirming that's what you said. So when Kim left you, she took a thumb drive full of evidence that could send you to jail."

"Not me. My —" He stops short and straightens. "It was my drive. I took the data from someone else. I'd been planning to use it but . . ."

I remember what Paul said. "It's the evidence against your family."

His head shoots up.

I go on. "I've done my homework. Six years ago, you offered evidence to the feds. Evidence against your family. Then you changed your mind. I'm guessing that was a tactic to spook your father, to get something you wanted."

He shakes his head. "No, it was a tactic to

374

get the hell away from my family, once and for all. Only it backfired. They threatened Kimmy. So I changed my mind. Then when Kimmy left, she took the drive. For insurance, I guess. I couldn't blame her. I just . . . The thought that she might have been pregnant? That she left because she was scared of my family?" He runs his hand through his hair. Then he throws it off and straightens again. "Does Hugh have my son?"

"Don't know. Right now, don't care. He has my husband, and that's my primary concern. So there's a USB drive that contains incriminating data you compiled after you got tired of working in the family business."

"I *never* worked in the family business." His voice is sharp, emphatic, eyes bright with anger.

"You ran an underage strip club —"

"I was young. I was stupid. I believed the girls when they said they were eighteen. Yeah, young and stupid, okay? A strip club with eighteen-year-olds isn't exactly a business to be proud of, but in my family, that bar's set pretty damned low. To me, that *was* going legit. It was also an enterprise my parents supported. They helped me set it up. Then I found out they were using it as a front for —" Again, he cuts himself off. "I found out my club wasn't as legal as I thought. So I closed it down and started the Zodiacs. Which *are* legit. Or they damned well better be. If Hugh . . ."

He gives his head a shake, that anger surging again. "What the hell am I saying? Of course my parents have their fingers in the Zodiacs. I was a damned fool. *Again.*"

He takes a deep breath and looks at me. "Hugh was my parents' employee. They gave him to me for the strip clubs. We became friends. He comes from the same place I do, just lower on the totem pole. He wanted out, too. Or so he said. So when I broke it off with my parents, Hugh came with me. I *trusted* him."

I'm still struggling to keep up here, to work it out, so I say, "You think he's been working for your parents all along. *They're* the ones who want the USB drive back, and they're using him to get it. He's doing this for them, not for you."

"Definitely not for me, that son of a bitch. I only wanted him to find my son. I thought he — Brandon — was out there somewhere, maybe taken by whoever killed Kimmy."

Zima pushes to his feet. I jump forward with "Uh-uh," gun still raised, and he seems to struggle to focus on it, as if he's distracted, forgetting the whole held-at-gunpoint situation.

When he realizes it, he waves me off. "You don't need that. I'm going to handle this. I'll call —"

I stop him as he reaches for his phone. "Explain first."

"The main thing right now is getting your husband and Brandon back. I'm going to call Hugh. He might be my parents' man, but I've got enough dirt on him to make him give back whoever he has."

I nod. "Go ahead, but I'm listening."

"I know." He hits speed dial. Listens. Then curses and hangs up. Tries again. Curses again.

"Not answering, is he?" I say.

"No, and I won't even bother leaving a message. That was his one and only chance to straighten this out. Now I go to my parents."

"They're in Chicago?"

He nods. "They came to celebrate the opening. Or I *thought* that's why they were here."

I'm putting it all together. "Hugh saw Kim in Chicago. He called your father, who had her killed."

Zima goes still. His hand reaches blindly, finding and gripping the desktop. He looks as if he's going to be sick, and I realize he hadn't connected the dots that far. He closes his eyes and takes a deep breath, composing himself.

When he speaks again his voice is low and controlled but strumming with anger. "I will handle this."

"I really don't have any idea where that drive is. Hugh is convinced I knew Kim, and that she told me about it. But I only met her once. I just got caught up in this."

He nods but doesn't seem to hear me, still lost in his thoughts, in his grief and anger.

"I don't care about the drive," he says. "This is about my son."

"And my husband."

He nods, but again, it's distracted. "I'll get him back for you. Everything will be fine. My father will listen to me. I'll straighten this out."

He walks away before I can say another word.

THIRTY-SIX

I go after Zima . . . at least to make sure we exchange numbers. Then he's gone, hell-bent on his mission.

I don't trust him.

But I do believe him when he says he had nothing to do with killing Kim or kidnapping Paul. His confusion and anger and grief were genuine. His story is true. The part I don't trust is him saying he'll get Paul back for me. Oh, he'll try, but that's not his priority. Brandon is. Zima's family is his responsibility, and my family is mine.

Orbec calls as I reach the car. Again I try reasoning with him. Try telling him I don't know anything about this "data." He won't even hear me out. I have one more hour to find it. One more hour until he calls. Then I'm out of time.

I need that USB drive. I have no damned idea where it is. I can't imagine Kim stashing it in the farmhouse. She'd find a safe place where they'd never look. . . .

I flash back to that first day in the park, when I met Kim. She'd been playing a hiding game with Brandon, and I'd noticed, thinking it'd be a fine game to play with Charlotte. I'd watched her hiding a small object . . . an object the size of a USB drive.

She'd been trying to find just the right spot for the drive. One Brandon couldn't easily figure out . . . meaning no one would accidentally see it. But also, I think, letting Brandon know where it was, in case it came to this, a situation where his life might depend on being able to find that drive. She made it an absolute last resort. If something happened to her and he was taken into safe custody, then he was better off not knowing about the drive. But if he was taken hostage and questioned properly — *do you remember Mommy hiding something about this size* — he'd think of the park.

It was an imperfect plan. So imperfect that clearly it'd gone wrong. Either his captors weren't asking Brandon the right questions or he wasn't around to —

No, I wouldn't think of that.

Get the data. That was my goal. Pray that I wasn't making wild and desperate connections. Pray that USB drive was where I thought it would be.

■ ■ ■ ■

I'm in the park. I've driven back to Oxford, watching to be sure I'm not tailed. Laila has called twice. I haven't heard from Zima. I doubt I will. I suspect that even if he manages to get Paul away from Orbec, I'll hear from Paul instead, Zima too concerned with finding his son and settling a score with his parents.

I saw Kim play her hiding game in a small patch of forest. On the drive here, I mentally move past the "finding the USB" part and on to planning my next move. That's how easy I expected this search to be. It's a quarter acre of forest. I know what I'm looking for. It's a simple matter of retrieving the drive.

It is not a simple matter. A quarter acre seems tiny when you're playing with a child. I remember once walking through this "forest" with Charlotte and laughing as she darted from tree to tree, hoping to spot a deer or fox. I remember thinking I really needed to get my daughter out of the city more often if this was her idea of wilderness.

Yes, this patch wouldn't hide a herd of deer, but it's more than a few trees. It's dozens of them, plus fallen logs and piles of dead leaves and pockets of brush. After ten minutes of wild searching — under this log, in this knothole — I stop and force myself to proceed methodically. Check every tree for knotholes. Lift every log and fallen branch. Forget the leaf piles for now — if I were Kim, I'd pick a spot he'd remember, and a random leaf pile wasn't good enough.

I'm still searching when my phone rings. I think it'll be Laila again, and I'm ready to ignore it when I see that it's Orbec. I check the clock. It's been fifty-five minutes.

"You said an hour," I say when I answer.

He gives a chuckle. It sounds strained, but it's probably just the connection. "If you don't have it by now, you won't have it in the next five minutes, Aubrey. Did I make a mistake taking your *estranged* husband? Are you hoping I'll kill him? Save you the hassle of a divorce?"

"If that's a joke, it's not funny."

"Good. I read the situation correctly. You want him back, which means you have the drive —"

"I don't have your drive, asshole. I met Kim *once*. Maybe you can't imagine a stranger getting involved in this, but take a closer look at your life and consider the possibility that's just you."

"No, I'm quite certain it's not. If you're stalling —"

"Yes." I check yet another knothole. "Yes, I *am* stalling. Because I'm hunting for this damned drive. I have a good idea where it is. That's detective work, not insider information. I'm searching for it right now."

"I don't believe you."

I let out a string of profanity that makes him chuckle again.

"You have quite the mouth on you, Aubrey. Not exactly the nice little librarian you pretend to be."

"Give me another half hour."

"I'm not giving you another half minute —"

I let out a grunt of pain that stops him short. I've stubbed my toe, walking with my gaze on the trees. I look down to see a rock. A rock beside a depression. A rock that has been moved.

While Orbec blusters, I bend and move the rock. There, under it, is a small black box. My hands shake as I take it out. I open it to see . . .

"I found it!" I say. "I have the drive."

I swear I hear Orbec exhale in relief. Apparently, I'm not the only one who needs this data. If he doesn't get it, he'll be in deep trouble with his boss . . . a guy who solves problems with bullets.

"Describe it," he says.

"Thumb drive. Silver swing top. Blue base. There's lettering . . . Zima Auto Body."

He definitely exhales now. "That's it. Bring —"

"I want to speak to my husband."

"You'll *see* him soon."

"I don't trust you. Let me speak to him, or I turn this over to the feds."

A growl of frustration. Footsteps. A door creaks.

"Mr. Finch, please tell your wife you are fine."

"Aubrey?" Paul's voice comes from the distance. "Call the police. I don't care what he's told you. Just call —"

The door slams shut. Orbec walks away, and Paul's muffled voice falls to silence.

"I trust you will not take his advice," Orbec says.

"Not unless I have to," I say. "But I'll be ready to. You give me the slightest reason to think you're going to screw me over, and I have the cops on speed dial."

I expect him to threaten me, but he only says, "Fine. I'm not going to cheat you, Aubrey. Like you said, you know who I am. This is a dangerous game we're both playing, and we just want it over with. I'm going to give you an address and exactly enough time to get there. You'll give me the drive. I'll give you your husband. If you don't do anything stupid, this will be painless. You have my word on that."

I try not to snort. Then I say, "And Brandon?"

"We'll discuss that."

"Do you have Brandon?"

"He's fine. Now, meet me —"

"If it's a back alley in Chicago, the answer is no."

"This isn't a gangster movie, Aubrey. I have nothing to gain by hurting you or your husband. I just want the drive. Give me that, and everyone's life gets a whole lot easier. Mine included. We're going to meet in a park. You seem to like parks."

I say nothing.

He tells me which park and which visitor lot, and then says, "It's a public enough place. I'm not driving up with your hubby in a gag and cuffs. He'll be riding shotgun. I'll park. You'll pull in beside me. We'll do the exchange there, and for all anyone will know, it's just a guy switching cars. No cloak-and-dagger crap. Okay?"

"Okay."

I drive straight to the park. When I enter

the visitors' lot, I see Orbec's Charger pull into a spot, as if he timed my arrival. He's down at the end, under a huge oak, away from the other cars. There's one couple tugging a jogging stroller from their SUV. Otherwise, while the lot is dotted with cars, there are no people. Relatively public, like he promised.

I pull in beside his car. Paul's in the passenger seat. He tries to smile for me. It's strained, but he looks fine.

Orbec lowers the passenger window. "See? He's okay. Now, he's going to reach out, and you're going to put the drive in his hand. He passes it to me. Then he gets out."

I look at Paul. He finds that weak smile again and mouths, "It's okay."

"Where's Brandon?" I ask.

Orbec sighs. "You just don't give up, do you? Brandon is fine. Hubby here has seen him, yes?"

Paul nods.

Orbec continues. "I have the number for his aunt Ellie, from Beth. As soon as I've verified the data on this drive, I'll place that call, and Ellie can come and get him."

"Not good enough."

His brows arch. "Excuse me?"

"I don't trust you, so here's the new plan. I give you the drive, and you let Paul go. He leaves with this car. I go with you to verify the drive, and then I take Brandon for Ellie."

Paul's mouth opens, and I brace for him to object. But then he meets my gaze, and he nods. He knows I need to do this, and he will not interfere, and God, I love him for that.

Orbec is muttering under his breath. Uncomplimentary things, I'm sure, but he doesn't object either. He just glares at me and says, "If you *aren't* a friend of Kim's, then you're a crazy bitch, you know that?"

"No, I'm a mom. And since Brandon's mother can't help him get home, I will."

He goes quiet at that and then nods. A moment of silence, before he sighs and looks past Paul to me. His voice is softer when he says, "Look, I know how this seems, but it's not like that. You don't need to come with me. I'll get Brandon to his auntie. All I need is that USB drive, and everyone will be safe."

"I don't care. I can't trust you."

"Fine. Paul, get that drive from your wife, and then you two swap places."

Paul shakes his head. "If Aubrey goes, I go."

"What?" Orbec says.

"You heard me. If Aubrey goes with you,

so do I."

"Oh, hell, you two make a great pair. So I get the USB and an *extra* hostage? You do understand that's not how ransom works, right?"

"If Paul stays, that's his choice," I say. "But I'm not handing over the drive. I'm getting into your backseat with it. You'll take me to Brandon, where I will verify integrity of the drive while you watch. Then I walk away with Brandon."

Orbec throws up his hands. "Fine. You're both nuts, but fine. Let's do this."

THIRTY-SEVEN

Paul insists on sitting in the backseat with me. He holds my hand, and I try to apologize, but he stops me.

"I'm all right," he says, our voices quiet, muffled by the rumble of the car. "Everything's all right. Brandon's fine. I've seen him. Whatever's going on here, he's not in danger. He's a bargaining chip. That's all."

"Gayle's okay, too," I say, whispering so Orbec doesn't overhear.

He makes a face, like he's about to say he doesn't care before he stops himself.

"I know what she did," I say, "with the video."

He leans in to whisper back. "I should have told you when I thought I recognized her car. I just couldn't believe it. I had to confront her." He shakes his head and continues, his voice still low. "Gayle wasn't . . . I'm not even sure what she was. She pursued me, and I gave in, and I hope part of it wasn't me trying to make you jealous, but I honestly don't know."

"I think, to be jealous, I'd have to feel like I could compete. She seemed perfect for you. After what I did to you, I wanted to make amends, and if that meant forcing myself to be happy that you were with someone who made *you* happy . . ."

"She didn't."

His hand tightens again, holding mine tighter now. Am I hoping for more? A declaration? Of course I am. But what I have is this — that he's coming with me, staying at my side, holding my hand. That's enough for now.

We take a convoluted route to our destination. I'm watching the position of the sun, and I can tell the car loops back on its route a few times. I try not to worry about that — it makes sense that Orbec wouldn't follow a straight path.

We leave the city and eventually arrive at a farmhouse not unlike the one where Kim had been living. It's a ramshackle two-story home surrounded by forest and field. Paul nods to me, confirming this is where he'd been before. Orbec takes us inside without preamble. He steps in and calls, "Lynn?"

A young woman opens a door and peeks

out warily.

"Bring the boy," he says.

She retreats and returns with Brandon. He looks wan, with dark circles under his eyes, but he's obviously been cared for, his clothing new, his hair and face clean. When he sees Paul, he smiles and runs over. Then he spots me and skids to a stop. He blinks.

"You're . . . you're the mom from the park," he says. "You did cartwheels."

I nod. "I am."

The smile fades as he eyes me.

"This is my wife, Aubrey," Paul says. "She's here to get you back to your aunt Ellie."

Brandon perks up. "Aunt Ellie's here?"

"She's in the city," I say. "First, though . . . Before you saw me in the park, had you ever met me before, Brandon?"

His face scrunches in confusion. "No . . ."

I shoot a glare at Orbec, who only shrugs. Then Orbec says, "Go back with Lynn, Brandon. The grown-ups need to talk, and then Paul and Aubrey can take you home."

"I'll stay with him," Paul says. "I believe we have a game of Chutes and Ladders to finish."

Brandon lights up and takes Paul's hand, leading him to the other room. The young woman follows and starts to close the door

391

behind them.

"Leave it open," I say.

She looks at Orbec, who nods. Once she's gone, I say, "Okay, get me a computer. I'll open the drive and confirm its integrity."

"Integrity?"

"Make sure the drive and the files aren't corrupted."

I can tell he still has no idea what I'm talking about, but he nods as if he does. Which tells me that if I do find problems, I don't need to let *him* know.

He brings out a laptop. I plug in the USB and confirm there are files on the drive. I run a quick disk scan. Everything comes up clean, and I show him the results.

"The drive is undamaged," I say. "Now open a few files to be sure it's the right one. I'll turn around. I don't even want to *see* what's on those."

I turn. After a few clicks, he says, "Yeah, it's the data."

"Good, so I get Brandon and you can deliver the drive to your boss."

He snorts. "My boss is the guy who made this damned drive. Denis. The idiot. Six years ago, I tried to tell him it was a stupid idea, but did he listen to me? Hell, no."

"I mean you can give it to your real boss. Denis's father."

"My *boss* is Denis Zima, Ms. Finch. I work for him, not his old man."

I look over sharply. "So Denis *was* behind this? *He* wants this drive?"

"He might, but it's going to his parents. Denis is my friend, and I look after my friends."

"I can see that. Was killing Kim and kidnapping Brandon for his own good, too? With friends like you, Denis Zima sure as hell doesn't need enemies."

Orbec glares at me. "You think you've got it all figured out, don't you? I'm the thug here. I'm the bad guy. The one who murders innocent girls and kidnaps their babies. You look at me, and you think you know all about me."

He steps toward me. "I don't work for Denis's parents. I didn't kill Kimmy. I didn't want to take her little boy. You tell me you got caught up in this, stuck in the middle of someone else's problem? Well, maybe you aren't the only one."

He eases back. "Papa Zima found out Kimmy was living near Chicago. I still have friends in his organization, and they warned me. I tried to warn her. I offered to help, but no, she had her own plans. She didn't trust me. I knew whatever plans Kimmy had, they weren't good enough. So I used her phone records to track down Beth Kenner. When I couldn't make *her* see reason either, I intercepted their plans for Brandon. Beth was supposed to pick him up at the park, but I beat her to it. Beth started listening to me then . . . or she did after those bastards got to Kimmy."

"So you and Beth Kenner have been working together to hold Brandon in protective custody. Until when? What was your end game?"

He waves the drive. "This, obviously. Find the data. Give it to Papa Zima. Back him off. Then call Kimmy's sister and give her the boy, preferably without Denis ever knowing he had a son. Which is a lousy thing to do to a friend, but it was for the kid's own good. Denis's, too. Denis's parents would hold the kid over his head, leverage to get Denis back into the fold."

"And now that Denis knows about Brandon?"

"We'll figure that one out. For now, I have this." He raises the drive. "And you can have the boy. I'll give you a lift back to the city."

"Thanks, but no. I think we'll take it from here."

He shrugs. "Suit yourself. Brandon? Come on out. It's time to go home."

■ ■ ■ ■

We have Brandon. Orbec offers again to drive us to the city, but he doesn't seem surprised when we refuse. Whatever his motivations, he is still the one who took Paul and threatened me, and now that I have what I came for, I'm getting the hell out. Paul agrees.

We walk onto the front porch.

"At the end of the drive, turn left," Orbec says as he steps onto the porch with us. "It's about a mile to a gas station. You can get a cab to pick you up there. Don't get any ideas about calling the cops. Please. That'll just make this a lot more complicated than it needs to be."

"I have what I wanted," I say.

"Good. Then get going —"

"Yes," says a voice behind me. "You and your husband should go. The boy stays with me."

Paul and I both wheel to see a woman walking from the forest. She's about fifty, tall and sturdy . . . and flanked by two men with guns. Two more men appear around the other side of the house.

"Don't, Hugh," she says. "You know that's a very bad idea."

Orbec goes still, hand poised over his gun. He slowly withdraws it.

"Mama Zima," Orbec says. "I was just about to come see you and Papa. I have something you want."

He holds up the USB drive.

"Excellent," she says. "But you actually have *two* things I want. I'll take the drive . . . and I'll take my grandson."

Orbec shakes his head. "He's not your grandson, Mama. He's just Kimmy's kid. She got knocked up after she left Denis. I took him, in hopes she'd turn over the drive in exchange, but someone else got to her first. Luckily, these two cared enough about the brat to make the trade."

"So this isn't my son's boy?"

"If Denis got Kimmy knocked up, she'd have ridden that train to the end. Sunk her hooks even deeper into Denis and never let go. Nah, this is just some brat —"

"Liar."

I don't see the gun in Mama Zima's hand until that hand rises, that gun firing. I wheel toward Paul and Brandon. Paul's lunging to shield me, but the shot whizzes past. Orbec falls. I scoop up Brandon, who's frozen. Paul shoves us both back through the still-open door. I'm running for cover when I realize Paul isn't behind me. I wheel, nearly dropping Brandon. Paul's there, slamming shut the dead bolt.

Outside, Mama Zima laughs. "Do you really think that's going to help? Give me my grandson, and I'll let you leave, but if I have to come in there after you . . ."

She doesn't bother finishing the threat. I give Brandon to Paul and take out my gun as I yank open an interior door. Behind it, Lynn stumbles back through what looks like a living room. She has her hands raised.

"Pl-please, don't —" she begins.

I shush her and whisper, "Where's the basement?"

She points. So do I . . . with the gun, aiming it at her.

"Where *exactly*?" I say.

She tells me.

I shove her toward the sofa. "Hide there. Don't come out."

I race into the hall, where Paul's waiting. Outside, Mama Zima is ordering her men to surround the house.

"Basement," I call to Paul, then I shut the living room door . . . and hustle them to the stairs leading up instead.

Paul has Brandon in his arms. The boy hasn't said a word. He's spent his lifetime hiding, and he only peeks at me over Paul's shoulder, and then buries his face in it as

Paul whispers reassurances.

We get up the stairs just as the front door opens. Paul glances back at me, but I only motion for him to move farther down the hall. Then I stop him and start checking rooms. Below, I hear someone say, "It's me."

Lynn comes out from her hiding place and starts talking quickly to Mama Zima, telling her we're in the basement. Is she ratting us out in hopes of winning her freedom? Or is she the one who *brought* Denis's mother here? Either is equally likely, and I'm not the least bit surprised to hear her.

The third door opens to another staircase, ascending into a dark attic. I wave Paul over.

"Take him up there," I whisper. "I'll handle this."

"I'll find him a place to hide," Paul says. "Then I'm coming to help you."

I shake my head. He opens his mouth to protest, but I grip his arm.

"I have a gun," I say. "You do not. I need you to stay with Brandon. Please. Call the police and stay with him."

He still hesitates, and I know he wants to argue, but he also knows this is the right plan. Finally, he gives an abrupt nod and says, "Don't engage. Just stall."

I nod and start to go.

He grips my arm. "Be careful."
I lean in to kiss his cheek. "I will."

Thirty-Eight

Below, Mama Zima is telling someone to check downstairs. Two sets of heavy footfalls retreat. That means two men are in the house and two are patrolling outside. Mama herself stays on the main level. Once the footsteps retreat down the steps, she says to Lynn, "Go outside. Wait in the car."

Lynn's footsteps head toward the front door. A shot fires. A body thuds to the floor, and I close my eyes, forcing my hammering heart to slow.

Mama Zima shot Orbec. Killed him without warning. Now she's killed a girl who helped her, a girl who'd probably been on her payroll the whole time.

She will not hesitate to shoot me.

Shoot me. Then go after Paul and Brandon, and if she does that, I have no doubt of what will happen to Paul. Another loose end to be clipped off. That's all he is to her. All we are.

What the hell have I done? What have I gotten my family into?

I thought I had this under control. I thought Hugh Orbec was the worst thing I had to deal with, and he was the sort of person I'd dealt with before. A thug. A man who would use force to get his way, but a man who could be reasoned with, a man who had no justification for killing me and therefore would not.

That isn't what I'm dealing with now.

I have never encountered anything like what I'm dealing with now.

I am not prepared for it. I don't know how to prepare for it. I don't know —

Breathe. Just breathe.

Two options here.

Retreat upstairs and hope Paul managed to contact the police, and they are on their way and will arrive before Mama Zima's thugs find us.

Or confront the problem.

I'm not a fool. I know I can't take on five armed criminals. The police are my best bet, and the only question is how I'll stall. Whether my best hope for stalling is defense or offense.

Offense.

I don't really have a choice here. To retreat puts Paul at risk. To confront means putting myself at risk, and praying that will buy enough time for the police to arrive. If that costs me my life, well, it's better than costing us both ours. Better than robbing our daughter of both her parents.

Distract. Stall.

Pray.

I start my descent. The problem with coming down a set of stairs? Mama Zima below will see my feet long before I spot *her.* So I try to angle myself away from the bannister, and with every step, I duck to get a look. I also listen. I can hear the men downstairs. I don't know how big the basement is, but there's a limited amount of time they'll spend down there before realizing they've been duped.

What I don't hear is Mama Zima. I take another two steps and then spot her shadow stretching across the floor. She's right around the corner. As soon as I come down, she'll see me.

So much for the element of surprise.

I'll need to go big. Hope to startle her and dodge and keep dodging.

While she shoots at me? While the sound of my running feet brings the thugs racing upstairs?

This isn't going to work. It cannot —

Deep breath.

I take out my phone. I need to text Paul. Make sure he's summoned the police and maybe find out how long —

There's no cell signal.

My phone has no signal.

No.

Oh God, no.

Either there's no signal here or they've blocked it.

Of course they've blocked it, you idiot. Otherwise they wouldn't be taking their time searching. They'd know we would call for help.

Movement flickers below. It's Mama Zima's shadow . . . moving away.

I close my eyes and strain to listen. For a big woman, she walks with very little noise, but she's definitely moving in the opposite direction.

Maybe if she continues into another room —

No maybes. No hopes. No prayers.

No waiting for the perfect opportunity.

I fly down the stairs as fast as I can. I'm leaping off the bottom step when she hears me. She starts to turn. I'm halfway to her, only a few feet left to go, but she's spinning, gun going up —

I slam into her. It's like hitting a brick wall, and all I can think is *You're a fool, Aubrey Finch. A stupid, senseless fool.* I've

403

played my ace, throwing my entire body into hers, and she's barely stumbling.

Except she still does stumble. It's only a slight stagger, but I've caught her as she was turning, and her feet twist, and it's enough. I've knocked her off-balance. I slam into her again, and we go down with a crash.

Her gun flies up. I hit her arm and the gun snaps backward, but she doesn't drop it. I strike again, and this time, I'm off-target. I barely hit her. But her hand opens, eyes widening, and I realize I've struck her ulnar nerve.

The gun falls.

It clacks to the hardwood floor, but I only dimly hear it over the footsteps thundering up the stairs. The thugs have heard us fall, and they're coming.

I knock her gun away and yank out my own. Beneath me, she's struggling, bucking with formidable strength. But I have her pinned. Then I have the gun, pointed at her forehead, just as the basement door flies open.

"Stop!" I shout. "Guns down, or I pull this trigger."

The first man through the door hesitates. I press the gun into Mama Zima's head. She glowers at me and doesn't even flinch. But the thug notices. He sees my expression. And he holsters his gun.

"No," I say. "You're going to drop that. Then you'll go outside. Get your comrades. They'll toss their guns through the front door. Then you'll let us leave. All three of us."

"Do you really think they'll let you leave?" Mama Zima says.

"They will if I take you with me," I say.

"Then you'll need to deal with *me*."

"I guess I will." I look at the man. "Outside. Now."

He goes, and the other thug follows. Neither looks over at Mama Zima, who's shooting them death glares and cursing in Russian.

"Hey, they're saving your life," I say.

"If they think so, they are mistaken." She raises her voice so they can hear. "You see that girl on the floor? That will be you."

"Maybe," I say. "But this gives them a chance to plead their case with your husband. Otherwise, if you don't survive this, I suspect they'll have more to worry about than a bullet in the back of the head."

"My husband is not the Zima they should worry about. They should know that. I am the one here for my grandson. You understand that. You are here with me, and I see no sign of *your* husband."

"Maybe so," I say as the door closes behind the two men, "but apparently, they don't dare go home without you. Now, you're going to roll over and put your hands —"

She bucks. I'm ready for it — I've been ready the whole time she's been talking — but when I go to shove her down, she kicks up instead, and that *does* catch me off-guard. When I teeter, she goes for the gun. I swing it against the side of her skull. It hits with a thwack, her head snapping sideways, but she only snarls and grabs my ponytail.

She yanks my head back. I let out a gasp and try to jerk free, but she's got my hair wrapped around her hand. Her other hand goes for the gun. I swing it up, out of her reach. At the last second, her hand chops downward instead, smacking me in the ribs.

I fall to the side. I'm focused on keeping the gun. That's all I care about. She never goes for it, though. She rolls from under me and lunges for her gun, lying on the floor.

I hear the thud of footsteps. I glance over just in time to see Paul running for her. He's going for the gun, to kick it away, but he's not close enough. Her fingers wrap around it, and she swings it up, barrel heading his way. I throw myself on her. The gun fires. With both hands, I grab her gun arm and wrench it back, thudding into the floor.

Mama Zima fights with everything she has, kicking and scratching. Paul has the gun, and he's staying far from the barrel as he pries her fingers away. She fires again. The shot goes wild, but the sound startles Paul. He relaxes his hold just enough for her to turn the gun his way —

I slam her arm into the floor. Paul wrenches the gun from her hand. Outside, there's a commotion. Shouting. Running footfalls. I scramble for my dropped gun, and I swing it up just as the door opens —

"Police!" Laila Jackson shouts. "Drop your weapons."

More officers push in behind her, and I still hear more outside, handling the thugs. I lift my hands and drop to my knees as the police rush in.

THIRTY-NINE

Laila gets Paul and me away from our guns. Then she focuses on Mama Zima and the thugs, letting us slip off to the side.

"Don't go *anywhere,*" she says.

I nod. When I turn to Paul, I say, "You *did* call them."

"Actually, no." His voice wavers. He takes a deep breath and shakes it off. "I couldn't. When I realized I didn't have cell service, I found a spot to hide Brandon and snuck to the steps to make sure you were okay. You weren't, so I came down armed with . . ." He points at a broken chair leg, dropped by the fight scene, and gives me a wry smile.

"Thank you." I put my arms around his neck and kiss him. Then I pull back fast. "Sorry. I —"

He cuts me off with a deep kiss. A moment later, a throat clears behind us. We turn to see Laila.

"Mind if I interrupt?" she says.

"Yes," I say.

She gives me a hard look and waves for us to follow her.

"Brandon," Paul says. "He's hiding in the attic. May we get him? With an officer escort, of course."

Laila agrees and sends Paul to do it. I'm not going anywhere, apparently. Once he's gone, she leads me outside. Paramedics are loading Hugh Orbec into an ambulance.

"Is he . . . ?" I begin.

"Alive. For now." She turns her back on the paramedics and faces me. "Before you ask, it was Ellie Milano. She finally contacted me, and only because she was worried about you. Took me a while to get permission to track your cell to its last location. I'd like to say you're lucky we showed up but . . ." She glances back at the house and then says, grudgingly, "You seemed to be doing okay."

"No, trust me, I'm still glad you showed up."

"I could have helped a whole lot sooner," she says. "And I'd love to give you hell for that, but . . ." She sighs as she scans the yard, the officers taking the thugs into custody. "We got off to a bad start. I just didn't want you getting caught up in something dangerous. Glad to see *that* didn't happen."

"I'm sorry."

She shakes her head and keeps surveying the situation. "Helluva mess. Didn't know what you got yourself into, did you?"

"Nope, but I'm guessing you didn't either. No one's ever really prepared for gun-toting, mobster grannies."

She snorts at that. "I've heard stories about Mama Zima, but I'd almost be impressed . . . if she wasn't such a cold-blooded bitch."

Laila's about to speak again when Brandon appears at the doorway, clutching Paul's hand.

"And there's the cause of all this commotion," she says. "Looks pretty good for an imaginary boy. Poor kid. His aunt should be here —"

A police car rolls into the drive, the passenger door opening before it even stops. Ellie leaps out, and Laila says, "Perfect timing."

Paul lets go of Brandon, and he runs for his aunt, who scoops him up in a bear hug. As we watch, another car appears, this one a BMW roaring into the drive. Laila swears. Before she can move, Cooper appears at a jog, shouting orders. Officers train their weapons on the vehicle as Cooper yells for the driver to get out of it. He already is, and seeing him, Laila curses again.

It's Denis Zima. He has his hands on his head, but he's stepping away from the car. Cooper shouts for him to stop.

"He's okay," I say. "Or I think he is. Oh, hell, at this point, I'm not even sure."

"I just want to see my —" Zima begins. Then he spots Brandon. He stops and stares, and he wobbles, just a little. There's a moment of absolute silence. Then he turns to Cooper. "I was speaking to my father. He had no idea what I was talking about. That's when I realized he wasn't the one behind this."

Zima's gaze shoots to the front door as it opens, his mother coming out in handcuffs. Zima surges forward, fists clenched, but Cooper gets in his path. Zima rocks back. Then his gaze goes to Brandon.

"May I see . . . ?" he begins.

Ellie picks Brandon up again and heads toward Zima. I turn away and glance at Paul, who passes me a smile and starts for me.

"Go on," Laila says, jerking her chin toward Brandon. "Join the reunion. You're the one who made it possible."

I shake my head. "I'm done. This part's for them."

I walk to Paul instead, and he takes my hand as I collapse against his shoulder.

We don't just get to walk away after this. We have to give statements at the station, and it's hours before I'm released.

As I'm leaving, Laila comes jogging after me.

"You still owe me," she says.

I turn. "What?"

"You owe me a link to that sword-fighting class. You probably also owe me a lift to it. The least you can do, really, since I saved your ass."

"You saved my ass about as much as I solved your case, which is, I believe, about fifty-fifty of each. We're taking turns driving to class."

She gives me her personal email address, and we talk for another minute, and as I walk away, I think back to that moment in the park with Kim, when I thought she was someone I could talk to, someone I could relate to. I may have actually found that, just not in the place I expected.

I walk out to find Paul waiting. He says nothing, just takes my hand, fingers inter-locking with mine, and leads me to the parking lot, where the officers let us bring our car earlier.

"How are you doing?" he asks when we reach the car.

"I'm glad it worked out but . . ." I shake my head and climb in the passenger side.

When he's in, I say, "I'm sorry. Yes, it all worked out, but I could have gotten you killed. I was in over my head. Way over my head."

He manages a smile. "Seems like you were swimming just fine. You didn't drag me in, Bree. We both underestimated the situation, but neither of us went in with our eyes closed. I'm a lawyer. I knew I was getting involved in something potentially dangerous, and I chose to do so."

I nod and say nothing, just turn to stare out the window.

He backs the car out. "I'm fine. Charlie's fine. You're fine. And so is Brandon."

I nod again.

He drives from the lot. A couple of minutes pass, and then he starts to say something, but I'm already speaking, saying, "Does this change anything?"

His fingers tighten on the wheel.

"I don't mean with us," I say. "You stuck by me, and you can't imagine how much I appreciated that, but I know it doesn't mean things have changed. I'm talking about Charlie. You knew what I was . . . and now

413

you've seen what I can be. What I'm capable of. Does that change anything with her? With the custody? I know that after what's happened, you might not think I'm the most responsible parent, but I swear, I would never have done any of this with her around."

He nods. That's all he does. He nods, and my heart hammers.

"Paul —"

"We'll discuss that later." He makes a sharp right. "First, I want to show you something."

As we ride in silence, I can barely breathe. When I asked if this changed his opinion of me as a mother, I was hoping he'd say of course not, that he'd acknowledge that I'd looked after Charlotte first, that he'd say he knows I'm a good mother. Instead, he's made that sharp — angry? — turn and ended the conversation.

He takes us to a new subdivision on the edge of Oxford. It's one I've never seen before. He drives onto a street of duplexes, a few inhabited, some still under construction. He pulls into the drive of a finished one with darkened windows. Then he gets out.

When I don't follow, he waves for me. I carefully climb from the car.

"What do you think?" he says.

It takes me a moment to realize he's talking about the duplex.

"It's . . . nice?" I say. "Is this . . . ? Do you mean as a possible place for me?"

He nods. I just keep looking from him to the duplex. Is this his way of saying he still wants to support me? Or is he changing the subject, distracting me from talk of custody?

"I . . . I'm not sure I could afford it," I say. "I have the down payment, but I should wait until I have a new job. I'll get a full-time one. I should — since I don't have Charlie to look after."

"Do you want Charlie to look after?"

My heart leaps, but I keep my expression neutral.

"In an ideal world, Bree, what would you want?" he says. "No pressure. No judgment. Full-time job? Full-time parent? Part-time both? Go back to school?"

"I . . ."

"Perfect world. Just tell me."

"I loved being home full-time but . . ."

"No judgment."

I take a deep breath. "In a perfect world, I'd stay home with Charlie and go back to school part-time. I'd let her go to daycare a couple of days a week because I think it's been good for her."

"Then that's what you'll do."

I nod. "Okay, I'll find a better apartment —"

"I'd like you to live here, Aubrey. The left-hand unit has a nice sunroom you can use as a study. The right-hand one is better for me — the office has a lousy view, which will keep me from getting distracted."

I turn to look at him.

"This is for us," he says. He steps toward me. "You're concerned that I don't want you parenting our daughter anymore. This is my answer. I found it yesterday, and I haven't changed my mind. I would like to change the custody arrangement. To this." He nods at the duplex. "Extreme co-parenting. If you'd be interested."

Tears prickle my eyelids. "I would absolutely be interested."

He shoves his hands into his pockets. "I'd love to just ask you to move back into the house, so we can try again, but even if you want to try again —"

"I do."

"Then I think we need to get to know each other first. Start over, and let me meet the real Aubrey." He looks up at the house. "Which will be a lot easier like this."

"I get to date the boy next door?"

He smiles. "Yes, I guess you do. And if it

works . . ." He shrugs. "The neighborhood is a work in progress. It's a good investment. Easy to sell if we want closer quarters. I just don't want to rush. I'm sorry. I know that's not the most romantic solution —"

I throw my arms around his neck. "It's the perfect solution. Thank you."

He kisses me, a long and passionate kiss. When he pulls back, he says, "Will you come with me to get Charlie?"

"That depends. Think we can find a hotel along the way?"

His brows arch.

I grin. "Well, you did say you want to get to know me again. Not to rush or anything . . ."

"That doesn't sound like rushing at all. Perfectly logical." He puts his arm around my waist and leads me back to the car. "I'll tell my mother to expect us first thing in the morning."

ABOUT THE AUTHOR

Kelley Armstrong graduated with a degree in psychology and then studied computer programming. Now she is a full-time writer and parent, and she lives with her husband and three children in rural Ontario, Canada. Kelley is a #1 *New York Times* bestselling author of both YA and adult novels, including the Otherworld series and the Rockton novels.

The employees of Thorndike Press hope you have enjoyed this Large Print book. All our Thorndike, Wheeler, and Kennebec Large Print titles are designed for easy reading, and all our books are made to last. Other Thorndike Press Large Print books are available at your library, through selected bookstores, or directly from us.

For information about titles, please call:
(800) 223-1244

or visit our website at:
gale.com/thorndike

To share your comments, please write:
Publisher
Thorndike Press
10 Water St., Suite 310
Waterville, ME 04901